"I'm not ...
you can j..."

"I'd never compare you to a cow, Jessie." His lazy smile aggravated her even more. "You're more like a pretty little mustang mare, running wild and free."

"Who wants to stay that way."

"Even a mustang doesn't like to be alone."

"So she's supposed to follow the first stallion who nickers sweet nothings and nuzzles her neck?" A sudden image sprang to mind—Cade lifting her hair away from her open collar with one powerful hand; the other at her waist, his touch firm yet gentle.

Cade glanced at her throat and groaned softly. When he looked up, an unmistakable fire burned in his eyes. "No, she has a choice. But he also has to let the other males know he wants her. Stake his claim."

He was going to kiss her, but heaven help her…she wanted him to!

* * *

McKinnon's Bride
Harlequin Historical #652—April 2003

Praise for author
Sharon Harlow

"Ms. Harlow creates a richly detailed world where the
good guys don't need white hats to be heroes—
they just need the love of a good woman."
—*Romantic Times*

The Wedding Wager
"Ms. Harlow's enthusiasm for life and love
draws readers in and causes their hearts
and imaginations to soar."
—*Romantic Times*

McKinnon's Bride

SHARON HARLOW

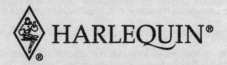
HARLEQUIN®

TORONTO • NEW YORK • LONDON
AMSTERDAM • PARIS • SYDNEY • HAMBURG
STOCKHOLM • ATHENS • TOKYO • MILAN • MADRID
PRAGUE • WARSAW • BUDAPEST • AUCKLAND

ISBN 0-373-29252-X

McKINNON'S BRIDE

Copyright © 2003 by Sharon Gillenwater

This edition published by arrangement with Harlequin Books S.A.

® and TM are trademarks of the publisher. Trademarks indicated with
® are registered in the United States Patent and Trademark Office, the
Canadian Trade Marks Office and in other countries.

Visit us at www.eHarlequin.com

Printed in U.S.A.

Please address questions and book requests to:
Harlequin Reader Service
U.S.: 3010 Walden Ave., P.O. Box 1325, Buffalo, NY 14269
Canadian: P.O. Box 609, Fort Erie, Ont. L2A 5X3

Dedication:

In memory of my mom and dad.
You are deeply loved and greatly missed.
What a joy it will be to see you again someday.

And to my husband, Gene, for having the love and grace
to let me take another crack at this writing thing.

Acknowledgments:

A special thank-you to my dear friends on the
Harlequin Historical Authors Loop for your friendship
and encouragement, especially during my long dry spell.

Another thank-you to my dear PQALS—
Lynn Bulock, Annie Jones and Diane Noble.
I would have been lost without you.

My heartfelt thanks to two more special people,
my agent Karen Solem and my editor Patience Smith,
for believing in me even when I didn't.

Chapter One

West Texas, 1883

"Are we ever gonna get there?"

Jessie Monroe smiled as her four-year-old daughter grimaced and shifted on the wagon seat. Ellie had asked the same question every afternoon since they had left their home in East Texas almost three months earlier.

"We should see the ranch headquarters any minute. I don't think the house will be more than a mile or two from the road." Jessie looked over Ellie's head at her son, Brad.

He met her gaze, his blue eyes filled with concern. "Do you think Uncle Quintin will be glad to see us?"

"I'm sure he will, honey." She smiled in reassurance. Only nine, the boy should have been excited, thinking of the adventures awaiting him, instead of being worried. "Won't he be surprised? Can't you just see him standing there with his mouth open and a dumb look on his face?"

Brad returned her smile, but it obviously took effort. "Then he'll grin all silly, like he did last time he came to see us and made such a fuss over how big I was."

"He'll make an even bigger fuss this time." *And it won't*

just be over how much you've grown. Quint would be mad as a hornet because she had made the trip on her own. He would understand why she had, but he wouldn't like it. "You're at least two inches taller."

Their old mare plodded along, following the road around a lazy curve and down a long, slight slope, a gentle reminder that though the land appeared flat, it wasn't.

During the past several days, they had crossed the same general terrain—a broad prairie stretching as far as the eye could see, broken by scattered hills but unhampered by the sprinkling of humanity who dared call it home. Tall grass draped most of the landscape in a cloak of green, but the high, steep-sided mesas of rugged gray rock and scarred brown dirt stood proudly bare.

It was so different from the East Texas woods she had known all her life. Jessie saw the beauty in the vast, barely tamed land, but that very wildness made her uneasy. Each creak of the old, shoddy wagon reminded her of how ill prepared she had been for such a journey.

But we made it, she thought with a twinge of pride and much relief. Even if the wagon completely fell apart, they could walk the rest of the way. Though she certainly hoped they didn't have to. Not with about fifty sandy-brown and mottled longhorn cattle grazing nearby, some with horns reaching six feet from tip to tip. A few of the cows raised their heads and watched the wagon's progress down the road, but they appeared more interested in the grass than in them.

They topped a small rise, and the headquarters of the McKinnon Ranch came into view.

"Does Uncle Quint live there?" Ellie pointed to the one-story ranch house. Sparkling with a fresh coat of white paint, the house was bigger and nicer than anything they had ever called home.

"No, honey. He lives in the bunkhouse with the rest of the cowboys. Probably that long building near the corrals."

"Where are we gonna stay?"

"I don't know. Maybe in the barn." Jessie really didn't care as long as they had a roof over their heads and four walls to shelter them. She had spent too many lonely, black nights dozing beside the wagon, a shotgun across her lap, guarding against predators—both the two-legged and the four-legged kind.

"Remember your uncle talking about Mr. McKinnon? He lives in the ranch house."

"Does he have a wife?" Ellie asked.

"No, unless he got married in the last six months."

The little girl frowned thoughtfully. "I hope not. Married people are sad a lot."

Pain stabbed Jessie's heart, but a swell of love soothed the ache as she looked down at her daughter. Ellie watched her intently, her small face mirroring her love and concern.

"Not all married couples have as many problems as your daddy and I did," said Jessie. "We just couldn't seem to get along."

Because he got along all too well with other women. Or threw away what little money they had on cards and liquor. She didn't know if her pain—or shame—would ever disappear. Maybe she shouldn't want them to. Only a fool would forget lessons so harshly learned.

She drew the horse to a halt in front of the house. No one was in sight, there or around the corrals and bunkhouse. There wasn't a single weed or blade of grass in the wide strip of dark earth surrounding the house. The whole area in front of the porch had been swept clean. Quintin told her that many ranchers preferred a bare yard because it made snakes easier to spot. It also served as a firebreak in the event of a prairie fire.

Jessie turned sideways, handing the reins to her son, and looked at Ellie. "Wait here with Brad."

"Can I tickle him?" Ellie grinned, an impish sparkle dancing in her big brown eyes.

Jessie smiled. "Not while he's handling Valentine. Now behave yourself, little miss." Jessie frowned, hoping the child could understand. "We really need a place to stay until I can find work. So be a good girl and put on your company manners."

"Can I take them off after supper?"

Jessie gently touched her daughter's cheek beneath the faded red calico sunbonnet. "I imagine you'd better wear them for a while. I don't like to depend on Mr. McKinnon's hospitality, but right now, looks like we have to. We mustn't do anything that will make him send us away."

"He won't send you away, Mama. Not if you help with the cookin'. You're the bestest cook in the whole world."

"Thank you, sweetie, but how do you know? Did you go around the world when I wasn't lookin'?"

Ellie stood on the floorboard and rubbed her posterior. "Feels like it."

Brad gave her one of his rare, spontaneous smiles, and Jessie laughed. "You scamp. A lady doesn't rub her backside, even when it's sore from riding too long."

"I ain't a lady. I'm just a kid."

"It's never too early to learn how to be polite."

Ellie sighed. "Yes, ma'am."

"That's my girl." Jessie hugged her, then climbed down from the wagon and walked up onto the porch.

Seconds after she knocked, a tall, handsome man answered the door. Curiosity lurked in his dark brown eyes as he smiled. "Good afternoon, ma'am."

"Mr. McKinnon?"

"Yes." His smile widened. "Though maybe not the one

you're looking for. I'm Ty. My brother Cade and I are partners, but he runs the ranch. He's not here right now.''

She knew that Ty lived in town. He and his brother also owned a large general store, which he ran. ''Actually, I'm looking for my brother, Quintin Webb. I'm Jessie Monroe.''

A frown creased his brow. ''I'm sorry, Mrs. Monroe. He isn't here. Cade fired him three weeks ago.''

Jessie's heart sank and weakness swept over her. Until that moment, she had not realized how much she had been counting on her brother's help and loving reassurance. Bewildered, she shook her head. Quintin wasn't a saint, but he had never lost a job before. ''Fired him? Why?''

''He picked a fight with Cade in front of the men. Just blew up and started swinging.''

Her brother seldom backed down from a fight, but Jessie had never known him to start one. Especially not with the man he considered his best friend. She couldn't imagine what Cade had done to make him so angry. ''That doesn't sound like Quintin.''

''Wasn't like him at all. Cade hated lettin' him go, but he had to be firm in front of the other men. He didn't have any choice.''

Jessie wasn't so sure about that. ''Do you know where he is?''

''No. He stayed in town for a few days, then took off. I don't know if anybody has seen him since.'' He glanced at the wagon, frowning again. ''Are you and the children alone? Your husband isn't with you?''

''He was killed a little over three months ago.'' She noted his questioning glance at her worn light blue cotton dress. Stiffening her spine, Jessie met his gaze. ''I'm sorry he's dead, but I won't mourn for him.''

McKinnon shrugged. ''Some men don't deserve it. We

have plenty of room. You and your family can stay here for a while, rest up and figure out what to do next.''

''I can't impose.'' It would have been hard enough for Jessie to depend on their hospitality with Quintin there. Under the circumstances, she found it nigh impossible. ''If we could sleep in the barn a few nights, though, I'd be grateful. Then we won't bother you anymore.''

''I won't hear of putting you and those young'uns down in the barn. I'm sure Cade won't, either. He had a disagreement with Quint, not you. Besides, cowboys welcome strangers to their campfire.'' He grinned and motioned toward the house. ''Ours just happens to be surrounded by four walls and covered with a roof.''

Quintin had never spoken an ill word about either of the McKinnons. She instinctively knew they would be safe there, far safer than at any time on the journey.

''If you're certain it's not any trouble, that would be a blessing. We've been on the road much too long. Poor Valentine couldn't go very far at a time.''

His gaze shifted to the horse. ''It's a wonder that she made it at all. I bet you fed her better than you did yourself.''

''At times,'' Jessie said with a tiny smile.

He looked back at her, studying her thoughtfully. ''How's your cooking?''

''According to my daughter, I'm the bestest cook in the world. Of course, her world is pretty small.''

He chuckled. ''Cade's housekeeper got married a couple of months ago, and he about killed himself with his own cooking. He finally resorted to eating down at the bunkhouse with the men. We have a good cook for them, but Cade likes eating at his own table. I reckon he'd gladly provide the food if you don't mind preparing it.''

''I don't mind at all.''

"I have to head back to town in a few minutes, but you come on in and make yourselves at home." McKinnon's gaze swept over her, his eyes twinkling. "Cade was planning to advertise for a housekeeper in next week's paper, but if you fix a decent supper, you'll save him the trouble."

Right that minute, Jessie didn't know whether or not she wanted to work for Cade McKinnon. But the thought of something besides jerky or beans made her mouth water. If nothing else, she would earn their supper and a place to sleep.

"Tell your son to take the wagon down to the barn. A couple of the men are down there someplace. They'll help put it away and see to the horse." He smiled, looking at the children. "You'd better send your little girl with him and let her run around a bit. She's tryin' to sit still, but she's liable to bust if she doesn't get down pretty soon."

Jessie turned toward the wagon. As usual, Brad sat quietly, watching them with a cool, detached air. She ached for him, knowing the pain he had buried deep inside. Ellie grinned, and though she sat perfectly ladylike, an elf couldn't have looked more mischievous. "The trip has been hard on her."

"It must have been hard on all of you. There are some new kittens in the barn. Tell her to ask one of the cowboys to show them to her. They opened their eyes last week, so their mama still stays close. She's a friendly old cat and doesn't mind sharing them with us if we're careful."

"I'll tell them." Jessie smiled, relieved that they hadn't been turned away. "Thank you."

"You're welcome. By the way, that house comes with the job." He pointed to a smaller house about twenty yards away, set back a bit from the ranch house. "It's empty except for a kitchen stove, but we have beds at the store.

Anything else you need, we'll pick up at the furniture store in town.''

"I'll keep that in mind." She returned to the wagon, explaining the situation to the children.

"I don't want to stay here without Uncle Quint," said Brad with a scowl. "I thought him and Mr. McKinnon were good friends."

"They were, honey. His brother said he didn't want to fire Quintin, but he had to."

"Why?"

Jessie considered how to answer. "An employer has to have authority over the people who work for him. Quintin challenged that. If Mr. McKinnon let him stay, some of the other men might slack off on their work or do something he doesn't want them to do."

She sighed and reached into the back for the battered satchels containing their clothes. "Take the wagon to the barn. Mr. McKinnon said there should be someone down there to help you put it away and tend to Valentine." She winked at Ellie. "He said to ask one of the men to show you the new kittens."

"Kittens!" The little girl jumped up and down, clapping her hands.

"Be careful with them. And mind the cowboys. Don't go anywhere unless one of them says it's all right."

"Yes, ma'am." Ellie sat down, looking at her brother. "Hurry up."

"Behave yourself. Brad, watch your sister."

He rolled his eyes. "Yes, ma'am."

Jessie carried the bags to the porch and waited on one end of it to keep an eye on the children. She breathed a soft prayer of thanks that they would be snug and warm inside the house, even if only for a few days.

She didn't think she could have faced another endless

stretch of road, knowing the wagon could fall to pieces any moment or the mare might pull up lame or even die of old age in the middle of nowhere. Jessie had worried enough in more populated areas, but out here, she had lived with the constant fear that one of them might get hurt, or they might become stranded and she wouldn't be able to find help.

Even a month at the ranch might not be enough. Brad was as travel weary as she was, and Ellie had been ready to stop two days after they started. The child would throw a hissy fit if she told her they had to leave right away.

A stocky cowboy came out of the barn and walked up to Ellie's side of the wagon. A minute later, he held out his hands and she jumped into them. He strolled around to the side of the barn. Balancing her daughter on one arm, he pulled open two wide doors, revealing a buggy shed. He and Ellie went inside, with Brad driving the horse and wagon in behind them.

The argument between Quintin and Cade troubled Jessie, but she couldn't afford to judge him too harshly, not when she had half a dollar to her name and only enough beans for one more meal.

She ached with disappointment at not finding her brother and struggled with fear of the unknown. But as she had done so many times in the past, she buried those feelings, covering them with the determined will of a survivor. She had learned years ago to take care of herself and to provide for her children. She hadn't expected Quintin to do it. She needed him to ease the burdens of her heart far more than to help with their financial situation.

Moving to the other end of the porch, her gaze settled on the house across the yard. She walked over to it, noting that the roof appeared solid. It had a wide porch running along the front, with a nice view of the prairie and distant hills. Opening the door, she stepped inside, gasping at the heat. "Well, it's good and tight."

But there were windows on all sides that would let in the breeze. The combined kitchen and living room covered the length of the house, with a kitchen stove and a doorway leading to a small side porch at one end. Two bedrooms occupied the other side of the house. Ellie could sleep with her. And Brad could have his own room.

Sudden tears stung her eyes. Though half the size of the ranch house, it was better than what she had lived in the whole time she'd been married. Her children had never had a bedroom. They'd slept on a mattress in one corner of the kitchen. When Neil stayed home, she and her husband had shared the one tiny bedroom.

If Cade offered her a job, they would be guaranteed a place to live. There was no such certainty if she tried to find something in Willow Grove. She knew it was a thriving town, born of the arrival of the railroad and the cattlemen. In his last letter, Quintin had mentioned that houses and business couldn't be built fast enough to provide for the growing population. She might find a place to work but have no place to live.

"When I find Quint, I'll rant and rave and gripe for a week. Today, I have to earn that housekeeping job." Jessie walked out of the house, closing the door behind her. When she turned, she found Ty watching her from the ranch house porch. He gave her a nod, then picked up their bags and carried them inside.

Squaring her shoulders, Jessie marched across the yard. If worse came to worst, she wasn't too proud to beg for the job. Pride might help sustain a person's dignity, but it was about as worthless as a leaky milk bucket when it came to filling a child's empty belly.

Chapter Two

Cade rode in at dusk, tired and hungry as a coyote with a toothache. All he wanted was supper, his big comfortable chair and a nap.

Drawing Mischief to a halt in front of the corral, he dismounted and opened the wide wooden gate. He waited patiently while the animal moseyed on inside, then he shut the gate. When his horse nickered softly, Cade looked over his shoulder as an old mare stepped out of the barn. She answered the greeting and placidly watched as they walked toward her.

Cade rubbed the side of her neck, chuckling as Mischief peered around him to inspect the newcomer. "Don't mind this ol' boy. He won't give you any trouble. Where did you come from?"

"Belongs to Quintin Webb's sister." Asa Noble, wagon boss of the McKinnon Ranch, eased his stocky frame over the fence and dropped to the ground, crossing the soft dirt inside the corral with a tired stride.

Cade looked at him in surprise. "Jessie?"

Asa nodded. "Her and the kids pulled in about four hours ago."

"So she finally left that no-account husband of hers."

Quintin had confided to Cade that his brother-in-law was a drunk, a cheat and a liar. He suspected he was a womanizer, as well. Quint had tried for years to get her to leave him, but she was a woman who believed in keeping her word—especially a vow made before God—even if her husband didn't.

"No. The little girl said he got killed. At first she couldn't remember how. Later she said he had some kind of accident. A tree fell on him or somethin'."

More likely shot for cheating at cards, Cade thought.

"Little Ellie is quite a talker. Pretty as a speckled pup, too. Tagged around after me for a spell, askin' all kinds of questions about cows and horses. Provided a bit more information."

"Such as?" Cade unsaddled Mischief, carrying his gear to the tack room.

Asa followed with the bridle. "That she's four, but will be five before long. Her brother, Brad, is nine, and her mama is old." He smiled ruefully. "But not as old as me."

Cade set the saddle and blanket on the stand as Asa hung up the bridle. He scooped up a bucket of oats before they went back outside.

"Didn't seem like her pa being dead bothered her none," said Asa. "Guess she's too little to really understand. The boy, now, he's another matter. Hardly said a word. Just watched me like a hawk around his sister. He did say that Miz Monroe had planned on Quintin helpin' her get settled some place. Reckon he didn't know they were comin'."

"Probably not." If he had, he would still be at the ranch. Not off trying to join a band of rustlers and help capture them. Neither Cade nor the sheriff had heard from him in the three weeks since he left. Hopefully, Quint was just being extra cautious, but they were worried about him.

The outlaws had almost killed an old friend of Quintin's

a week before he left, and he was bent on revenge. The sheriff convinced him that capturing the gang and stopping them before they actually murdered someone was the best retribution. Cade thought the plan was too risky, but they hadn't been able to come up with anything better. So they staged a fight, and he made a big show of firing Quint to lend credibility to his reasons for joining the rustlers.

In the corral, Cade poured the oats in a wooden trough and stepped over to the old mare while Mischief rolled in the dirt, soaking up the sweat from his run. The mare shifted a couple of steps, her joints creaking when she moved. Cade ran his hand along her bony shoulder. She was well cared for, but certainly not overfed. She reminded him of a fragile, elderly woman. "This lady got a name?"

"Yep. Valentine. Ellie said they'd had her as long as she could remember." Asa smiled, looking at the horse with respect. "Probably as long as her mama can remember, too. Reckon she just about used herself up gettin' here."

"Love and loyalty pulled that wagon, not strength."

Asa nodded. "She couldn't have gone much farther."

Cade agreed. "Any sign of Hercules?" He'd bought a prized Hereford bull, hoping to improve his herd, but the animal didn't appreciate being fenced in. He wanted to roam the range like the longhorns and choose his own ladies. Unfortunately, he hadn't limited his harem to cows bearing the McKinnon Ranch brand.

"Picked up his trail near the canyons, but lost it again in the rocks."

"He's goin' to wind up on the supper table."

Asa laughed, pulling off his hat and wiping his forehead on his sleeve. "That'd be a mighty high priced barbecue, boss."

Cade grimaced. "Too high. And that dang bull knows it. I'll go with you tomorrow. See you in the morning."

"You may change your mind." Asa glanced toward the ranch house.

"Why?"

"I wandered up to the house with the young'uns. Thought I'd take me a look-see at their mama."

"You would."

"In this country, a man has to take an opportunity when it comes along."

True. Single women were far and few between. "And?"

"It was worth the walk." Asa grinned as he started toward the gate. He glanced back over his shoulder. "Mighty fine lookin' female, even if I did just peek through the window." He turned around, walking backward. "If you take a hankerin' for her, you'd better stake your claim early."

Quint would have Cade's hide if he let anyone bother his sister. "Stay away from her. Tell the other men to do the same."

Asa glared at him. "You take all the fun out of life."

"Start actin' your age."

"I am actin' my age—all thirty-seven years of it. If I'm goin' to settle down with a wife, I'd better do it before I'm too stove up to enjoy it. You looked in the mirror lately, Cade? You ain't no young buck anymore yourself."

"I'm younger than you." By a whole two years, as if that meant much. He followed Asa out the corral gate. Cade wasn't about to admit that one reason he worked as hard as he did was so he could sleep at night instead of tossing and turning in his lonely, empty bed. He often stayed awake half the night, doing paperwork, reading or, just as likely, pacing the floor.

He stopped by the buggy shed to see if Jessie's wagon was as old as the horse. It was. Probably older. Bailing wire held the back end to the sides, and the seat tilted to the left. One wheel was slightly warped and another leaned at an odd angle, ready to break if it hit a rock just right. A homemade quilted pad covered the seat, but it was threadbare in places.

He lifted the heavy tarp covering the back and looked over Jessie Monroe's worldly goods, at least the ones she'd been able to bring with her. Cooking utensils, three bedrolls and pillows, a laundry tub, a couple of water buckets, several canteens, a small trunk, and boxes of dishes, linens, and other household items, along with a rocking chair. And one old but clean double-barreled shotgun. It wasn't much. The way things were piled in the boxes gave him the impression that they'd left in a big hurry. He frowned at the almost empty box of foodstuff. A couple of pieces of jerky and maybe enough beans for one meal—if they had small appetites.

Cade tucked the tarp back into place and headed for the house, sick at the thought of all the things that could have happened to someone so poorly equipped. Bad enough if it had been a man, but a woman traveling alone that way was unthinkable. Often days passed without anyone going along the main road. In places, it was a stretch to even call it a road. They could have been stranded without enough food or water, possibly even have died. The woman had to be stupid or desperate. Considering how Quintin bragged on his sister, she wasn't stupid.

Cade quietly walked up the back steps and stopped by the kitchen window, looking in. The children were sprawled on the floor, playing a game of checkers.

He let his gaze drift to the woman bending over the stove, taking a pan of cookies from the oven. Jessie Monroe was slim, and if the loose fit of her dress was any indication, she'd lost weight since it was made. Probably lost it on the trip.

Opening the door, he stepped into the room as she turned toward him and set the pan on a rack on the table. For a few seconds Cade couldn't move, then he pushed the door closed behind him, forcing himself not to stare. But he wanted to. Lord have mercy, how he wanted to.

Threads of pale gold glinted in her medium brown hair, coiled into a thick bun at the nape of her neck. A few little wispy curls had come loose, framing her face. He had the urge to slowly remove the pins one by one and comb his fingers through the shiny strands until they fell across her shoulders.

Her eyes were the same deep blue-gray as a thundercloud and, for an instant, as her gaze met his, just as turbulent. Did he see attraction in their depths? Or did he only wish for it? Her skin was smooth and lightly tanned, her cheeks slightly flushed from the warmth of the stove. Under his intense gaze, her color deepened. Regret nudged him for embarrassing her, and he looked away.

Cade pulled off his hat and hooked it on a peg by the door before looking back at her. He nodded politely and smiled. "Welcome to McKinnon Ranch, Mrs. Monroe."

She nervously wiped her hands on her apron. "Thank you."

The fragrance of the spicy cookies lingered in the room, and his stomach rumbled. "Those smell mighty good."

"They're oatmeal raisin. I hope you like them."

"One of my favorites." He didn't mention that he liked just about every kind of cookie he'd ever tried.

Jessie cleared her throat. "Your brother said we could spend the night and that you wouldn't mind providing the food if I cooked."

"I think I got the best part of that bargain." Cade grinned. "And after I've eaten, I suspect I'll appreciate it even more."

Brad moved to stand slightly in front of his mother, his stance tense, protective. The boy watched him closely, his expression guarded.

Cade crossed the room and held out his hand to him. "Cade McKinnon."

The boy hesitated, then shook his hand. "Brad Monroe."

He had a good firm handshake. Cade liked that. "Pleased to meet you."

He looked down at the little girl, thinking she was probably the most beautiful child he had ever seen. He squatted in front of her so his face was level with hers. "What's your name?"

"Ellen, but everybody calls me Ellie." A sparkle lit her large brown eyes and, when she smiled, two dimples appeared in her rosy cheeks.

Cade's heart melted into a big puddle. "A pretty name for a mighty pretty lady."

She giggled. "I'm not a lady. But Mama says I have to wear my company manners."

He heard Jessie take a soft, quick breath. He looked up and winked at her, then turned back to her daughter. "They're very nice manners."

"Thanks."

Cade's stomach growled, and Ellie giggled again. "Your tummy's noisy."

"Sure is. It's so empty, my belly button's rubbin' a blister on my backbone."

She laughed, wiggling a little in the process. "You'd better fill it up. Mama fixed a real good supper. We ain't had anything so good in a long time."

"Haven't, honey," Jessie corrected softly.

Ellie shrugged. "Well, it sure was good to eat something besides beans."

Cade chuckled as he stood.

Jessie glanced at her children. "I didn't know when you'd be here, so I had it ready about an hour ago. I hope you don't mind that we went ahead."

"Not a bit. I was later than usual. And it's not good to make hungry kids wait."

"I kept everything warm for you. I'll set it on the table while you wash up. Would you like coffee?"

"Yes, ma'am. Black." He turned to the washstand by the back door and rolled up his sleeves. Pouring water from the pitcher into the porcelain basin, he washed his hands and face. As he dried his face, he glanced in the foot-square mirror that hung at eye level. Brad asked Jessie if she wanted him to pour the coffee. Thanking him, she smiled at her son, her whole face lighting up. Cade was surprised and a little embarrassed by how much he wanted her to smile at him that way.

Drying his hands, he closed his eyes and listened to the comforting, homey sounds around him—the light click of Jessie's footsteps on the wooden floor, the muffled thumps as she took pans from the warming oven, and Ellie's crow of delight when she captured one of Brad's checkers while he was busy helping his mother.

Wondering why he had never noticed the soft swish of a skirt and petticoats as a woman moved around a kitchen, he opened his eyes and hung the towel on the washstand. Turning, he watched her go about putting his supper on the table. She worked quickly, but every movement was controlled to avoid noise. His former housekeeper had been a quick worker, too, but she hadn't cared how much racket she made. Whenever he was home, she had craved conversation to alleviate the boredom of living miles from the nearest neighbors.

He stood still a moment longer, heat racing through him.

If simply looking at her stirred such intense feelings, how would it be to touch her?

Walking across the room to the table, he pulled out the chair opposite his, pausing behind it. "Mrs. Monroe, why don't you come rest a spell. From the looks of this meal, you've been working for quite a while."

He moved around the table, waiting until Jessie sat down before he took his seat. "Asa said your husband had been killed. I'm sorry for your loss."

She murmured her thanks, not meeting his gaze.

He figured she didn't want to talk about it in front of the children. His mouth watered as he buttered a light-as-a-feather biscuit. He took a bite and almost groaned with pleasure. "Did y'all come all the way by yourselves?"

"Yes." The slight lifting of her chin told him she didn't want to hear how foolhardy she had been.

He frowned, tempering his words. "Dangerous." Especially for a woman as pretty as her.

She sighed. "Yes, it was. But we couldn't stay in Riverbend any longer." For a moment her thoughts seemed to drift, and pain filled her eyes.

"I understand." But he didn't, not completely. That brief expression and something in her tone indicated she'd had other reasons besides her husband's death for leaving East Texas. He ate a bite of ham hash, savoring the touch of onion and the crispy brown crust on the diced potatoes. "This is real tasty, ma'am. And the biscuits are the best I've ever eaten."

Jessie smiled, meeting his gaze. "Thank you."

Cade stared, a forkful of hash halfway to his mouth. Her face glowed softly as delicate color bloomed in her cheeks, like the mountain pinks that covered a rocky slope in late summer. Her eyes were no longer the dark blue-gray of a storm-tossed sky but had lightened to the blue of a clear summer day. Would her eyes be light and joyful when he kissed her, or would they grow dark with passion?

He came to his senses and poked the food into his mouth, chewing but barely tasting it. Unsettled, he focused his attention on his plate. When he kissed her. Not if. He'd never experienced such a strong reaction to a woman.

Lost in thought, he ate half a plate of food before he realized he was being rude. He looked up. Shoulders stooped in weariness, she methodically folded a dish towel into smaller and smaller squares. She had it down to six inches and seemed determined to make it three. Cade felt like a heel. She had to be bone tired and worrying herself sick, not only about Quint, but also wondering how she would provide for her family. And here he sat, thinking about things far less noble.

He laid the fork on the plate and relaxed against the back of the chair. "Mrs. Monroe, I expect you're probably anxious to find Quintin, but you and your family need a good rest. Why don't you stay here for a while, and I'll see if I can track him down."

Her hands stilled and she met his gaze, straightening her shoulders. "I can't take your charity, even though I thank you for the offer. I understand you are in need of a housekeeper. If you'll hire me, I'd welcome the opportunity." She clenched the dish towel and leaned forward, speaking softly. "I'm a hard worker, Mr. McKinnon. Your brother said the house next door came with the job, so I wouldn't expect much pay. It would be a big help, even though it's only temporary—until we find Quintin or you find someone else for the job."

Cade's heart constricted at the desperation in her eyes. *You don't have to beg, Jessie.* "The housekeeper's place is small. Only has three rooms."

"It's bigger than what we had." At the hasty admission, her face turned bright red.

"Would forty dollars a month plus room and board be agreeable?" The wage was high, equal to top pay for most cowboys, but he'd go even higher to keep Jessie Monroe around.

Eyes widening, she nodded. Relief and warmth flooded her face, and she whispered, "Thank you."

"I'll be the one to benefit. I'm a lousy cook." He thought of the mess in his bedroom. "And a worse house-keeper." He glanced around the room, noting the absence of the layer of dust that had covered everything for a couple of weeks. "But you've already noticed that." He smiled, holding her gaze. "And taken care of it."

She blushed again and shrugged lightly. "I just tidied up in here."

"I appreciate it. You'll need to sleep here for a few days. I gave just about everything that was in the little house to Nan when she got married. Saturday, we can go to town and get bedding and furniture. The house will probably need some cleaning, too."

Jessie laughed. "I've worked as a housekeeper and cook since I was fifteen. I'm good at cleaning."

Even if she wasn't, it would still be worth every cent to make certain she and the children were safe. He owed it to Quint.

She relaxed against the back of the chair with a grin. "You don't know how nice it will be not to sleep on the ground."

Cade chuckled and picked up his fork. "Oh, yes, ma'am, I do. Most cowboys would never own up to it, but person-ally, I'll take a comfortable bed over the hard ground most any time."

As her musical laughter floated around him, Cade pictured her smiling up at him, her lovely face framed by the soft white pillow on his bed. His throat went dry, and he silently admitted that his friendship with her brother had little to do with wanting to keep Jessie Monroe within arm's reach.

Chapter Three

Jessie pulled the sheet up over Ellie's shoulder, smiling as her sleeping daughter burrowed down in the middle of the soft mattress. Brad was already settled in the front bedroom. Though he had muttered something about not being able to sleep on something so soft, he'd been snoring lightly before she'd closed his door.

Turning down the coal-oil lamp on the nightstand, she left enough light to find her way around the room when she came to bed. She paused at the doorway, listening to Ellie's slow, even breathing, her heart catching at the sweetness of the sound.

She went into the front room, hoping to speak with her new employer, but the room was empty, the lamps blown out for the night. She assumed Cade had gone to bed until she noticed a lamp turned low in the kitchen, casting its soft light through the window onto the back porch.

Jessie spotted him standing by the porch railing, eating a cookie. Her brother had mentioned that he was a powerful man, not only in status but also in size. Still she had not expected him to hover around six foot two, plus another inch or so with his boots on. He had broad shoulders and a large frame to match.

In a rugged way, he was one of the most handsome men she had ever met. When he had arrived home and stepped into the kitchen, it hadn't mattered that a light layer of sweat and dust covered his face and clothes. Or that his hat had smashed his short, dark brown hair, leaving it with an unsightly crease. Her breath had caught at the sight of him.

After he ate, Cade took a pitcher of hot water into his room, emerging a few minutes later wearing a crisply ironed white shirt, his damp hair neatly combed. For a heartbeat, he had looked into Jessie's eyes, as if seeking her approval.

She shook her head ruefully. After the misery Neil put her through, how could she be attracted to another man? She didn't want to be. Yet her heart quickened at the memory of the heat in Cade's green eyes when he first looked at her. The desire that sprang to life beneath his intense gaze surprised and amazed her. Obviously, she wasn't as cold and useless as her husband had thought.

But you'd do well to pretend you are. And to remember that he is your boss.

Intent on asking him about Quintin, she went out to the porch, quietly closing the door. The chilly breeze surprised her, until she noticed lightning in the distance.

Cade turned with a smile. "The kids asleep already?"

She nodded. "They're both worn-out."

He leaned back against the railing, resting his hands on the wood. His gaze moved over her before settling on her face. "You look a mite weary yourself."

"It was a hard trip." She stood beside him, watching the approaching storm, careful to keep a wide space between them.

"You're lucky you made it."

"Yes, we were. God was gracious." She thought of a

few times when nothing else could have saved them from disaster. "Do you know where Quintin is?"

"No. I wish I did. He should know you're here." He sighed heavily. "I miss him. He's a good worker and a good friend."

"Then why did you fire him?" she asked, unable to hide her irritation.

"The danged fool didn't give me any choice. He was upset because an old friend of his, Jack Shepherd, was nearly killed by rustlers. Jack has a small ranch north of town. He's an old-timer Quint rode with when he first went to cowboyin'. Your brother had been snarling all week, almost locked horns several times with some of the other men. I knew better than to send him out with anybody. Someone would come back bloody. So I told him to go clear brush down by the river. Figured chopping wood might work off some of his anger."

Cade turned around, looking up at the stars. "But he didn't agree. He demanded that I send him out to move cattle instead." A sad smile flickered across his face. "I told him he was too riled up, that he'd ride all the fat off them. I figured he'd realize I was joshin' him, but he blew up. Punched me in the jaw."

"I don't understand it. Quintin doesn't usually act that way."

"No, he doesn't. If we'd been by ourselves, I would've taken him down and sat on him, and that'd been the end of it."

"But he challenged you in front of the men."

Cade searched her face in the faint light. "They all know we're good friends, but I'm still the boss. On something like this, I have to treat him just like I would anybody else."

"I expect he knows that, at least now that he's cooled off."

"I hope so. I sure hated knocking him out."

Jessie caught her breath. "You hit him?"

"Just a tap." He rubbed the back of his neck, his expression sheepish. "Well, a little harder than that. Otherwise, he would've kept pounding on me. I don't like being punched any more than the next guy."

Her husband's angry face flashed through her mind. Shouted curses and a hard shove. Raised fists. Mindnumbing fear. Agonizing pain...

A wave of nausea rolled through her. She gripped the railing, fighting down the bile that rose in her throat. Cade was much stronger; his hands much larger. She pictured her brother's face covered with blood and bruises, so swollen that it looked inhuman. It took a moment before she could whisper, "Did you break anything?"

Cade frowned. "I didn't hit him that hard."

But you could have, she thought, understanding what he left unsaid.

He studied her face. "Why didn't you let Quintin know you wanted to move out here? I would have given him as much time off as he needed to travel with you."

She looked into his discerning eyes, then quickly glanced away. She doubted he missed much. "Ellie thinks her daddy was killed when a tree fell on him, but he wasn't. He was shot."

"Card game?"

She shook her head and swallowed hard. "No."

"An angry husband?"

She barely contained a gasp. Had Neil been right? Was it her fault that he needed other women? Was she so lacking that even a stranger could see it?

"Yes," she whispered, choked by pain and embarrassment.

"I understand how difficult it must have been."

No, he didn't. He couldn't.

"But you should have gone somewhere else and sent for Quint. Taking off across Texas in a dilapidated wagon, pulled by a half-dead horse is bad enough." His irritation surprised her. "Coming by yourselves, without protection or adequate provisions was just plain stupid. You don't seem like a woman who would put her children in danger, but you did. And yourself, too."

How dare he judge her. Hurt and shame gave way to indignation.

Glaring, Jessie turned toward him, crossing her arms. "I didn't have any choice. The mayor caught him in bed with his wife and shot him on the spot. The whole town was in an uproar. Ellie is too young to understand the gossip, but Brad isn't. It was tearing him apart."

And her, too.

Cade straightened and faced her, moving closer. Silhouetted against the lantern light, he loomed over her. "You should have sent for your brother." A thread of anger vibrated in his low voice.

She couldn't see his face clearly but easily imagined his scowl. Fear shot through her. Heart pounding, Jessie stepped back, only to be stopped at the end of the porch by another railing. When he lifted his hand, she reacted automatically. Bringing her hands up to protect her face, she turned her head, scrunched up her shoulders and braced for the first blow.

"Good Lord..."

She barely heard his ragged whisper above the roar in her ears. He touched her arm, and she flinched, jerking backward, slamming against the railing.

"Jessie, I'm not going to hurt you." He spoke quietly, his tone deep and soothing. "You don't ever have to be afraid of me. I've never hit a woman in my life."

After a few seconds his words sank in, but overcoming the fear took a little longer. Relief, clouded by embarrassment, washed through her. Lowering her trembling hands, she hid them in the folds of her skirt and straightened, looking out into the darkness. Anywhere but at him. She hadn't been able to hide what Neil had done to her. Most people had viewed her with pity or scorn. She couldn't bear to see either in Cade's eyes.

"You looked cold." His voice dropped even lower. "I only moved closer to block the wind."

A simple, thoughtful act by a kind and considerate man.

"And swatted at a mosquito." He sighed. "I'm sorry, Jessie. I know my size bothers people sometimes."

Tears of humiliation stung her eyes. How could she have been such an idiot? "I'm the one who should apologize. You haven't given me any reason to believe you would hurt me. I'm just tired and not thinking straight."

"Who did this to you?"

She shook her head, not wanting to admit that the man who had once professed to love her had grown to despise her. If she'd somehow done better, maybe Neil would have, too.

"Who hurt you, Jessie?"

She was so angry with herself she wanted to scream. Why couldn't she have acted normally and hidden the sordidness of her life from him? She'd dreamed of starting over here and leaving the past behind them. But if she kept behaving like this, she would destroy any chance of that.

He waited patiently. Finally she worked past the tightness in her throat. "My husband."

"Why did you stay with him? You know Quintin would have helped you."

She forced herself to look at him. Confusion mingled with tenderness in his face. His fingers twitched, as if he wanted to touch her but was afraid to. To her surprise, she realized she wanted him to wrap his arms around her and cradle her against his wide, solid chest. She yearned to lose herself in his strength, to lean on him for just a moment. *I barely know him.* That didn't stop the longing.

She turned toward the yard, averting her face lest he read her thoughts. "I couldn't tell Quint. If he knew Neil had hit me, he would have killed him. The sheriff is my husband's cousin. When Neil was killed, he wouldn't go against the mayor and jeopardize his own career. But if Quintin had done it, he would have seen to it that he was hanged, with or without a trial."

Cade lightly gripped her shoulders and carefully turned her to face him. Fury glittered in his eyes, but she sensed it was not directed at her. "According to the law, a woman doesn't have to stay with a cruel or indecent man. Quintin suspected your husband was running around on you. That was reason enough for you to leave and for him to help you."

Mortified, Jessie could barely speak. "He knew about the women?"

Cade nodded.

"But I never told him."

He brushed his thumb back and forth across her collarbone. "Quintin heard rumors when he visited you, but he didn't want to mention it to you unless he knew it was true. He didn't want to hurt you with only suspicions, and he couldn't prove it. Evidently, your husband temporarily mended his ways when he was around. Quint had a hard talk with him, but it obviously didn't do any good."

Jessie closed her eyes against the pain. How long had her brother known? How long had her foolish pride and guilt kept her and her children in torment when they didn't have to be?

"Neil liked to gamble and drink. Gradually he spent more and more evenings away from home, then all night." She shrugged, staring blankly at a button on Cade's shirt.

"At first he stayed at the saloons. Later there were a couple of widows and a string of married women." She hadn't needed to wait for the gossip to learn about them. He liked to brag about how much better he was in bed than their husbands. And how much better at everything the other women were than her. "He always had a hot temper, but he didn't hit me until six months ago."

Cade tightened his fingers on her shoulders, but there was only strength in his touch, not pain. "How bad did he hurt you?"

"Split my lip and bloodied my nose." She hung her head. "Gave me two black eyes. I thought for a few days that he had broken my jaw. But it healed up pretty quick. He didn't hit me any more after that. Just threatening me was enough."

He eased his arms around her and drew her close. "No woman should have to put up with that kind of mistreatment." He held her against him with one hand, lightly running his other hand up and down her back.

Jessie didn't resist, though she knew she should. Turning her head, she rested her cheek against his chest and listened to the strong, steady beat of his heart. His warmth surrounded her, chasing away the chill of the evening, whispering against the cold, empty shadows of her soul. How could such a big man's touch be so gentle?

She'd tried to be strong, protecting her children from Neil, working hard to pay their bills, and holding on to her dignity when it was all she had. But in the end, he had destroyed that, too.

Was it wrong to take Cade's comfort, to cherish the healing balm of tenderness? Would he read too much in her acceptance of his embrace and think she was offering him more? Or was she so jaded by men that she expected all of them to yield to their baser natures? Over the past few years, she'd lost count of the men who had been all too willing to console her by sharing her bed.

Even as she worried about what he might think, desire slowly coiled through her, filling her with a sweet hunger she had never known. The movement of his hand stilled, and his muscles tensed slightly. Beneath her ear, his heartbeat quickened. She thought she heard him whisper her name, but perhaps it was only a trick of the wind.

Her lonely heart told her to stay within the warm circle of his arms, but common sense ordered her to move away. She straightened, and when she pushed lightly against his chest, he released her, although she sensed his reluctance.

"I tried to leave him after I healed."

Cade stepped back, stuffing his hands into his pockets. "Why did you go back to him?"

"He sent the sheriff after me for stealing the horse and wagon."

"That's illegal. This is a community property state."

"The wagon and horse were his before we were married, so I had no legal claim to them." She drew a shaky breath. "The sheriff hauled me back and threw me in jail. I was there for two weeks before the judge came to town. Neil brought the children to see me every day. Not out of kindness, but because he knew it would make Ellie cry when I couldn't hold her or go home with them." Her voice cracked, and she turned toward the yard, gazing at the lightning as it moved closer. "I could only touch her sweet face through the bars. Brad never cried. He never begged me to come home. He just looked at me with a sadness no child should ever know.

"At my trial, the judge said if I didn't go back to my husband, he'd send me to prison for five years for theft and kidnapping. He wanted to make an example of me, so other wives wouldn't think they could take their children and walk out on their husbands."

"That judge ought to be horsewhipped. And the sheriff, too." Cade jerked his hands free, curling them into fists. "It's a shame that sorry excuse for a husband got himself killed. Right this minute, I think I could put a plug in him myself."

"Neil wasn't always bad. Our first few years together were reasonably happy. But he changed after I had Brad. Started going to the saloon more often. He became worse after Ellie was born. I think he resented them."

"You couldn't cater to his every whim," he said in disgust, though he relaxed his fingers. "Children take time and energy. They need plenty of love and attention."

Jessie sighed. "So does a husband." The same thoughts and doubts had churned through her mind for years. "If I'd tried harder to show him more love and attention, maybe he wouldn't have been so unhappy."

"With a growing family, a man has to change, too. How could you possibly do things like you did before you had children? Were you working for someone else, too?"

"Yes. Neil's job wasn't steady, so I cleaned houses two or three days a week. A neighbor watched the kids for me. When Ellie was a year old, I got a full-time housekeeping job." She looked up at him. "For the mayor and his wife."

Shock flashed across his face. "You were still working for them when he shot your husband?"

"Yes. For once, Neil hadn't told me about his latest conquest. I guess, trying to keep me from finding out made it that much more exciting for both him and Mrs. Drake.'' She laughed derisively, the sound brittle with pain. ''It was two days before payday, but I couldn't bring myself to go ask for my wages.''

He reached toward her, then pulled his hand back, resting it on the rail instead. ''So you were broke.''

''Almost. I didn't have enough to stay anywhere else. Since we had to live out of the wagon, I figured it might as well be moving. I just wanted to get as far away from there as I could.'' She sighed softly, sadness filling her heart. ''I should have stayed for Neil's funeral. Someday, Brad will regret that he wasn't there.''

''I doubt it. Like you said, he's old enough to understand what was going on. You were right not to put him through any more misery. When he's older, he'll find his way back there if he needs to. Judging from the way he tries to protect you, he doesn't hold much love for his father.''

''Neil never gave him any reason to.''

They stood quietly for a few minutes, watching the lightning dance across the sky. He gently laid his hand on her shoulder. ''You should get some sleep. That storm is headed our way, so we'll be awake again in an hour or so.''

''Ellie is terrified of thunderstorms.'' Jessie closed her eyes for a heartbeat, focusing on his touch. ''She's always been afraid of them, but it's worse now. An awful storm hit one night while we were camped out in the middle of nowhere. We all hid under the wagon, praying that the lightning wouldn't hit us or Valentine.''

''She should feel safer inside the house.''

''Maybe.''

He slanted her a glance. ''You don't think that will help?''

"I hope so. When she's really upset, she doesn't just cry. She screams." Sometimes the child kept it up for hours, but Jessie didn't think it prudent to mention that. They might wind up in the little house without a bed after all.

"Then you'd better rest while you can."

Jessie glanced at the storm cloud with a sigh. It would be a long night. "I hope she doesn't bother you too much."

"She won't. I'll be busy watching the storm."

The man obviously had not spent much time around frightened little girls. Jessie eased away and turned toward the door.

"Jessie…"

She looked up, halting at the tenderness and compassion in his beautiful green eyes.

"Most of us have things in our past we'd like to keep there," he said quietly. "I won't tell Quintin, or anyone else, about what happened tonight or about your husband hitting you.

"I don't expect that anyone around here will give you any trouble." A smile teased the corners of his mouth. "Women are so scarce, men hold them in high regard. But if anyone bothers you for any reason, you tell me." A strand of hair blew across her cheek, and he brushed it aside with his fingertip, lingering a second longer than necessary. A tingle rippled across her skin and her heart skipped a beat. "I'll take care of it."

"Thank you." She had the notion that he could take care of just about anything—except what troubled her most. She didn't know if even Cade McKinnon could mend a broken heart or heal a battered soul.

Two hours later, Cade stuck his index finger in his ear and wiggled it, wondering if his ears would ever stop ring-

ing. He had been eyeball to eyeball with snarling mountain
lions that didn't shriek as loud as one tiny girl.

Ellie had been at it for a good half hour. Lightning lit
up the living room, and thunder rattled the windows. She
let loose with another wail that would have sent a weaker
man hightailing it to the bunkhouse.

"At this rate, we'll all go deaf," he muttered, stomping
across the floor and knocking on Jessie's bedroom door.
Scowling when she didn't answer, he pounded again, almost shaking it from the hinges. Seconds later, the door
flew open. One look at Jessie's wide, frightened eyes made
him feel like a heel. "Sorry, I didn't figure you'd hear a
normal knock."

"I couldn't." Shifting her sobbing daughter to her other
shoulder, Jessie sighed, patting the little girl's back.

Lightning flashed, and Jessie tensed. So did Cade. As the
thunder rumbled overhead, Ellie screamed, tightening her
arms around her mother's neck. "Shh, honey, it's only
thunder. It won't hurt us."

Cade studied the trembling child and her mother's hag-
gard expression. She looked ready to drop. "Let me take
her for a while."

"That's okay." Jessie watched him warily, turning sideways to put her daughter out of his reach.

Though she seemed to move without thinking, Cade
hated the fear and distrust in her eyes. "Jessie, let me
help."

Two small red circles blazed in her pale cheeks. She
looked down at the floor. "I don't know if she'll go to
you."

Cade stepped into the room and rested his hand on the
child's back, leaning over until he could see her face. She
clung to Jessie, her eyes squeezed shut, breathing in shuddering little sniffs. "Ellie, will you let me hold you for a

while?'' When she didn't respond, Cade caressed her soft cheek with his thumb. "Sweetheart, your mama is plumb wore-out. Would you let me rock you?''

Ellie opened her eyes, staring forlornly at him.

He tipped his head and smiled at her. He pointed toward the rocking chair in the corner of the front room and the lamp burning nearby. "We can sit out here, and I'll sing to you. Songs cowboys sing to the cattle so the critters won't be scared of the storm.''

Ellie raised her head, studied him for a minute, then leaned toward him, holding out her arms. A swell of emotion took him by surprise, and he wondered how he could teach her mama to accept him with childlike trust. Cade carefully lifted her and cleared the lump from his throat. He glanced at Jessie. She looked dumbfounded. He settled Ellie comfortably in his arms, her head nestled against his shoulder, and walked toward the rocker. As they reached it, the lightning and thunder hit once more.

Ellie shrieked and began sobbing all over again. Murmuring gentle words into her ear, Cade rubbed her back and sat down. He rested his cheek against her dark brown curls and started to sing quietly, rocking in rhythm with the song.

Jessie followed them into the room and sank down on the sofa, curling her bare feet up on the cushion beneath her skirt. She hadn't changed into her nightclothes, though she had unpinned her hair and brushed it. Cade wanted to sift his fingers through the thick strands, starting at her temple and ending at the soft waves curling around her waist. He ached to smooth away the lines of worry on her brow and reassure her that, like the storm and her daughter's fear, the heartache of her past would fade away.

By the time he finished the third verse of "Goodbye, Old Paint," Ellie had quit sobbing, but she still breathed in little gasping sniffs. He brushed a kiss on her forehead, thinking how the tiny, frightened sprite had captured a place in his heart. Looking at Jessie, he saw tears glisten in her eyes. So he composed a few more verses to the song, silly nonsense that made her smile.

Then he sang "Colorado Trail," holding her gaze with his, changing the girl's name in the song to one he liked better.

> "Eyes like the morning star,
> Cheeks like a rose,
> Jessie is a pretty girl,
> God almighty knows."

When she blushed, he winked and continued singing.

Ellie's breathing slowed until it became normal. He shifted her a bit, and she mumbled, "More." So he obliged her with one he had learned trailing a herd to Kansas.

> "Whoopee ti-yi-yo, git along little dogies,
> It's your misfortune and none of my own,
> Whoopee ti-yi-yo, git along little dogies,
> For you know Montana will be your new home."

Long before he reached the last chorus, the child was sound asleep, her breath warming his neck, her small hand curled against his jaw. He looked at Jessie, wanting to share the precious moment.

She, too, was sound asleep, her head resting on the arm of the sofa. The lamplight caught the blond in her hair until it shone like spun gold. The worry lines had vanished from her forehead, leaving her face soft and inviting. Did she have any idea how beautiful she was? He doubted it. A

woman needed to be told of her beauty, needed it to be
appreciated by her man.

He rocked Ellie a while longer, indulging in the opportunity to look at her mama. Jessie frowned in her sleep,
making a tiny sound of anguish in her throat. Did she dream
of her husband? Of the pain he had inflicted, both physical
and emotional? Or did some unspoken fear haunt her?

He had made a bit of headway toward earning her trust,
but what would she do when she learned he was lying to
her? He couldn't tell her that he had faked the fight with
her brother or that firing him had merely been for show. It
would only worry her more if she knew what Quint was
doing, and the knowledge might put her in danger. Even if
she understood his reasons, his deception could destroy
what little faith she had in him.

The best he could do for now was watch over her and
her family, be alert for anyone who might pose a threat to
them. Including himself. He wanted Jessie Monroe, pure
and simple. But she wasn't the kind of woman to be a
man's mistress. Nor was he the kind of man to have one.
He had always scoffed at the notion of love at first sight—
until he opened the back door, looked into Jessie's beautiful
eyes and saw the other half of his soul.

He figured she'd laugh in his face if he suggested such
a thing, though he could tell she was attracted to him. After
what she had been through, she wouldn't be all that interested in marrying again. And with something as important
as a wife and family, he should move slowly, even when
he didn't want to.

She was as skittish as a new colt and as distrustful as a
whipped pup. Gentleness and patience would be crucial to
winning her trust and her heart. He could handle gentleness.
Patience was another thing entirely. Once he made up his

mind about something, he usually stormed ahead like a herd of stampeding longhorns. He'd have to work on that.

He rose and carried Ellie into the bedroom. Laying her on the bed, Cade pulled the sheet and blanket up, tucking them around her shoulders. He kissed her forehead, smiling when she wiggled and pulled her arms out from underneath the covers.

Going back to the parlor, he stopped beside the sofa, looking down at Jessie, and felt a twinge of regret. He shouldn't have watched her for so long. Come morning, she was liable to have a crick in her neck. Maybe he'd offer to rub it out. She would politely refuse, but he would insist. He grinned, anticipating winning that small battle.

He leaned down and carefully slid one arm beneath her back and the other under her knees. He held his breath and straightened slowly, lifting her from the sofa. When she didn't awaken, he exhaled in relief and cradled her against his chest. She laid her head on his shoulder and curled her hand around his neck, sighing softly.

He stood there for a minute, savoring the feeling of her in his arms. Walking as quietly as he could, he carried her toward the bedroom.

Her eyelids fluttered, and she looked up at him in sleepy confusion. "Cade?"

"You fell asleep on the sofa." He stopped beside the bed but was in no hurry to put her down. "I didn't want to wake you."

"Mmm." She yawned and snuggled closer, her hair brushing his jaw.

Pleasure spiraled through him, though he figured she would be mortified if she realized what she was doing. He held her a moment longer. "The storm is over, and Ellie's all tucked in, sleeping like a little angel."

He reluctantly laid her down, taking delight in how slowly she withdrew her hand from around his neck.

"Thank you," she mumbled as he pulled the cover up to her waist.

Pausing, he touched a lock of her hair. "You're welcome."

He blew out the lamp and waited for his eyes to adjust to the darkness. The storm had passed, and moonlight frolicked across the bed, illuminating Jessie's face in a soft glow.

Cade caught his breath. Eyes closed, her lips parted slightly in sleep, she was almost more of a temptation than he could resist. He smoothed the back of his knuckles along her jaw. At her tiny sound of pleasure, he lightly brushed his thumb across her lips and felt a jolt all the way to his toes.

"Good night, darlin'," he whispered, and walked quietly from the room. As he pulled the door closed, he heard her soft gasp.

He didn't wait around for her to sort things out.

Chapter Four

Jessie awoke to the warmth of sunshine on her face. Curled up on her side, she lay still for a moment, enjoying the comfort of the mattress and the fresh, clean scent of the pillowcase. Ellie slept soundly on the other side of the bed, her arm wrapped around one corner of the pillow.

Turning over onto her back, Jessie smiled and stretched her arms above her head, breathing the pleasant aroma of coffee and bacon. *Coffee? Bacon?* "Merciful heavens!"

She threw off the sheet and light blanket, scrambling from the bed. Grabbing a clean pair of stockings from her satchel, she plopped down on the ladder-back chair beside the washstand and pulled them on. She shoved her feet into the boots she had worn on the journey, though her high-button shoes would have been more appropriate for working inside.

"Working?" she mumbled as she stood and poured cold water from the pitcher into the basin on the washstand. Splashing her face, she jerked the towel off the rod and wiped the sleep from her eyes. "I'll be lucky if I still have a job."

Hanging up the towel, she winced at a twinge in her neck. She'd gotten used to having all sorts of kinks in the

morning from sleeping on the ground, but hadn't expected
one from a good bed. As her gaze fell on her image in the
mirror above the washstand, she realized it probably hadn't
been from the bed at all. The last thing she remembered
clearly was curling up on the sofa, laying her head against
the arm of it, listening as Cade sang to Ellie.

And to her. His gentleness with Ellie had touched her
deeply, but other memories brought heat to her cheeks. His
smile and wink as he substituted her name in the song,
calling her "a pretty girl." The solid strength of his chest
and arms when he carried her to bed, as if she weighed no
more than her child. The hint of soap on his skin. The warm
whisper of his breath on her cheek, and the faint tug on her
hair as it brushed across the light stubble of his beard. Jessie
closed her eyes in dismay. Had she really snuggled closer?

Oh, yes. And she had wanted to stay there.

She stared in the mirror at her rumpled dress and disheveled hair, which she usually controlled with a loose
braid at night. Picking up her brush, she tugged it through
her hair, grimacing at a stubborn tangle.

Surely she had only dreamed the touch of his thumb on
her lips, a caress so like a kiss that even now it quickened
her heart. Of course, he hadn't called her "darlin'." That,
too, had been a dream, hadn't it?

Quiet humming came from the kitchen, a cheerful tune
in a beautiful deep voice. How could a man be so happy
cooking his own breakfast when he had hired a housekeeper
the night before?

Because he's not thinking about breakfast.

Jessie groaned softly. She should be angry with him for
taking such liberties, not wishing he would touch her again.
Gathering up her hair, she twisted it into a knot at the nape
of her neck, angrily jabbing the hairpins into place. "Quit

acting like a love-starved old maid," she whispered. "You fell for a sweet-talkin' man once. Don't do it again."

Cade wasn't anything like her husband, but he could still hurt her. Any man could. She didn't know if she had the strength to survive another broken heart.

Squaring her shoulders, Jessie walked out of the bedroom, closing the door softly behind her. She took a deep, fortifying breath, cutting across the corner of the living room and through the doorway into the kitchen.

"Good morning." He set his empty plate in the dry sink and looked up with a smile, the warmth in his eyes making her heart do a little shuffle step.

"Good morning." She picked up an empty cup from the table, moved to the stove and poured a cup of coffee.

He leaned against the dry sink, holding his coffee cup, and watched as she savored her first sip. "I left you some bacon but figured you'd want to cook your own eggs."

"Thank you." She peeked into the warming oven, her mouth watering at the plate of crisp bacon sitting there. "Mr. McKinnon, I believe you lied to me."

Frowning, he met her gaze, concern flickering through his eyes. "Why?"

"You said you couldn't cook."

Relief swept across his face. "I can manage coffee, bacon and eggs. It's everything else that gives me trouble, including biscuits. All we have this morning is bread from the bakery in town."

"A nice change from biscuits." Until last night, Jessie and the kids hadn't even had biscuits in over two weeks. She couldn't remember the last time they had bakery bread. "I'm sorry you had to cook your own breakfast. It won't happen again. I usually wake up at the crack of dawn."

"Not a problem." The corner of his lip twitched. "I left you the dishes. Besides, you had a rough night."

"So did you."

"Once my ears quit ringing, it was pretty nice."

She didn't dare let him know that she agreed. "I appreciate you helping me with Ellie."

"I'm glad I could."

She smiled up at him. "She likes you."

"I kind of figured that." His smile held a hint of pride. "I like both your kids, though Ellie's such a charmer I don't think anyone could resist her."

No one but her father, Jessie thought bitterly. At least he had simply ignored her. It could have been worse. He could have taken a razor strop to her like he had Brad. Thankfully, most of the time, even that had been more of an effort than he wanted to make.

"She can be a little scamp, but a lovable one."

"I can imagine." He set his cup beside the empty plate. "I probably won't be in until supper time. We have to go look for a wayward bull."

"Did he run off during the storm?"

"No, he's been gone for a few days. He's a prize Hereford. I had a good-sized pen fenced off for him, but he keeps breaking out. He wants to wander with the other cattle. Unfortunately, he isn't particular about the company he keeps."

"How will you keep him here once you find him?"

"Build a bigger pasture and use barbed wire this time instead of wood." He paused, his expression thoughtful. "Some folks won't like that, but Ty and I have been thinking that we should start fencing the ranch. Keeping our herd contained—and other cattle out—is the only way to improve our stock. A few of the bigger ranches are stringing wire, so we won't be the first. But we'll ease into it, just the same."

Feeling the twinge in her neck again, she rotated her

shoulders, then leaned her head to one side, trying to stretch it.

"Sore neck?"

"A little."

"Want me to try to rub the kink out?"

Her heart took a little leap. "No, thanks. It's feeling better already. Guess I'm not used to a real bed."

"I shouldn't have let you sleep so long using the arm of the sofa for a pillow."

"You were busy with Ellie."

"I could have put her to bed sooner." He hesitated, his gaze moving over her face like a caress, settling on her mouth.

Longing stole her breath, and she quickly lowered her head to keep him from seeing her reaction.

He slowly raised his hand, lightly nudging her chin upward with his knuckle until she looked into his eyes. "But I was watching you. Do you have any idea how beautiful you are?"

"Cade, don't..." she whispered.

"Don't tell the truth?"

Don't tempt me. She closed her eyes for a heartbeat, then stepped back, away from his touch, away from the invisible web of desire and loneliness threatening to trap them both.

Jessie turned to the table, picked up a long knife and cut off a slice of bread from the loaf sitting there. "Is there anything in particular you want done in the house today?"

"No." He walked over to a cabinet and took out a jar of jerky. She watched him from the corner of her eye, relieved when he didn't seem angry. He removed a few pieces of the dried meat and wrapped them in a small cloth. "We'll be going to town tomorrow, so you should tend to your house today. It will need a good sweeping. There are probably some cobwebs, too. Nan washed the windows and curtains before she left.''

''I need to do our laundry, so I'll do yours, too.''

''I take mine to the Chinese laundry in town.''

She waved away the notion. ''There's no need for that.''

''Yes, there is.''

''Mr. McKinnon, I'm perfectly capable of doing your laundry.''

He frowned and crossed the room, stopping in front of her. ''A minute ago you called me Cade. I like that better.''

So did she, but she would be wiser to keep things more formal. ''It was highly improper of me. You're my employer.''

He smiled ruefully. ''I'm aware of that, ma'am.''

''Then you'll do well to remember it.'' She pointed her nose in the air—which unfortunately only meant she was looking right up at him—and pursed her lips in what she hoped was a reproachful expression.

A devilish twinkle lit his eyes. ''That'll be a mite difficult if you keep puckerin' up for a kiss.''

''I do not want to kiss you!'' It took a great deal of effort to keep her voice low. Heaven forbid they wake the children.

''Liar,'' he murmured.

''That was a prudish look.''

''Fooled me.'' His expression changed to the picture of innocence.

She felt the tug of laughter and finally gave in, grinning at him. ''Well, it worked for the banker's wife.''

''Let me guess—tall, skinny and a face like a horse?''

She nodded, deciding to relax and enjoy their banter. ''That's her.''

''I can see where she could pull it off. But you bring to mind something else entirely.'' He tilted his head thoughtfully. "Of course, maybe that's because I've been studying on it for a spell already."

Warmth flooded her face. "You have better things to do."

He chuckled and shook his head. "Can't think of any."

She was digging herself in deeper by the second. "Go find your bull, Mr. McKinnon. I have work to tend to."

He sighed, looking hound-dog mournful. "I'd much rather stay here and pester you."

She laughed in spite of herself. "I'm sure you would."

"But I reckon I'd better head out before Asa starts speculatin' as to why I'm taking so long." He strolled to the back door and plucked his hat from the rack. When he opened the door, he paused, looking back. "Though, in a way, it's all his fault."

She moved toward him so they could carry on the conversation quietly. "Why?"

"He told me if I took a hankering to you, I'd better stake my claim early." He eased the hat on his head and walked outside.

"Of all the arrogant..." Jessie sputtered for a second before following him, closing the door behind her. He waited on the porch, his back to the railing, arms crossed, calm as you please. Settling her hands on her hips, she glared at him. "I'll have you know, Cade McKinnon, that I'm not a stray cow you can just claim."

"I'd never compare you to a cow, Jessie." His lazy smile aggravated her even more. "You're more like a pretty little mustang mare, running wild and free."

"Who wants to stay that way."

"Even a mustang doesn't like to be alone."

"So she's supposed to follow the first stallion who nickers sweet nothings and nuzzles her neck?" A sudden image sprang to mind—Cade lifting her hair away from her open collar with one powerful hand; the other at her waist, his touch firm yet gentle through the calico. Tiny kisses down her neck and throat, soft lips and warm breath against her skin. Jessie shivered, her mouth going dry.

Cade glanced at her throat and groaned softly. When he looked up, an unmistakable fire burned in his eyes. He straightened, shifting away from the rail. "No, she has a choice. He has to gain her interest and prove that he can provide for her and protect her. But he also has to let the other males know he wants her. Stake his claim." He leaned toward her, sliding one hand around her waist. "And fight to keep it, or one of them might steal her away."

He was going to kiss her. Right out here in the open. It was foolish, but heaven help her, she wanted him to. She raised her hand—whether to push him away or draw him closer, she honestly didn't know.

A discreet cough and the creak of saddle leather stopped him. Startled, Jessie looked toward the yard to find a horse and rider waiting nearby. It was the same man who had helped the children with the wagon the day before. He led another saddled horse, obviously for Cade.

Cade muttered a mild oath and slowly raised his head, releasing her. He looked so disgusted Jessie didn't know what to say.

He turned toward the rider, but she noted that he stayed close to her. "Mrs. Monroe, this is Asa Noble, wagon boss of the McKinnon Ranch. Asa, this is Mrs. Jessie Monroe."

The cowboy nodded politely. "Welcome to West Texas, ma'am."

"Thank you. I appreciate you helping Brad yesterday and watching Ellie for a while. They enjoyed it."

"So did I. They're fine youngsters. Real polite." Asa looked at Cade. "You ready to go, boss?"

"In a minute. I'll meet you at the barn." Cade's irritation

was obvious. He waited until the other man nodded, turned the horses around and moved away. He shifted so that his back was to Asa, blocking the cowboy from her view, and her from his, which she figured was more his intention.

"Jessie, I'm sorry for embarrassing you. Asa usually waits in the bunkhouse or at the corrals. I never really thought he would come up here." A tiny wry smile touched his face. "Guess I wasn't thinking much at all, except about how much I want to kiss you."

Want. Not wanted. "You barely know me."

"Quint talked about you so often I feel we've been acquainted for a long time."

"He talked about you, too." When she thought about it, she knew a great deal about Cade McKinnon, most of it admirable. But that didn't mean she wanted any kind of relationship with him other than as her employer. She glanced up at his handsome face and amended the thought. She might want something more, even ache for it, but she would be twice the fool if she allowed it.

"I'm your housekeeper, Mr. McKinnon. I can't be anything more."

"Guess it's up to me to rectify that situation."

She stared at him in amazement. "You're crazy."

He nodded. "Plumb loco. And stubborn as a mule."

Jessie shook her head. "I need to get to work."

"Don't do my washing." When she opened her mouth to argue, he lightly laid his finger against her lips, silencing her. "If I take my laundry to Sam Sing, others will, too. He needs the business."

When he moved his finger away, she felt a twinge of disappointment. *Idiot.* "In that case, I'll leave it."

He grinned and started down the steps. "See you by supper time. There are some canned peaches in the pantry. Maybe you could make a cobbler if you have time."

"It's liable to be burnt," she snapped, annoyed that he could dismiss her protests so easily. And that a traitorous part of her was glad for it.

He stopped, turned slightly and met her gaze. "I'm good at pealing off crusty layers to get to the sweet." Giving her a wink, he went on about his business.

What if there isn't any sweet left, she thought sadly, but only bitter ashes?

Chapter Five

A couple of hours after they left ranch headquarters, Cade and Asa spotted Hercules lumbering toward home. When he saw them, the big Hereford let out a bellow and stopped, waiting for them.

"Well, I'll be dad-gummed," said Asa. "I think he's glad to see us."

"Maybe he doesn't like thunderstorms." Cade nudged Mischief to a trot. When he reached the bull, he circled him slowly, checking for injuries. "Well, old man, I don't know how you did it, but looks like you came away unscathed. Must not have run into any jealous longhorns. Though you have lost a little weight."

Hercules snorted and started on his way back to the ranch.

Laughing, Asa shook his head as they followed. "He wants to get back to that extra grub you've been feeding him."

"If he runs off again, he's on his own. Nothin' but grass." Cade nodded toward a nearby creek. "He could probably use some water."

They herded the bull toward the creek, stopping in the light shade of a mesquite. Dismounting, they let the animals drink their fill. Hercules found a patch of thick, green grass on the creek bank, content to stay put for the moment. Cade tied his horse's reins to a branch on the tree where the gelding could graze. Taking his canteen with him, he sat down in the shade, leaning against a big rock.

Asa shot him a questioning look, then did the same. "I figured you'd be all fired up to get back to the house."

It was his first reference to Jessie that morning, though Cade had explained to the men that she was going to be working as his housekeeper. He wasn't sure how much his friend had witnessed, but it had to be enough for Asa to know he was interested in her.

"Jessie's cleaning her house and doing their laundry. She's not expecting us back until this afternoon, so she probably isn't fixing much to eat. Wouldn't be very nice to come in right at dinnertime."

"Mighty considerate of you." Asa took a drink from his canteen, wiping his mouth on his sleeve.

"After this morning, I'd better be considerate."

"Things did look interesting out there on the porch. I was tempted to just wait and see where it went, but figured you'd have my hide if I did."

"You got that one right. You could have just turned around and gone back where you came from."

"And miss the chance of watching that little lady put you in your place?"

"I think I was winning."

"Maybe. I had the feeling she couldn't make up her mind whether to kiss you or shove you off the porch. Either one would have been more entertainment than I've had in a month of Sundays."

"Life must be getting dull in town."

"You know I don't like saloon gals any more than you do. What we need is a place to meet decent women."

Cade grinned and scratched an itch on the back of his ear. "Go to church." He opened his canteen and took a long drink.

"Been thinking I might do just that."

Cade choked, spewing water all over his pants. When he quit coughing, he wiped the tears from his eyes, cleared his throat a couple of times and took a deep, wheezy breath. "You ever been to church?"

Asa jerked off his hat and swatted at a fly that kept buzzing past his nose. "Nope. But there's a whole crop of them springing up in town, so they must not be all bad, especially since they seem to attract the respectable womenfolk."

"They do at that. Just make sure you don't fall asleep and start snoring."

"Reckon I have to find a preacher who hollers a lot."

Cade laughed and stood. "Asking a pretty lady to sit next to you and nudge you in the ribs would be a lot more pleasant."

"That's a fact." Asa pushed himself up to stand. He untied his horse's reins and mounted, his expression turning serious. "Most of the time I don't envy you."

Cade swung up into the saddle with a frown. "What's different now?"

"I'd give half of Texas to have Jessie Monroe look at me the way she was lookin' at you this morning."

Cade felt uncomfortable under Asa's hard-edged gaze. Hidden beneath that easygoing manner was one tough hombre. "You might change your mind if you'd seen her spittin' nails a few minutes earlier."

"If you take advantage of her, Quint won't be the only one you'll have to answer to."

A spurt of anger shot through Cade. He narrowed his eyes and gave Asa a hard look of his own. "How long have you known me?"

"A little over ten years."

"Have I ever taken advantage of a woman?"

"No, but I ain't ever seen you with so bad an itch, either."

He had him there. Cade guided Mischief around behind Hercules, encouraging him to move. Grabbing one last bite of grass, the bull started off at a slow walk, which suited Cade just fine. "An itch I don't intend to scratch until she has my ring on her finger."

"Then we'd all better hope for a short courtship, because you're going to be one cantankerous son of a gun before long."

After a quiet supper filled with an underlying tension that Cade hoped the kids didn't sense, Jessie hustled them to their new house for baths.

He offered to haul over his bathtub for them to use, but she refused. "The washtub will work just fine, thank you."

Maybe for her. If there had been any liquor in the house, it would have driven him to drink. He stood in the darkness at the end of his back porch and studied the little house across the yard, particularly the lantern light glowing softly through the window. He had never noticed how the thin curtains only partially concealed what was going on inside—probably because, until tonight, he hadn't been looking. His former housekeeper was almost sixty years old and wide as the door.

He watched as Jessie lifted Ellie from the tub and set her on the floor. She reached for a towel, then vanished from view as she knelt down to dry her off. In a few minutes, she popped up again, her daughter in her arms, and walked out of sight. Brad climbed into the tub, visible from the chest up, then disappeared when he sat down.

Before long, it would be Jessie's turn. Cade had experienced bathing in a washtub and knew it was too small to allow Jessie to sit down. It would be bad enough if she only appeared in the window briefly as Brad had done, but she'd have to stand in the tub, the upper half of her body hidden only behind a gauzy veil. She would bend down and dip out a pan full of water, straighten and pour it over herself. Then she would pick up the soap....

His body tightened and his mouth went dry. He wouldn't be able to see every detail, but he could easily imagine them. *And you call yourself an honorable man?* He shook his head in disgust. She wouldn't have any idea that she was performing an erotic shadow dance for his benefit.

Or for anyone who wandered by.

"Dang it, honey." Cade stomped into the house and gathered up a stack of clean sheets. He went back out to the porch, waiting until he spotted Brad climb out of the tub. When he figured the boy had had enough time to dress, he made a beeline for their back door and knocked. "Jessie, it's Cade."

She opened the door, glancing at the sheets with a puzzled expression. "Yes?"

"You need thicker curtains," he said gruffly.

Her gaze skittered to the window and back to his frown. "Oh, dear."

He pushed the door farther open with his shoulder, careful not to bump her in the process. Walking over to the window facing his house, he was unable to keep his gaze from darting to that blasted washtub. When she followed, he shoved the sheets at her. "Hold these."

He grabbed one from the stack, unfurled it with a snap and folded it in half again. Draping it over the curtain rod, he tugged it down until it covered the curtain on both sides. By the time they had methodically taken care of all the windows in the front room, most of his annoyance and some of his frustration had abated.

"I didn't realize...." Jessie's subdued tone tugged at him.

For the first time since coming into the house, he looked her square in the eye. Delicate color filled her face, but he suspected it had been much redder a few minutes earlier.

"I know you didn't. I hadn't noticed it, either. Never paid any attention when Nan lived here. We have some heavier curtains at the store. We'll pick some up tomorrow."

Cade turned to the children, who were staring at them with wide eyes. "Why don't you two run on over to the house and have some of your mama's cobbler." He glanced at Jessie. "If she doesn't mind."

"Can we, Mama?" Ellie inched toward the door.

"Yes, as long as you don't take too much. Let Brad dish it up for you."

"I will. Come on, Brad."

The boy held back, watching Cade suspiciously. "You want some cobbler, Mr. McKinnon?"

"Yep. A nice big bowlful." He looked at Jessie again. "It's real tasty, not a burnt spot on it."

"She never burns anything."

"I'm sure she doesn't." Cade shifted his attention back to Brad. He had seen the boy inspecting the bookcase earlier, whispering some of the titles to himself. "Pick out a book. You can read for a while after we eat."

Brad shook his head. "I only got through the third reader. Those are too hard for me."

"You find one that looks interesting, and I'll read to you and your sister. Pick something you think she'll like, too."

The youngster studied him for a minute, as if trying to decide whether or not he meant what he said. Suddenly his face broke into a smile, the first one Cade had seen. "Yes, sir. Come on, Ellie." He grabbed her hand, and they raced out the door.

"I'll be along directly," called Cade.

"That's very kind of you."

"Kindness doesn't have much to do with it. I'll enjoy the company. Come evening, that house gets mighty lonely." He glanced pointedly at the washtub, then let his gaze slowly roam down to her bare toes peeking from beneath the hem of her dress and back up again, making no attempt to hide the desire in his eyes. "And I need the distraction."

She drew a shaky breath, glancing at his mouth before looking up at the makeshift curtain. "Thank you for being so considerate. For being a gentleman."

"I was tempted not to be."

Her gaze clashed with his.

"Until tonight, I'd never realized how easy it is to see in your window from my back porch. I stood there in the dark, imagining you bathing, barely hidden by that thin curtain. For a minute or two, I almost gave in to the temptation to watch, and that made me feel lower than a snake's belt buckle. You deserve a whole lot more respect, Jessie. Then it occurred to me that if one of the men wandered by and saw you, I'd have to shoot him."

Jessie smiled, even as color flooded her cheeks again. "And good cowboys are hard to find."

He nodded. "So are good women."

"Go eat your cobbler, McKinnon." Her soft voice wafted over him like a cool evening breeze, pleasant and peaceful.

"Yes, ma'am." He smiled down at her, glad he had done the right thing. Lord willing, there would be other nights when he could watch her all he wanted to. "Leave the water in the washtub, and I'll empty it later."

"Cade, you're going to spoil me."

"It's time someone did." He traced the line of her jaw with his fingertip. "Hurry, so you won't miss much of the story."

"Eat slow."

He laughed and headed for the door, amazed because she thought him emptying the washtub was spoiling her. *Darlin', I haven't even started.*

Chapter Six

Disconcerted by Cade's comments, Jessie rushed through her bath. Despite her husband's assertion that she was too skinny to bother looking at, she knew better. She'd had enough untoward offers to know men found her attractive, even though she was repulsed by their advances.

Surprisingly, Cade's honest admission that he had been tempted to watch her bathe was not offensive. Instead, it stirred thoughts—and a hunger—that she had never experienced. Jessie shook her head as she dried with the threadbare towel. "And I thought I knew how things were between a man and a woman." She suspected Cade could teach her much more about her own desire than she had ever imagined.

She changed into clean undergarments but put on the same dress she had worn most of the day. Her other two dresses were clean and nicely ironed, hanging up in the bedroom. Hesitating a moment, she contemplated lugging the washtub out the back door and dumping the water, but decided to take Cade up on his offer to empty it.

Carrying the lantern, she returned to the ranch house, letting herself in the back door. She set the lamp on the kitchen table, turning the flame down low before going to the living room.

Though Cade had told the children he would read to them, the sight of them huddled on the sofa brought her to an abrupt halt. Ellie sat in Cade's lap, leaning back against his chest. His arms encircled her as he held the book at a slight angle so Brad could see it, too. Her son sat right beside them, with only a tiny space between him and the big rancher.

Engrossed in the story, Cade kept reading, his deep voice strong one minute, lowering almost to a whisper the next, reflecting the action of the story. Suddenly he stopped and looked up with a smile that warmed her from head to toe.

"Did I miss much?"

"No. We picked *Around the World in Eighty Days*. Have you read it?"

She shook her head and moved to the closest chair and sat down.

"It's about some people who are going to fly around the world in a hot-air balloon," said Brad in an awed voice.

"Goodness, I didn't know that was possible."

"I'm not sure it is," said Cade. "It's written by Jules Verne, so it's fiction."

"What's that?" asked Ellie, looking up at him.

"It means that it's just a story somebody made up. But there *are* hot-air balloons. I've even ridden in one."

"You did?" Brad stared wide-eyed at Cade. Jessie figured his respect for the rancher went up about five notches before his next question. "Was it fun?"

"Yes and no. It was exciting to be up in the air and see everything down below. Except it was Kansas and it all pretty much looked the same. We went about ten miles in less than an hour, so that was fun. But when we started to come down, the wind shifted, and we landed right smack-dab in the middle of a trail drive. Spooked the cattle and almost caused a stampede. That riled the cowboys. I had to do some fast talking to keep them from shooting the balloon full of holes. It didn't take much to convinced the balloon owner to give them all a free ride.''

Jessie laughed softly, and the children giggled. Cade met her gaze and winked, then started to read again. He finished the chapter and closed the book. ''That's all for tonight. We'll read the next chapter after we come home from town.''

''But then we'll be staying in our house,'' said Brad, his expression crestfallen. ''It's no fun to only hear part of a story.''

''Well, I figure we can still read a chapter every night. You'll be eating supper over here anyway.'' Cade met Jessie's gaze. ''Just because you're going to sleep over there doesn't mean we can't spend some time together in the evening.''

Brad looked wistfully at Jessie. There had been little time for reading in the evenings and then only from someone else's cast-off magazines or books. The magazine stories were sometimes published in serial form, and all too often, they would start an exciting story only to miss later chapters.

Jessie's heart twisted at how little she had been able to give her children. ''I expect that will be all right. And, if for some reason, Mr. McKinnon can't read to you, I'm sure he would let me borrow the book.''

''Of course.'' He set the book on a table at the end of the sofa. ''Now, you young'uns better go to bed. We have to get up early tomorrow and head for town so we can buy some furniture for your house.''

''Can't we just stay here?'' Ellie shifted, looking up at

him. "I like it here." She rested her head against his shoulder, curling her arm around his neck.

Cade closed his eyes for a second, giving her a gentle hug. "And I like having you here, quarter pint. But it's better for you and your mama to have a place of your own." He glanced at Jessie again. "For now."

Jessie's heart skipped a beat.

Ellie straightened, frowning up at him. "Why?"

"It's a matter of propriety, honey," said Jessie.

"What's pro…pretty?"

Cade got a mischievous twinkle in his eyes, and Jessie gave him a warning frown. He ignored her. "It's rules made up by a bunch of nosy women and stuffy men telling everybody else how they should behave."

Ellie nodded. "Like when Mama tells me to put on my company manners?"

Jessie smiled and Cade chuckled. "Something like that." He grew serious. "The thing is, sweetheart, most decent folk live by these rules, even if they are aggravating sometimes. Those people might think bad things about your mother if y'all keep staying here with me."

"Why?"

He shot Jessie a panicked look, but she merely crossed her arms and relaxed. "You started this."

"Uh…well…most people don't think a man and woman should live in the same house unless they're married."

Jessie held her breath, waiting for Ellie's response.

"Oh. And since Mama says nothin' on God's green earth could make her get married again, we have to move." Ellie played with the collar of Cade's shirt, then looked up at him sadly. "My daddy was mean. He hurted Mama and Brad."

Brad stiffened, his face contorting with anger. When he looked at Jessie, she shook her head slightly, realizing she needed to tell him that Cade knew about Neil. His small hands curled into fists, but he kept quiet.

"I know he did, honey. Did your daddy hurt you?" Cade spoke so gently it made Jessie's heart ache.

"Nope. He told Mama he didn't want nothin' to do with me 'cause I was somebody else's whelp."

At Cade's startled expression, Jessie caught her breath. She didn't know Ellie had heard Neil's vile accusation and desperately hoped her daughter didn't understand what he meant. Unable to keep her voice steady, she said, "Your daddy was wrong, honey."

"I know that, Mama." Ellie grinned. "I'm a little girl."

"A sweet little girl who needs to get to bed." Jessie stood, holding out her hand.

When Cade started to lift her down, Ellie twisted around and slid her arms around his neck, giving him a quick hug. "Night."

"Good night, sweetheart." He hugged her back, then set her feet on the floor. "Sleep tight."

"Don't let the bedbugs bite." Ellie giggled and grabbed her mother's hand.

"I'll just squish 'em." Cade winked at her, then smiled at Brad when he hopped off the sofa. "Good night. We'll see if we can find you a pair of boots tomorrow."

"Don't like wearin' shoes." Brad looked down at his bare feet, his expression mulish.

"Don't like shoes much myself. Boots are different, though, and they're a necessity for a cowboy."

Brad looked up, wariness in his eyes. "I ain't a cowboy."

"Not yet. Can you ride a horse?"

He shook his head.

"Would you like to learn?"

"Yes, sir."

"Then you'll need some boots."

Jessie wished she owned a pair of pointy-toed cowboy boots so she could give Cade a sharp kick in the shin. He knew she didn't have the money to buy a pair of socks, much less boots.

"I want some new shoes, too," said Ellie, tugging on her mother's hand. "Shiny black ones."

"I'm sorry, honey, but you'll have to wear the ones you have until I get paid at the end of the month." Jessie smiled apologetically at her child, then sent Cade a dagger-filled glance over her head.

"But they hurt." Tears filled Ellie's big brown eyes.

Jessie fought down a sharp pang of guilt and remorse, momentarily at a loss for what to say.

"We'll get you some shoes tomorrow, too." Cade's expression warned Jessie not to argue with him. "Your mother and I'll work it out."

"Shiny black ones?"

"I think we have some at the store, unless Ty sold them already. I expect we can find something you like."

Torn between anger at his high-handed ways and the need to clothe her child, Jessie pointed Ellie toward the kitchen. "Brad, I left the lantern on the table. Will you take Ellie to the outhouse?"

"Yes, ma'am." He motioned toward his sister, who followed him out of the room.

Jessie turned to Cade, who remained on the sofa. "I'll expect you to take the cost of the children's shoes and boots from my wages."

"I suppose I could."

"No supposing about it. You will." She crossed her arms, not bothering to hide her irritation. "You should have talked to me first."

"You wouldn't have let me buy them."

"So you brought it up in front of the children, knowing I couldn't refuse?"

"I deliberated on it for about a minute." He stood, closing the distance between them in one stride.

Jessie resisted the urge to step back, rigidly holding her ground, and lowered her arms. "I don't want to indebted to anyone."

"You don't have to be."

Jessie caught her breath, praying that she had been right about him, that he hadn't deceived her with noble words and feigned consideration. Because, for the first time in her life, if he suggested a way to repay her debt without money, she might be tempted. She couldn't explain the desire that danced between them like lightning in a distant thundercloud, filling her with anticipation of the approaching storm. "I don't want your charity."

"Gifts, Jessie, not charity. Gifts with nothing expected in return."

"There is no such thing. Everyone wants something."

He studied her for a moment, and she thought she saw regret in his eyes.

"I want to make you happy," he said softly. "I need to."

"Why?"

He shrugged, his expression bemused. "I haven't quite figured that out." A tiny smile lifted one corner of his mouth. "But I guarantee it has nothing to do with charity. Maybe it's pure selfishness. I like seeing Ellie get all excited about new shoes. And that little glimmer of anticipation in Brad's eyes at the thought of learning to be a cowboy reminds me of how I felt when it was all new to me."

He moved a step closer. "Mostly, though, I like the way your eyes sparkle and your face lights up when you smile.

I like the sound of your laughter and the way it warms the cold emptiness of my heart.

"I know how it feels to have shoes that are too small and not have the money for more. To be broke and hungry." His voice dropped to barely more than a whisper, raw with emotion. "To see my father go off to war and watch my mother die from lack of food and medicine because I couldn't provide for her."

Quick, unexpected moisture stung Jessie's eyes at his pain, still deep and harsh. "How old were you?"

"Thirteen. Ty was eleven. At least I had him. I didn't have to face the pain and fear alone." He touched her cheek with his fingertip, capturing the lone tear that had slipped from her eyes. "Let me help you take care of your family, Jessie."

And help heal his own wounds. "Just until I find Quint."

"Unless I can change your mind by then and convince you to stay here."

"Not likely."

"Give me time, darlin'." Hearing the children in the kitchen, he smiled and moved away from her. "I usually spend Saturday night in town and go to church on Sunday. We can get a couple of rooms at Campbell's Hotel." When she started to protest, he held up his hand. "I'll pay for it. Whenever I send a man to town for supplies, I cover his meals and hotel. Since you'll be grocery shopping for me, I should do the same for you." He paused to take a deep breath. "But if you'd rather come home tomorrow, we can."

She wondered if, like the mayor of Riverbend, he went to church merely because it was politically beneficial. She was instantly ashamed of herself. He wasn't anything like her former employer. She tried to imagine Cade snoring during the sermon, but the thought was so silly it made her smile.

"What? Me going to church is amusing?" Cade tipped his head, looking disappointed.

"No. I think it's nice. And I'd like to go. We haven't been in a long time." She'd grown tired of the whispers and pitying glances. Here no one knew about her past, though if she and the children went with Cade, it likely would cause talk.

"Good. I particularly want to be there this week, since Asa's been thinking about going."

"And you want to encourage him. How thoughtful."

Cade grinned, his eyes dancing with mischief. "Not exactly. He's never set foot in a church before. I want to see how well the roof holds up."

Jessie laughed as Ellie ran into the room. She picked up the little girl, giving her a big hug and smiling at Cade. "Good night."

"Good night."

As she carried her daughter into the bedroom, Ellie leaned back and looked at her. "I like Mr. McKinnon."

"Because he's going to buy you new shoes?" teased Jessie.

She nodded, her expression filled with pure sweetness. "But mostly 'cause he makes you laugh."

"Yes, he does." But was that good or bad?

"And he gives good hugs."

Very good hugs.

That was definitely bad.

Chapter Seven

They didn't have to wait until Sunday morning for Jessie's presence with Cade to cause talk. It began the minute they drove down Main Street, Jessie sitting beside him on the seat of the freight wagon and the kids perched on boxes and a folded quilt in the back. Heads turned. Men gaped. Women leaned close together in a flurry of whispers.

Cade glanced at her as he drew the team to a halt in front of what appeared to be the largest store in town. Equally large letters painted across the second story proclaimed it to be McKinnon Brothers, General Merchandise. "Don't let folks bother you. They're always curious when someone new comes to town."

"Especially a woman and children with the most eligible man in the county," Jessie said wryly.

He chuckled and set the brake on the wagon. "I suppose you pegged that one right, though some folks think Ty deserves the title. We flip a coin once a month for braggin' rights."

Jessie laughed, appreciating his effort to set her at ease. She looked around at the bustle of activity. Across the street, bricklayers stood high on a scaffold laying a row of bricks on the second story of a new building. Two men on the ground below used a rope and pulley to hoist up another flat box of bricks. She counted six businesses on that side of the block, three of them saloons, which seemed to have plenty of customers even at nine in the morning.

There were two saloons on their side of the street, one only three stores down from Cade and Ty's, as well as a dressmaker, millinery, drugstore and a large restaurant. She was surprised to see an empty lot next to McKinnon's store. "Why hasn't someone built there?" She nodded to the grassy plot of ground.

"We were waiting to see if we needed it for storage, but the merchandise moves out so quickly, we've decided to put up another building and rent it out. We'll start on it in a couple of months."

"Do you own the whole block?" Quintin had told her that Cade and Ty were successful businessmen as well as ranchers, but she hadn't realized how well-off they were. She wasn't sure which bothered her more—his wealth or the idea of him renting out space for saloons.

He smiled and shook his head. "Not the whole thing. We bought the lots on this side of the street on this block and the next one as soon as the town was laid out. We've sold the extra ones on this block but still own the other land. We haven't decided what to do with it yet."

Across the street on the next block, a two-story building was finished, with a sign hanging out front that indicated it was the courthouse. "Isn't that a little small for a courthouse?"

"Yes. We want to purchase the empty block one street down and build a real one, but the owner is trying to gouge us. So everyone in town has banded together and refused to buy any lots from him. We've been successful at heading off any other potential buyers, too. I think he'll see reason before long. We could put it some other place, but everyone likes that block the best. We'll wait a little longer, then move on something else if he doesn't come through.''

More buildings were going up, a mix of wooden and brick structures. All were one story high, but some had a false front, giving the illusion of another story. The shouts of the workmen and the sound of pounding hammers rang in the air, intermingled with the creak of wagon wheels and jingling harnesses as people went about their Saturday shopping. Two wagons piled high with goods, hitched together and pulled by a team of ten oxen slowly rambling by drew her gaze.

"Supplies for one of the big ranches in the Panhandle. They bought most of it right here at our store," Cade said with a note of pride. He glanced over his shoulder, smiling at Brad and Ellie as they stood behind the seat, taking in the sights. "What do you think of Willow Grove?"

"It's bigger than I thought it would be," said Brad. "There sure is a lot going on."

Ellie nodded in wide-eyed amazement. "Can we look in all the stores?"

"Not all of them today," said Jessie. "But I'm sure we will see plenty."

Cade climbed down and walked around the back of the wagon to Jessie's side, waiving at Asa as he drove by with another wagon. He planned to leave it in front of the furniture store down the street. Cade looked up at her. "Ready to do some shopping?"

She patted her purse. "I have the grocery list all made out. You didn't have many staples in the pantry."

"I haven't bought much since Nan left."

"Is there anything you don't care for?"

"Nope. And I expect you to get anything you and the kids like, too."

When he reached up to help her down, Jessie leaned

forward, resting her hands on his shoulders. He curled his hands around her waist and lifted her from the wagon with ease, setting her lightly on her feet. He released her the instant she was on the ground, and she moved her hands away just as quickly. To even the most keen observer, it would have appeared as nothing more than the common courtesy of a gentleman assisting a lady from a wagon.

But no one else saw the flare of heat in his eyes when she touched him, or his gaze drop to her lips as he lowered her from the wagon. No one else felt the tiny pressure of his thumbs as they brushed along her rib cage before he released her. Or caught the little hitch in his breathing and the promise in his eyes as he looked up once again. He dragged in a deep breath, silently telling her that his heart was probably pounding as much as hers, then sidestepped and reached up to help Brad down.

When he lifted Ellie out of the wagon bed, instead of putting her down, he tucked one arm beneath her to serve as a seat, gently keeping her steady with his other hand. She grinned and rested her arm along his shoulder as if he had been carrying her for years. Jessie was again struck by the natural trust her daughter held for Cade and the instant affection between them. It would hurt the child when they moved away from the ranch, she thought sadly.

They walked up the steps to the boardwalk in front of the store, Brad leading the way. When a man came out of Talbot's Saloon, heading toward them with a big smile, Cade drew to a halt. Tall and lanky, wearing a white western-style shirt, dark pants, boots and a cream-colored Stetson typical of West Texas, he would have passed for a regular cowboy except for the shiny five-pointed star on his black leather vest.

"Good morning, Sheriff." Cade shifted Ellie slightly and shook hands with him.

"Mornin'." The lawman touched the brim of his hat, nodding a greeting to Jessie. Amusement crinkled his eyes as he smiled at the children. "You been holding out on us, Cade?"

Cade laughed and shook his head. "Sheriff Procter, I'd like you to meet Mrs. Jessie Monroe and her children, Brad and Ellie. Mrs. Monroe is Quintin Webb's sister."

"Pleased to meet you, ma'am. I didn't realize Webb had a sister living out this way."

"He didn't until day before yesterday," Jessie said with a smile. "He's been after me to move here from East Texas for a couple of years. I thought I'd surprise him, but the surprise was mine when I arrived at Mr. McKinnon's ranch and learned that Quint isn't working there anymore. Have you seen him lately?"

"Not since he was in town about three weeks ago." The sheriff glanced at Cade.

"She knows about the fight and that I fired him. If you run into him, tell him that he can have his job back if he wants it."

"I'll be sure to do that. Are you staying here in town, Mrs. Monroe?" His quick, appraising glance at her well-worn dress probably told him all he needed to know about her financial situation.

"No, sir. Mr. McKinnon has hired me as his house-keeper, at least until I hear from Quintin."

"Good."

Jessie thought she detected a great deal of relief in that one word. When the sheriff glanced at Cade again, she had the oddest feeling that there was some kind of unspoken communication passing between the two men. Did they know something about Quintin that they didn't want her to find out? "If you see my brother, will you please tell him that I'm at the ranch?"

"Of course." The sheriff rubbed his jaw absentmindedly. "I'm glad you're staying out there, ma'am. We're short on housing here in town, unless you bunk at one of the hotels, and to be honest, I wouldn't be too comfortable with that. For the most part, the men are respectful to the womenfolk, but some of them get ornery, especially when they've had too much to drink. And we have some unsavory characters pass through on occasion. A pretty, young woman all alone might not be totally safe." He frowned, studying her so closely that Jessie shifted uncomfortably. "Your husband isn't with you?"

"I'm a widow."

"I'm sorry for your loss, ma'am." He paused thoughtfully. "You say you arrived Thursday?"

Jessie nodded.

"I didn't see you get off the train." He smiled ruefully. "I must not be as sharp as I used to be. I should have noticed you and your family."

"We didn't come in on the train." Jessie stiffened her spine. "The children and I made the journey by wagon."

"Just the three of them," said Cade quietly.

Was that a tinge of pride she heard in his voice? Jessie looked at him, but he was watching the sheriff.

"You came alone?" Sheriff Procter's smile turned into a scowl. "From East Texas?"

"Yes, near Navasota in Grimes County."

He stared at her incredulously. "Do you have any idea of what could have happened to you?"

"Of course I do." She felt Cade move a tiny bit closer and glanced up at him. Though he agreed with the sheriff about the foolishness of her journey, she sensed that he would stand up for her if needed. Warmth stole through her heart, softening her response to the officer. "But nothing terrible happened, so it doesn't do any good to fret about it now.'' She glanced pointedly at her children.

The sheriff took a deep breath. *Biting his tongue, perhaps?* Jessie hid a smile.

''Well, Mrs. Monroe, if you decide to go back to East Texas—or anywhere—tell me. I'll make sure you have a proper escort.''

''No need,'' said Cade. ''I'll take care of it.''

The sheriff nodded as if that was the end of it, which it was. It wouldn't do any good to argue with him or Cade. To be honest, Jessie did not want to travel anywhere alone again. Despite what she told the lawman, there had been many frightening moments on their journey. Long, lonely nights listening to the howl of coyotes and shriek of mountain lions. Thunderstorms, treacherous rivers and even more treacherous men. More than once, it had taken a steady hand on her shotgun to send them on their way.

Cade edged toward the door of the store. ''We'd best get on with our shopping. I know a couple of kids who need some new moccasins.''

Ellie shook her head. ''Not mosscasins. Shoes.''

Sheriff Procter laughed. ''Reckon you'd better see to it. Nice to meet you and your family, Mrs. Monroe. Welcome to Willow Grove. If you need anything you let me know.'' His gaze slid to Cade. ''Drop by the office if you have time.''

It was clear he meant for Cade to go see him, whether he had time or not.

''Won't be until this afternoon.''

''I'll be there.''

When the sheriff walked away, Cade opened the door, waiting for Jessie and Brad to walk through before he and Ellie followed them.

''What was that about?'' Jessie asked.

"Cattle rustling, most likely. There has been quite a bit of it the last few months."

"Have you lost any cattle?"

"No. They're working to the north and west of here. Unless they've moved. No one's been able to track them far enough to catch them."

"How come?" asked Brad.

"They drive the cattle into the breaks—rugged and rocky terrain—so they don't leave any prints. There are miles of that type of country across a good portion of West Texas."

"But the rustlers can wait." He tickled Ellie's tummy, making her giggle. "We need to get down to serious business." Looking around the store, he spotted Ty up on a ladder, handing a bolt of cloth down to one of his clerks. Cade raised his voice loud enough for his brother to hear him. "Why can't a man find a shoe salesman when he needs one?"

Ty looked up and grinned. "Your feet growing again?"

"Not mine, but these young'uns are sproutin' up like weeds."

Ty climbed down the ladder and walked across the store to join them. "Good morning, Mrs. Monroe." He smiled at Jessie, then the kids. "What can I show you?"

"Ellie needs some new shoes. Preferably shiny black ones," Jessie added with a smile at her daughter. "And Brad needs some cowboy boots. Mr. McKinnon is going to teach him how to ride."

"And be a cowboy." Brad smiled shyly, first at Ty, then at Cade.

"Then you're planning to stay on a while." Ty nodded in satisfaction. "Was he smart enough to hire you as his housekeeper?"

Jessie sent Cade a mischievous glance. He blinked, then

grinned back. "I don't know how smart he is, but I'm the new housekeeper."

Ty laughed and nudged his brother with an elbow. "She's already puttin' you in your place."

"Makes me mind my manners." *Even when I don't want to.* He hadn't spoken the words out loud, but the look in his eyes and his lazy smile whispered them to her heart.

"Somebody needs to." Ty winked at Jessie. "You let me know if he misbehaves and—"

An image of Cade on the back porch the previous morning sprang to mind—handsome, confident, sexy and far too appealing. It was followed by another memory—his confession that he had been tempted to watch her bathe. Tender and noble. Hungry and needy. Stirring her senses like no one ever had.

To her dismay, a hot flush stole up her cheeks. She felt Cade's gaze and looked up. She suspected he was dealing with memories of his own, and her face burned even more.

"—I'll hog-tie him."

A tiny frown wrinkled Cade's brow, and he shifted his stance, drawing Ty's attention. "You and who else?"

Ty picked up the banter, but Jessie barely heard it. Neil would have jumped at the chance to say something crude, fiendishly delighting in making a scene. Once again, Cade had come to her rescue, distracting his brother to ease her embarrassment.

So different from her husband.

Chapter Eight

Ty looked down at Brad. "My neighbor, Will, is ten. I told him you might be in town today. He and a couple of other boys play baseball in the empty lots behind us. He thought you might want to join them later this afternoon. Do you like baseball?"

Brad shrugged. "I can hit and throw okay. I'm not so good at catching the ball."

"Do you have a mitt?" asked Ty.

Brad shook his head. "Store in Riverbend didn't have any."

Not that they'd had the money for it anyway. Jessie had planned to order one for his birthday in the fall. Now that she was working again, and at a better wage, she should be able to do it.

"We have some." Cade practically beamed. "It's not just the boys here in town who like the game. The young men have formed a couple of teams to play each other. Ty even gave it a try until they threw him off the team because he was so slow."

"They didn't throw me off. I quit." Ty grinned at Jessie. "It only took me a couple of practices to figure out that

I'm too old to be on a team. Still like to toss the ball around though.''

"We'll find you a mitt after we get your boots," said Cade, resting his hand on Brad's shoulder.

Jessie opened her mouth to protest, but shut it again on seeing the hesitant anticipation on Brad's face and the excitement on Cade's. What would it hurt to let him give her child another present? Other than Quint, Cade was the first man to take an interest in the boy, the first one to show him kindness and affection. When Brad looked at her, she nodded her approval.

Cade set Ellie on the floor. "Why don't you and Brad go look at the shoes and boots and see if you find any you like."

She scampered down the aisle, with Brad ambling along behind her.

"Mrs. Monroe, if you take Ed your list, he'll start gathering up the supplies." Ty gestured toward a man stocking the grocery shelves. "He boxes everything up for folks so they can browse." Smiling, he glanced at the only other customers, two older women, who were on the other side of the store discussing lace with a young female clerk. "They buy more that way."

Jessie laughed. "I expect they do. I won't be buying anything until payday. But I'll enjoy looking."

"If you find something you want, let me or Miss Hemphill know, and we'll put it away for you."

"I couldn't ask you to do that."

"Yes, you can," said Cade, moving beside her. "We supply a big territory, so the merchandise doesn't stay long. Something you find today probably won't be here next Saturday."

"My goodness. No wonder there are so many new stores being built."

"It's a boomtown, sure enough," said Ty. "Five years ago the buffalo and Kiowa roamed this range, along with a few ranchers. Now there are dozens of ranches in the territory, and we're bringing civilization to the cowboys."

"Whether they want it or not." Cade chuckled and cupped her elbow, gently nudging her toward the grocery department. "Ty, if you'll help the kids, we'll get Ed started."

Ty nodded and headed toward the shoes.

Jessie pulled the list out of her purse. "Do you want to look over it?"

Cade took the sheet of paper, scanning it as they walked across the store. "We'll need to go to the meat market and grocer for some things, but most of it we have right here. Looks a little sparse though."

"Is there anything in particular I should add?"

"Candy."

"What kind?" She glanced at the jars of brightly colored stick candy.

"Anything you and the kids like." He smiled down at her, his thumb moving in a little circle against the inside of her elbow. His gaze dipped to her mouth for a heartbeat. "I just have a fondness for sweets."

The man was driving her crazy. She took a deep breath and looked away. "I forgot to check the coal oil. Do we need some?"

"Wouldn't hurt. And some matches, too."

He introduced her to the clerk, then excused himself. "I'll go see how Ty is doing with the kids. Why don't you look around and see what else you want? Try anything you like."

Jessie handed the list to Ed, discussing a few things with him, then did as Cade suggested. She was amazed at the variety of foodstuff in the store. In Riverbend, the mayor's wife had to special-order many things, but it seemed as if McKinnon's had almost everything imaginable in stock.

Dried currents, purchased by the pound, were available, as well as canned ones. There were lemons from Sicily, peanuts from Tennessee and London raisins. Fresh bananas, plums, peaches, green apples and tomatoes. Grapes, dates and figs. Even pineapple and several kinds of nuts. The variety of canned goods was as good or better than what she had seen in any store, ranging from blackberries to expensive French sardines.

Recipes that she longed to try but had been unable to ran through her head. Some were her own ideas. Others, she had found in *The First Texas Cookbook,* published by the Ladies Association of the First Presbyterian Church of Houston. An acquaintance sent the cookbook to the mayor's wife, but Mrs. Drake had disdained something compiled by a bunch of churchwomen and tossed it out. Jessie had rescued it from the trash and found a treasure.

When she spotted fresh strawberries, she let out a little squeak of delight. She looked up to see Cade striding in her direction and felt silly. She tried to wave him away, but he ignored her.

"What's wrong?" he asked quietly, stopping next to her.

"Nothing." Grinning, she pointed to the strawberries. "I adore strawberries."

"The ones last week didn't have much flavor. Let's see if these are better." He picked up a big, bright red berry, checked to make sure it was clean, then lifted it to her mouth.

Jessie took a bite of the juicy fruit and sighed. "Delicious."

Cade grinned and held it up for her to eat, grasping it by the stem. She bit off the rest of the berry, accidentally brushing her lips against his fingers. A jolt shot through her, and he drew in a sharp breath.

He curled his hand into a fist, the strawberry stem clutched inside, and exhaled slowly. "Buy the whole box."

She shook her head. "We couldn't eat them all before they spoiled."

"But we'd sure have fun tryin'." A twinkle of amusement mingled with the heat in his gaze.

"Go away."

"Yes, ma'am." He turned abruptly, going back down the aisle.

Unable to look at the strawberries without her face heating up, Jessie went to the women's section of the store, inspecting a rack of ready-made dresses. They had a good assortment of styles and sizes, but a rose-pink one particularly drew her attention. She lifted it off the rack and held it up in front of her, checking her image in a cheval mirror standing nearby.

"It was made for you." The female clerk Ty had mentioned earlier replaced some spools of lace on a shelf, then joined her. She was an attractive young woman, in her early twenties, with blond hair and clear blue eyes.

Jessie smiled and looked back in the mirror. "I think it might fit."

"We have a dressing room right over here if you'd like to try it on."

"Yes, I would."

"I'm Lydia Hemphill." She led the way to a small room situated between the men and women's clothing sections. "Ty said you're Cade's new housekeeper. Mrs. Monroe, is it?"

"Yes. Jessie Monroe."

Lydia glanced across the store at Cade. "You'll be the envy of half the women in Willow Grove."

"I'm only his housekeeper," Jessie said sharply. "With separate living quarters."

"Of course. Everybody knows Nan had a place of her own. And he's too fine a man for anyone to believe he would do anything indecent. But the women will be jealous about the way he looks at you."

Taken aback, Jessie stopped in the dressing room doorway, staring at the young woman. "What do you mean, the way he looks at me?"

"Like you're the only woman in Texas."

Jessie laughed at the fanciful notion.

Miss Hemphill sighed softly. "Don't you realize the man is smitten?"

"Well, I don't know about smitten," Jessie said dryly. Other words came more readily to mind. *Persistent. Arrogant. Seductive.*

"Trust me, he is. He's always nice to the ladies, teases them and such. But when he looks at you...well, it's obvious he has deep feelings for you."

"Miss Hemphill, you're a romantic."

The young woman blushed slightly. "There's nothing wrong with that."

Jessie wanted to tell her that it was a foolish notion, that the harsh realities of life would break her heart. But who was she to shatter a young woman's dreams? Perhaps Miss Hemphill would never discover that romance was only an illusion. "As long as you don't expect the impossible."

"Oh, I don't. I'm practical," she said with a laugh. "When you've changed clothes, come out and check the dress in this mirror. The light is better here. If it needs any adjustments, I'll mark them for the seamstress. There's no charge for alterations." She pointed to a hook on the upper part of the door. "This will latch it, to keep anyone else from accidentally walking in on you."

Jessie went inside the fitting room and closed the door, fastening the latch. Though the walls went all the way to the floor and were about eight feet high, there was no ceiling. A full-length mirror was attached to the wall, with a chair in the corner. She hung the dress on a hook and began to unbutton her dress. Though she was certain no one could see inside the fitting room, removing her clothes in a public place felt strange, especially when she could easily hear Miss Hemphill and Asa Noble exchange greetings. She guessed they were only a few yards away from the cubical. She was not one to eavesdrop, but in this instance, she couldn't avoid it.

"Can I help you find something, Mr. Noble?"

"Yes, ma'am. I'm considerin' going to church tomorrow. I need something to wear, but I ain't real excited about gettin' all gussied up." His tone changed, gentled a bit. "I believe Cade mentioned that you attend the same church he does?"

Smiling, Jessie pulled her old dress above her head and draped it over another hook. Was the young lady the reason Asa had decided to get religion?

"Every Sunday," replied Miss Hemphill. Jessie imagined her smiling at the older but handsome cowboy.

"Do I need to buy a suit?" He sounded as if that would be a terrible thing.

"The Lord doesn't care what you wear, Mr. Noble. I'm sure He's just glad you'll be there. As am I," she added softly.

"Truly, ma'am?"

Jessie quickly pulled the rose dress over her head so she wouldn't miss the young lady's reply.

"It's always good for a man to have an interest in God."

"Even if I've never been to church before?"

"Never?"

"No, ma'am. Not once. Reckon that lowers your opinion of me." Disappointment threaded his voice.

Jessie barely knew Asa Noble, but what she had seen impressed her. He'd been kind to her children, respectful to her even when he caught her and Cade about to kiss on the back porch. Her fingers slowed as she buttoned up the dress.

"But you're planning to go now. That's the important thing," said Miss Hemphill, her voice slightly muffled. "Ah, here is it is. This white shirt, along with a good pair of trousers, would do nicely. No need for a suit. This one should fit you."

Slipping the last button through the buttonhole, Jessie looked in the mirror. Her mouth fell open. She had never worn anything so stylish. Nor could she remember any other dress making her look so attractive. It accented the curves of her bosom and small waist. The color brought a delicate pink to her cheeks and brightened her eyes.

She turned around, looking over her shoulder in the mirror. It was a perfect fit, right down to the length. As she stared at her reflection, the conversation between Mr. Noble and Miss Hemphill resumed.

"I'm a mite nervous about going," he said. "Not sure what to expect, or worse that I might doze off or something."

Miss Hemphill laughed. "You wouldn't be the first person to do that. Usually, the minister's sermons are interesting enough to keep my attention, but on a warm day, I sometimes get drowsy."

Mr. Noble chuckled. "Maybe we should sit together and keep each other awake."

"An excellent idea. I'll meet you outside the church about ten till eleven."

"I'll look forward to it. What kind of dress trousers do

you recommend?'' His voice trailed off as they moved away.

Jessie waited a few more minutes before opening the fitting-room door and walked out, going over to the mirror. Miss Hemphill had been right, the light was better there, and the dress even prettier in the sunlight. The patter of small, running feet caused her to turn around.

''Ellie, don't run in the store,'' she said with a smile.

Her daughter instantly slowed to a walk, an awed expression lighting her face. ''Mama, you're beautiful.'' She stared at Jessie for a minute, then turned to look up at Cade as he and Brad caught up with her. ''Isn't Mama beautiful, Mr. McKinnon?''

''Yes, she is, Ellie.'' His appreciative gaze swept over Jessie from head to toe, then moved back up to her face. ''She's lovely.''

Jessie's heart lurched. Everyone else in the store—even the store itself—seemed to disappear. Admiration glowed in his eyes, along with something so incredible she refused to give it a name.

''Are you gonna wear that to church tomorrow?'' asked Ellie.

''Not this Sunday. But I'll ask Mr. McKinnon to put it away for me until payday.''

''I'll buy it for you,'' said Cade quietly.

''Thank you, but I should wait.''

''We can just add it to the pile.'' When he moved his hands, Jessie realized his arms were full of things for her children. A pretty red dress, straw hat and black shoes for Ellie; along with a baseball bat and mitt, pair of new pants and a shirt for Brad. She glanced at her daughter, who was wearing a new pair of brown everyday shoes and carrying a baby doll. Brad had on his cowboy boots, a Stetson and carried a baseball mitt, baseball and his old shoes.

"Two mitts?"

Cade grinned. "One's for me."

"Cade, that's too much."

"But I need it so Brad and I can play catch."

Jessie shook her head, trying to ignore the sparkle of mischief in his eyes. "I wasn't talking about your mitt." She motioned at the other things. "I meant everything else."

"I'm having fun. And I'll be even happier if you let me buy that dress for you. You can pay me back. Besides, if I buy it, you can get it wholesale. Half price," he added with a grin.

That got her attention. "Half price?"

"Yep. Shouldn't pass up a deal like that."

Jessie hesitated for just a minute. "Oh, all right."

"That's my girl," he said softly.

Ellie tugged on his sleeve. "I thought I was your girl."

"You are, honey." He met Jessie's gaze as she turned around. "Reckon that makes your mother my woman."

Cade's woman. Jessie caught her breath as bittersweet yearning filled her soul. What would it be like to belong to this decent, honest man? A man she could believe in and trust. To be secure and cared for, teased and pampered. To know safety in his touch, gentleness in his caress. To be loved by him.

She shivered with longing, trembled in fear. Shaking her head in denial, Jessie turned and fled into the dressing room. Though she knew all too well life's harsh realities, she was still prone to foolish notions.

Even a broken heart could dream.

Chapter Nine

It had been almost two weeks since their first trip to town, and Cade had tried hard to not crowd Jessie. He hadn't missed the longing in her eyes when he called her his woman, but it had been overshadowed by fear. Fear that made her tremble and flee.

Afterward, she had been pleasant enough company but even more cautious than before. So he had trod carefully, been respectful and tried to make her laugh. He often succeeded, such as that first Sunday in church when Asa had walked in, and he'd glanced up at the ceiling to see if the roof held. Then he realized that his old friend was escorting Miss Hemphill and his mouth fell open. Jessie teased him about catching flies, making him chuckle, then smugly told him she had detected a budding interest between the two in the store the day before.

He had seen Lydia helping Asa find a shirt and trousers but hadn't noted any hint of anything else going on. Of course, he'd been clear across the store. Eventually, it dawned on him that Jessie had been in the dressing room and likely overheard their conversation. But when he started to ask her about it, she had already turned her attention to the minister, who picked that inconvenient time to begin the opening hymn. He doubted she would have shared what she overheard anyway, given her aversion to gossip.

He talked to Asa later, who told him he had just been following his advice about sitting with a pretty lady to keep him awake during the service. Cade wasn't sure how much of the sermon his friend heard.

Probably about as much as he did with Jessie sitting beside him, their arms brushing on occasion and his fingers touching hers as they held the hymnal. He'd actually been relieved when Ellie grew restless. He settled her on his lap and let her play his fingers like a piano. He still didn't hear much of the sermon, but at least he wasn't so focused on the lady beside him.

He'd come to town again for a regular meeting of the county commissioners court. Finished with business, he decided to stop by the store and see Ty. He found him in the office, writing up an order for another freight-car load of merchandise.

Cade paused in the doorway, resting his hand on the frame and grinned at his brother. "Spending all the money again?"

"Have to spend it to make it." Ty leaned back in his desk chair and stretched his arms over his head. "But that's all right. We're gettin' richer by the minute."

Chuckling, Cade wandered over to a second chair beside the desk and sat down. "Maybe I should quit ranching and open up another business."

"You'd go loco in a week."

"Yep. Start shootin' up the town and probably half the customers to boot. Though we could use another livery stable and wagon yard. Lowery's stable was full when I got here this morning. I had to tie Mischief in front of the courthouse for a while."

A speculative gleam lit his brother's eyes. "I don't know of anything special going on in town. If he's full in the middle of the week, what do people do on the weekend?"

"He said he's been stringing a line out back for the extra horses and putting the wagons in the vacant lot next to his. He seemed to think having too many customers is a nuisance." Cade grinned as Ty leaned forward and began to scribble something on a piece of paper. "Think he's more interested in expanding his freight business."

"He can have it. But I've been thinking about starting a stage line between here and Fort Concho." At Cade's raised eyebrow, Ty laughed. "This time we wouldn't have to fight Indians along the way. And I don't intend to drive. We can find someone else to take care of that part. A stable and wagon yard would fit right in."

Cade considered the plan, slowly nodding. "We could arrange with the ranches to keep the additional teams. You'd need some meal stops, maybe even an overnight one."

"Can't do it until we get a halfway decent road." Ty's eyes twinkled with merriment. "Know anybody on the commissioners court we could talk to?"

"Don't think you'll have to do much talking. We received a petition this morning from several folks south of us, asking for the road to be improved." Cade shook his head. "Lord knows it needs it. It's hardly more than a wide trail in some places. Every time I think about Jessie and the kids coming through that country by themselves, I feel sick. In fact, I'd planned to bring it up this morning, but Terrell and the other ranchers beat me to it."

"So what was the vote?"

"We're looking into the costs and how to go about it. But I don't doubt for a minute that it will be approved, along with at least two bridges over the creeks, possibly three if we can afford it. The country is settling up. If we want our town and county to keep growing, we have to build a good road to Fort Concho to get them here.''

''Can you persuade Tom Green County to take care of their part?''

''I think so. They would benefit, too. Since it's in my precinct, I have to go down there next week and convince them.''

''You don't sound too excited about it.''

Giving his brother a wry smile, Cade shrugged. ''I don't want be away from Jessie and the kids.''

''How are they?''

''Good. Brad is doing well with the riding lessons. We've spent most of the time in the corral, though yesterday we went for a little ride in the pasture. I thought I'd take him out for an hour or so tomorrow morning. Show him some of the ranch. Give him a chance to gallop.'' He settled more comfortably in the chair. ''Ellie's jealous. She's all set for a pony.''

''So you took her a dollhouse instead,'' said Ty with a laugh.

Cade laughed quietly. ''At first she didn't know whether to be mad because I said she was too young for a pony or tickled about the dollhouse. But she's been playing with it a lot, so guess she likes it. We've been reading every night. 'Bout finished with *Around the World in Eighty Days*.''

''You're becoming a regular family man.''

''Not as regular as I'd like.''

Ty studied him for a minute. ''You're serious.'' When Cade nodded, he continued, ''How are things between you and Jessie?''

''I don't know. I think I spooked her a little. Came on too strong. So I've been trying to go slow. I know there's something between us, but she's afraid.''

"Because of her first husband? She said something about not mourning for him, so I figured he wasn't worth much."

"Not worth a plug nickel. So I'm trying to show her that I am."

"Don't you think she could see that right off?"

"Some of it. But she needs a man who will love her and take care of her and the family. One she can trust and depend on."

Understanding dawned in Ty's eyes. "And you haven't told her about Quint."

"I know what he set out to do, but we haven't heard from him." Cade stood, pacing across the small office and back. "He might be dead."

"You have to find some way to explain it to her. The longer you wait, the worse it's going to be."

Cade sighed heavily. "I know. I'll figure out something. In the meantime, we can spread the word that Jessie is at the ranch. Maybe he'll hear about her and quit his foolishness."

Ty gave him an amused look. "The news about Jessie being at the ranch made the rounds the first weekend y'all came to town. Even some of the cowboys from ranches in the Panhandle have heard about it."

"What are they saying?"

"Most folks are speculating that you're about to get hitched."

"And the others?"

"A few men didn't think you needed to bother with marriage. Figured having her working for you and living right next door provided plenty of opportunity to take care of other needs besides grub and a clean house."

"Did you set them straight?"

"Of course. Told them she's a good, God-fearing woman who deserves their respect."

"Good." Cade paused, frowning. "You should have added that I wouldn't take that kind of advantage of a woman."

"I did. And I think most people believe it. But some of them, even the upright ones, look at Jessie and know they'd be hard-pressed to keep their hands off her."

Cade slowly smiled. "I didn't say I intended to. I don't know for certain yet, but I suspect even God-fearing women like to be kissed."

Ty's smile was bittersweet, and sadness filled his eyes. "Amanda did."

Cade wanted to kick himself. Ty's wife had died in childbirth three years earlier. The babe had only lived a few hours. "Sorry."

"Don't be. Like I told you before, you don't have to guard your words. I think about her every day anyway."

"She would be proud of you."

Ty smiled, a happy one this time. "Yes, she would be. Of both of us. She'd like Jessie, too. And she would scold you all day to Sunday for not telling her about Quint."

"I'll give him another week to contact me or the sheriff. Then, whether I've heard from him or not, I'll tell her what I know. Hopefully, it will be good news."

"You think that will make a difference?"

"Maybe a little. She'll probably be mad enough to kick a hog barefooted anyway."

Cade grabbed some dinner at the restaurant, then rode back to the ranch. He stopped at the house, looping Mischief's reins around the hitching post by the back porch. When he walked into the kitchen, Jessie stood beside the table, spreading chocolate frosting on a cake.

She looked up with a smile, and his heart gave a little kick. "How did your meeting go?"

"Good." But it didn't compare with coming home to her in his kitchen, asking about his day. He wanted every day to be like this, only with a welcome-home kiss along with her pretty smile. "We're looking into improving the road from here to Fort Concho."

"Heaven knows it needs it. We almost lost our way a couple of times."

He laid his hat on the table, walking around it to her side. "Every time I think about you out there on your own, I get a bellyache. I had planned to bring up the road today, but some of the folks south of here beat me to it. They were waiting with a petition asking us to do something about it."

She finished spreading the icing with a little swirl of the narrow spatula and dropped it into the empty bowl, absently admiring her handiwork. "You could use a few bridges, too."

"I already suggested it."

She rewarded his brilliance with another smile. "A good road will bring more settlers. I don't know how many people we talked to along the way who had the itch to move but hadn't worked up the courage to do it."

He swiped some icing off the side of the bowl. Licking the sweet chocolate off his fingertip, he looked up and caught his breath. Her eyes were focused on his mouth, her face filled with longing.

And not for chocolate.

"Unlike you," he murmured, sliding his hand around her waist.

She met his gaze, shifting minutely closer. "I was desperate."

"So am I." He slowly lowered his head. "For this."

He brushed his lips across hers, his heart soaring when she breathed a soft, contented sigh and slid her hands around his neck. *Be gentle.* He drew her closer, kissing her tenderly. Raising his head, he smiled at the delicate color in her cheeks and her soft, lush mouth. Her eyelids fluttered, and when she looked up, her eyes were dark gray with passion. Need and pride swept through him. If he didn't back off, the next kiss wouldn't be so gentle. "Where are the kids?"

"Playing with the kittens." She licked her lips, and he stifled a groan. "You taste like chocolate," she whispered.

"Too bad Ty didn't have any more strawberries."

"I'm not complaining." She closed her eyes and lifted her face toward his, inviting his touch.

When he captured her mouth again, she whimpered softly, her fingers tangling in the hair at the nape of his neck. Cade tightened his embrace, molding her against him, and deepened the kiss, giving and taking, seeking solace for two lonely hearts. Touching one corner of her lips, he whispered, "I wanted to kiss you the first time I saw you."

"I know."

"That obvious, huh?" He added a tiny kiss on the other side of her mouth.

"Yes." She caught her breath and tipped her head to the side as he feathered kisses down her neck. "Even then, you made me feel things I'd never felt before."

He straightened, searching her eyes with a frown. "Never?"

"Not like this. Not this sweet ache."

Cade drew in a ragged breath, smoothing a wisp of hair back from her forehead. Beautiful and strong, yet fragile, with a heart he could so easily shatter. "This is only the beginning of the pleasure we'll share, darlin'."

"It's a very nice beginning." She trembled as he skimmed his fingers along her jaw.

He nodded, lowering his hand to her waist and sliding it

around to the small of her back. "But I want moonlight whispers and morning sighs."

"Cade, I can't." She lowered her hands, resting them against his chest. "The children...it would be wrong."

He smiled tenderly. "I know. But someday, we'll make it right."

She shook her head, dropping her gaze. "I won't risk that kind of pain again." When she finally looked up, her eyes were filled with sorrow. "I couldn't bear to disappoint you."

"You won't. What happened with Neil wasn't your fault. It was his. He could never be satisfied with one woman."

"You don't know that."

"Honey, I'd wager the ranch on it. If he'd found someone who made him happy, he would have stayed with her." At the flicker of surprise in her eyes, he wondered if she had ever considered that. "But he kept moving on to someone new, didn't he?"

"Yes. He liked the challenge and the chase, but especially the conquest."

"Exactly. Some men can't ever go beyond that."

She searched his eyes with an intensity that unsettled him. "You like the challenge and the chase, too."

And the conquest. The unspoken words hovered between them.

He hesitated, considering how to answer. "Yes, I do. And I've done my share of playing the game in the past. But that ends with you." He cupped her face with his hand and grinned. "You're enough of a challenge to last a lifetime, and you'll still be leading me on a merry chase when I'm eighty. As for the conquest, I figure it'll be a draw." He sobered, lightly caressing her cheek with his thumb. "I want a lifetime with you, Jessie. I've wanted it since I held you that first night."

"I'm scared."

"I know. And I understand why. All I'm asking for is a chance to prove myself." He thought about Quint, and uneasiness trickled down his spine. *Kiss her senseless and then tell her. Maybe she won't be so mad.* He teased her lower lip. "Will you give me that?" he murmured against her mouth.

"Maybe."

He felt her smile. "Need a little more persuasion?"

"You do it so well."

He claimed her mouth, his kiss deep, full of passion and promises. Pulling her willing body against his, he gave in to his need for just a moment, his touch growing bolder. Her hands wound around his neck again, her desire matching his.

The slamming of the screen door startled them, causing them to abruptly end the kiss and jump apart. Brad stood just inside the doorway. He stared at Cade, his face red and contorted with rage. Shifting his gaze to his mother, tears welled in his eyes, anguish battling anger.

Jessie started toward him, holding out her hand. "Brad, it's all right."

"No, it's not!" He spun around, shoving the screen door open, and barreled through the doorway, knocking Ellie aside as she came across the porch. She landed on her bottom and let out a wail. He jumped off the porch and raced toward the creek.

Jessie ran out the door. "Brad, wait!"

He ran faster.

Chapter Ten

Cade clamped his hand on Jessie's shoulder, stopping her at the bottom of the steps. "Let me talk to him."

She tried to twist from his hold. "I need to." She glanced guiltily at Ellie, who sat sobbing on the porch. "Take care of Ellie for me."

Cade shook his head, instinct telling him that if he didn't talk to Brad there would be a chasm between them that he might never be able to cross. "Jessie, I have to set this straight with him. Or I might not ever be able to."

She hesitated, then nodded. "He's been hurt so much. By his father, the townspeople, the other children." Her voice caught. "Now, by me. Lord, what have I done?"

"Nothing wrong." He pulled her against him in a quick hug, caressing her shoulder. "Now go tend to Ellie. I'll be careful with him."

She stepped back, looking up with tears shimmering in her eyes. "He likes to sit under the big willow tree."

"I'll find him."

He hurried toward the creek, barely hearing Jessie's soothing words as she picked up her daughter. Brad's reaction surprised him. The boy was smart and wiser in the ways of the world than most his age. He had to have noticed the attraction between them. Cade had expected him to be wary but not angry. And especially not hurt by it. Maybe he thought Jessie wouldn't love her children anymore if Cade became part of her life.

Slowing as he approached the creek, he moved down the bank near the big willow tree, sliding the last few feet on the crumbling dirt. Ducking beneath the long, widespread feathery branches, he spotted Brad huddled against the trunk. The old tree was tall, allowing Cade to stand straight beneath the shady canopy.

"Go away!" Brad glared at him, swiping his tearstained face with his hand.

"Not until we have a little talk." Cade hunkered down, not quite in front him but close enough to grab him if he tried to bolt.

Resting his arms on his bent knees, Brad leaned forward, burying his face against them. "Go back to your whore," he mumbled miserably.

Shocked, Cade stared at him for a second. "Don't ever talk that way about your mother," he ordered.

"Pa said she was." Brad raised his head, shooting daggers from tear-swollen eyes.

"Your pa was an idiot and a fool." Cade settled down beside him, leaning back against the wide trunk, thinking of half a dozen other names he'd like to call the man. He wished he'd met up with him before the mayor ended his sorry life. "When did you start believing him about anything?"

"He said Ellie wasn't his. Other people talked about Mama, too." Brad took a deep, shuddering breath. "They said she deserved the way Pa ran around on her, that she wasn't no better than him."

Cade frowned, unable to reconcile the woman he knew

with that image. "Sounds like a rumor your father or his cronies started just for spite. Did you believe them?"

Brad was quiet for a few minutes, fighting to control his emotions. "No."

"Did you ever see her with another man?"

He shook his head. "But she was kissing you." Misery dripped from every word.

"That doesn't mean she's a bad woman, son."

"But she swore she wouldn't ever get married again."

Cade smiled slightly, understanding what the boy left unsaid. "I'm trying to change her mind. Kissing her is part of the strategy. She's a fine, upright woman, Brad, and I'm hoping she'll become my wife. You think I'd want to marry somebody who wasn't decent?"

Brad stared at the creek. "I don't reckon."

"Tell me something. Does Ellie look like your pa?"

"Yeah. His hair was dark brown and curly like hers." He paused thoughtfully, finally looking at Cade with a deep frown. "And her eyes are the same color brown as his. But why would he say he wasn't her pa?"

"I don't know. Maybe it was another way to hurt your mother. Maybe he just didn't want to take responsibility for her, didn't want to feel he needed to provide for her."

Brad snorted. "He didn't bring no money home anyway. He was always tearin' the house apart in case Mama hid some."

"And if he didn't find it?"

"He threw things around, then stomped out the door, yellin' a lot. Most of the time, after she paid the rent and bought groceries, there wasn't any left." He shuddered, not meeting Cade's gaze. "He beat her up once."

"She told me."

Brad swallowed hard. "I tried to stop him, but I couldn't."

"At least you tried. That's the best a man can do. Did he hurt you, too?"

"Yeah. That time, he threw me against the wall, knocked me out," he said in a matter-of-fact way.

Cade cringed. He had to clear his throat before he could ask, "And other times?"

"He'd take the razor strop to me. But he didn't do it much. Didn't want to work that hard." Brad looked up at him, his tears gone, his face solemn. "Would you use a razor strop on a kid?"

Cade pictured the leather one hanging by his washstand that he used to sharpen the straight razor. It had a handle on one end and a metal hook on the other. Those without hooks had a metal eyelet on the end opposite the handle. He couldn't imagine hitting a child with one. "No, I wouldn't. I might use a willow switch on occasion, but I don't hold with whippin' kids except for grave offenses." Even then, it would just about kill him. "I figure most of the time, if punishment is needed, we can come up with something better."

Brad swallowed and looked away. "Like washin' my mouth out with soap for what I said about Mama?"

"You were mighty upset. You didn't mean it, did you?"

"No, sir." He turned to Cade, his expression intense. "You won't tell her what I called her, will you?"

"Never. Son, I care very much for your mother. And that's why I like to kiss her." Cade hesitated, considering how much to say. He wanted to do a lot more than kiss her, but that probably wasn't something he should discuss with her son. "I think she cares for me a little, because she likes to kiss me, too."

"She sure does," Brad muttered, with more than a hint of disgust.

Cade managed not to smile. "It isn't wrong because we

have feelings for each other. But I promise you that I won't do anything that we shouldn't. I'll never do anything to harm your mother's good reputation. I respect her too much.''

''You promise not to hurt her?''

''I'd never hit your mother. Nothing on this earth would make me strike her.''

''Pa only did it once. But he made her cry a lot.''

''I can't promise that I won't ever make her cry.'' Unfortunately, that was liable to happen much too soon. ''But I'll try my best not to. I don't want to see her hurt any more than you do.''

Brad stood. ''I guess I have to go apologize.''

''That would be good.'' Cade stood also, brushing the twigs and dust off the seat of his pants. ''And I need to go change out of my city clothes. You'd better apologize to Ellie, too. She wasn't too happy about landing on her rump.''

Brad grimaced as he shoved a thin tree branch aside and walked out from beneath the big willow. ''I'll probably have to play with her and her dollhouse to make up for it.''

''Sounds like a good plan.''

''To you, maybe.''

Cade chuckled and ruffled his hair. ''Might as well learn early to appease the womenfolk. Makes life easier all the way around.''

Jessie glanced at the clock for the tenth time in as many minutes. Surely, Cade and Brad had been gone an hour, not less than a quarter of that time. She paced back and forth across the kitchen, looking out the back window whenever she crossed in front of it.

Ellie licked the last crumbs of chocolate cake from her fork, then took a big drink of milk, leaving a white mustache above her lip. "Maybe Brad fell in the creek," she said hopefully.

Jessie stopped by the table and handed her daughter a napkin. "That's not a nice thing to wish for."

"He wouldn't drown. The water don't even come up to my knees."

"Doesn't, honey."

"Yes, ma'am. Might cool him off." She climbed down from the chair and carried her plate and fork over to the basin in the dry sink. Jessie followed with her glass. "What was he so mad about anyway? He don't…doesn't hardly ever cry."

Jessie didn't bother to correct Ellie's grammar again. She'd been waiting for the question since her daughter calmed down, and she still didn't know how to answer her. "He saw Mr. McKinnon kiss me."

Ellie's mouth dropped open. "Mr. McKinnon kissed you? Why?"

Jessie felt her cheeks grow warm. "He likes me." A lot.

"Mr. Toad liked you, but you didn't have nothin' to do with him."

Jessie laughed in spite of herself. "Mr. Johnson, honey."

"Looked like a toad to me."

"Well, yes, he did."

"Was that why you didn't kiss him?"

"I was married then. And married women don't go around kissing men who aren't their husbands." The mayor's wife came to mind. "At least the decent ones don't." She could practically see the wheels turning in her daughter's head. "What?"

"But it's all right to kiss somebody if you aren't married?"

"Sometimes."

"What if Mr. Toad came callin' again?"

"I still wouldn't want anything to do with him."

"Good." Ellie wiggled in what Jessie thought was supposed to be a shiver. "I didn't like him."

"I didn't, either." Jessie glanced at the clock again. Almost fifteen minutes since she'd come into the house. That meant Brad had been gone at least twenty minutes. Maybe he had fallen into the creek. Or tried to push Cade in. The silliness of that idea brought a tiny smile.

"But you like Mr. McKinnon."

"Yes, I do." A lot.

"He'd make a good daddy."

"Yes, he probably would." When Jessie saw her daughter grin and look past her, she swallowed hard and turned around.

Cade stood in the doorway with Brad, his big hand resting affectionately on the boy's shoulder. Her son appeared uncomfortable, as if he were waiting for a scolding. Cade's tender smile was almost her undoing. Then he glanced at Ellie and winked. "Thanks for the compliment."

She tried to wink back, blinking both eyes. "You're welcome." Then she settled her hands on her hips and glared at her brother. "You knocked me down."

"I'm sorry. You all right?"

Ellie rubbed her backside. "Hurts."

"Ellie, that's not what you told me," Jessie chided softly.

"Well, it did." She stuck her tongue out at Brad.

Jessie frowned at her daughter. "That's enough. Why don't you take your dolly out onto the porch for some fresh air."

"She don't want any."

"Take her out anyway."

Ellie grimaced but did as she was told. When she was

out of the room, Jessie walked over to Brad. Cade backed through the doorway onto the porch, leaving them alone.

"Honey, I'm sorry." She brushed her son's hair back from his forehead.

"It's all right, Mama. I shouldn't have gotten all riled up. Mr. McKinnon explained that you weren't do nothin' wrong."

She lowered her hand, wondering how much her son knew about the ways between a man and a woman. "But you thought I was?" When he nodded reluctantly, she asked, "Why?"

He shrugged, looking down at the floor.

"Brad, please tell me."

He rubbed his bare foot against the smooth wooden floor. "When we were in Riverbend, Johnny said his daddy said you deserved for Pa to run around on you." He swallowed hard. "That you'd spent time with him. And some other men, too."

Stunned, Jessie found it hard to breathe. She knew people had talked, had even heard a few rumors herself. But nothing so vicious. She had never imagined that her child would hear such awful things. She laid her hands on his shoulders and looked him right in the eye. "Brad, Johnny's daddy lied. I don't know why, but he did."

"I know that, Mama. And that's what I told Johnny." A smile tugged at the corner of his mouth. "Punched him in the nose, too."

"That's why you didn't want to be friends with him anymore," she said sadly.

"He wasn't much fun most of the time anyway."

She released him and glanced away. "So when you saw Cade kissing me, you thought..." *Oh, Lord, how do I ask this?*

"You said you wouldn't ever marry again."

Jessie looked up. Brad's red face told her exactly what he had thought. "I'm not, uh, spending time with him. And I don't intend to."

"I know that now. Mr. McKinnon explained it to me. He said he was trying to change your mind about marrying again."

"Oh." Jessie felt her own face flush.

"And that he wouldn't ever do anything that made people talk about you, 'cause he respects you too much."

"He's a good man, Brad."

"Yes, ma'am. You gonna marry him?"

"I don't know." She closed her eyes for a second, then met his gaze with a tiny smile. "But I'm not quite as scared about the idea as I was yesterday."

Chapter Eleven

"If you need anything, holler at Asa. He'll stay around headquarters until I get back." Cade stopped on his back porch, waiting for Jessie to come outside. "Ty said he'd ride out tomorrow afternoon to see how things are going."

"We'll be fine." She gave him an indulgent smile. "I've been fending for myself a long time."

"But you don't have to now," he said, a stubborn set to his jaw. "Lock your doors at night." He frowned, glancing around the backyard. "I wish we had a dog."

We. He used the word without thinking, which made it all that much sweeter. And more unnerving. Her heart yearned to share her life with this man, but old fears were hard to conquer.

"I'm sure Asa and the other men will keep watch over us."

"They'd better." He looked over at her house. "Maybe I should have someone sleep on your porch."

"How about the front room?" Jessie narrowed her eyes and crossed her arms, growing impatient with his overprotectiveness.

"I'll have his hide," he growled. When she started tapping her foot, he turned his attention back to her. "Guess the porch was a silly suggestion."

"Almost as silly as the front room."

"You have your shotgun loaded?"

She nodded. "It's on the rack." He had suggested hanging it up to keep it from being accidentally knocked over and built her a rack by the back door. It was low enough for Jessie to reach easily but high enough that Ellie couldn't mess with it. Not that she would. The child was afraid of guns. She had been ever since Neil came home one night, shooting his pistol up in the air for fun. Still, Jessie liked the idea of having the gun handy but out of the way. She had also been touched by his concern and practical solution.

"You'd better get going."

"And quit wastin' daylight." He smiled, turning to Brad and Ellie, who stood nearby. "No squabbling while I'm gone, you hear?"

"Yes, sir," they said in unison. Ellie giggled and Brad shot her a grin.

Cade laughed. "Keep up that kind of cooperation and you'll do just fine. Brad, if you practice your roping, we'll try it on a real cow when I get home."

"Okay. But not one with big horns."

"I'll see if I can arrange that." Cade knelt down, holding his arms open to Ellie. "Come here and hug my neck, sweetheart."

She scampered across the porch, throwing her arms around his neck in a tight squeeze. He hugged her back and gave her a kiss on the cheek. "Be a good girl while I'm gone."

"I'm always good." She grinned impishly.

"Most of the time anyway." Cade smiled and stood, holding his hand out to Brad. "You wait to start *Treasure Island* till I get back."

Brad took his hand, shaking it firmly. "I will. Mama said we could read some from *Harper's Magazine* instead."

"I have a whole stack of them. They have some good stories. Interesting articles, too." Cade's gaze settled on Jessie. "Even some purty poetry."

Ellie giggled again and Brad rolled his eyes.

"Makes me think of your mama," Cade added, his voice dropping a notch deeper. Her eyes widened and heat filled her cheeks.

"Come on, Ellie, let's go look for grasshoppers," said Brad. "They're gonna get mushy again."

"Okay. Bye, Mr. McKinnon."

Since he had kissed Jessie a few times in front of the children, evidently it wasn't much of a novelty anymore. "Goodbye, honey. I'll see you at the end of the week." The little girl waved and ran off after her brother.

"Brad's right." Cade moved a step closer to Jessie. "I need a proper send-off."

"We should go inside."

"No, ma'am. We're staying right here so anybody that's watching will know you're my woman."

"You're getting cocky, cowboy." She wasn't about to admit that she liked it.

"Cattleman. The cowboys work for me."

"My, my. You better be careful when you try to mount your horse."

"Why?"

"Your head is so big, you're liable to just topple right on over."

Cade laughed and put his arms around her waist. "Merely pointing out that you'd be better off with me than anybody else on this ranch." He grinned cheekily. "Of course, that would be true even if I didn't own it."

Smiling, Jessie shook her head in bemusement. "Have you always been so sure of yourself?"

"Not always." Sadness flickered through his eyes, and Jessie remembered what he'd told her about being unable to care for his mother.

Without thinking, she laid her hand along his jaw. "Since you became a man, I mean."

He closed his eyes for a heartbeat, leaning ever so slightly against her hand. Turning his head, he pressed his lips against her palm. "I started out with more guts than sense."

She lowered her hand. "You have more sense now?"

"A lot more. I took one look at you and saw the other half of my soul. That's the most intelligent thing I've ever done."

"Oh, Cade…" Tears welled up in her eyes. She wished with all her heart that she could tell him the same thing. But this attraction was too strong, too quick. She feared it would be like fireworks on Independence Day—beautiful, exciting and over in a flash.

"Shh, darlin'. Send me off with a smile, not tears." He slowly pulled her closer. "And a kiss to keep me warm at night."

"It's June. You'll be warm anyway."

He chuckled and dropped a kiss on the tip of her nose. "You always gonna be this sassy, woman?"

"Probably."

"Good," he murmured, lowering his head.

The tenderness of his touch moved her as much as passion would have. Desire lay beneath the surface, carefully controlled, waiting for another time and place. He ended the kiss slowly and eased away. "I'll be back by Saturday. Friday afternoon if I can."

"Be careful."

"Always am. Have even more reason to be now." He moved down the steps toward Mischief as the horse waited patiently at the hitching post. "This ol' boy could get me home even if I fall asleep in the saddle." Cade untied the reins, patted him on the neck and mounted with the grace and ease that came from earning his living horseback. "He's done it many a time.

"An order of new dresses came in yesterday. Why don't you have Asa take you to town and pick up something pretty?" Earlier that morning, he had insisted on giving her what she had earned to date in case she needed money while he was gone. He had also given her some extra cash out of the household account to use for groceries or emergencies.

She had been equally insistent that he take out what she owed him from her wages. "I'm saving my money for a hat to go with the new dress I already have."

"It's two weeks old already."

Jessie laughed and leaned against the porch railing. "And I've only worn it twice. Still new to me."

He guided Mischief over next to the porch. "When we get married, I'll buy you a new dress every week. Two or three if you want them."

He had mentioned marriage other times, often in a way that sounded as if it were a foregone conclusion. She found it mildly annoying, yet also a compliment. "And where would I wear them?"

"To town. Or just for me. A couple of different ones every day."

"Two a day? That's a lot of bother."

He leaned close to her, resting his hand beside hers on the railing. "Not if I help you change." He kissed her hard and quick. When he pushed himself back upright in the saddle, he grinned devilishly. "Think about it."

The images his words evoked sent heat spiraling through her. "I will not."

His burning gaze settled on her scarlet face. "Darlin', you already are."

Jessie clung to the railing to keep from fanning her cheeks. "Cade McKinnon, you're a scoundrel."

"Yeah, but I'm lovable." He winked and nudged the horse to a walk.

Too lovable, thought Jessie, sad to see him leave.

She spent Monday cleaning all the nooks and crannies of Cade's house. On Tuesday, she checked his clothes, carefully sewing up a ripped seam in a work shirt, repairing a torn pocket on a pair of pants, and replaced a few buttons here and there. The task took longer than it should have. It seemed such a wifely thing to do, especially when she caught herself resting her cheek against one of his dress shirts, breathing in the faint scent of his cologne that lingered at the collar.

In the afternoon, Brad and Ellie took her fishing at the creek. According to Brad, Jessie had a nibble, but the fish stole her bait and swam away while she was daydreaming—probably about Cade. She didn't bother to deny it, but left the fishing up to her son while she and Ellie picked a small bouquet of wildflowers. He caught two good-sized catfish, which she fried for supper. Ty rode up just in time to eat, and they enjoyed a pleasant evening.

By Wednesday, she had cabin fever and asked Asa to take them to town. He happily obliged. If he hadn't been a gentleman, he would have dashed into McKinnon's store ahead of them. Instead, he held the door open politely and waited impatiently while Lydia finished ringing up a customer.

She gave in to Lydia's encouragement and bought a new

dress instead of the hat she had planned to purchase. She found a nice straw one at McKinnon's that would go with both dresses, at less than half the cost of the one she had spotted at the milliners. The new dress was an extravagance, but she wanted to please Cade.

On Thursday morning she did the family laundry. A pot of red beans, flavored with salt pork and a bit of onion simmered on the stove in her house. After hanging up the laundry on a clothesline Cade had built for her, she went inside and made a pan of cornbread. It still felt strange to spend the day in her own house, setting her own mismatched plates and bowls on the new oak table.

Jessie gazed slowly around the room at all Cade had bought for them. She had worried about the expense, but he pointed out that he needed to furnish the place regardless of who lived there. He also noted that though he bought good quality merchandise, it wasn't fancy, nor extravagant.

At least most of it. To Jessie, the five-foot-long plunge bath sitting in the corner of the kitchen and the beautiful screen shielding it from view were both luxuries she had only dreamed of. The hand-painted silk screen, with graceful white swans gliding amid green and white lily pads on a dark blue lake, was far prettier than the one the mayor's wife had in her bedroom.

She smiled, remembering when Cade had carried the tub out of the store. He'd shoved it along one side of the wagon bed, then turned to her with a stern expression. "Not a word, woman," he'd ordered quietly. "This is for my own peace of mind." His gaze slid over her and he sighed. "Don't know which is worse—this or that blasted washtub." He had never mentioned it again. But each time she delightfully soaked in the hot water, she wondered if he was thinking about her and if his imagination was as unsettling as hers.

Besides the table, other additions to the kitchen were four chairs, a pie safe and another cupboard. The living room portion of the long room held a small sofa, her rocker, another comfortable chair so he could visit, and two end tables.

Her trunk was tucked into a corner because there was no room for it in the bedroom. A narrow armoire, a dresser with a matching mirror, the bed and a washstand filled that room, leaving barely enough space to change clothes. Brad's room was furnished in a similar manner, only with a single bed and smaller dresser.

Cade had also surprised her with a special gift, meant for her, not the house. He had noticed her admiring a lovely china washbowl and pitcher, covered with delicate yellow roses. Sometime while they were moving the furniture into the house, he had slipped the set into her bedroom. It was by far the most beautiful gift she had ever been given, though she suspected she would have cherished it almost as much if it were gray graniteware.

After dinner, she ironed their clothes and put the rest of the dried laundry away. As evening approached and the air cooled, she and the children walked down to the creek for a spell. When they returned home, she read a story called "Fish and Men in the Maine Islands" from the August, 1880, issue of *Harper's Magazine*. The children particularly liked the drawings showing them a place and way of life they knew nothing about.

She tucked Brad and Ellie into bed, spending a little longer with each of them than usual. Late evening had become her time alone with Cade, sitting on the front porch away from the cowboys' curious eyes. They shared hugs and kisses, but equally important to her, they talked. About his life as a Texas Ranger, stage driver and cowboy. About her happy childhood until smallpox took her parents when she was fifteen and she went to work.

They talked about her hopes and dreams, as well as his for the ranch and the town. They discussed problems that came with settling a new part of the country. To her amazement, he often asked her opinion on things. He listened to her ideas and concerns with respect and admiration, making her feel intelligent and important, not only to him but to the community.

She missed him terribly. She tried to read first one story then another in the magazine, but nothing held her interest past the first few paragraphs. Finally she snuffed out the lamp and went outside to sit on the back porch.

Lamplight shone through the windows of the bunkhouse, and faint laughter reached her ears. A horse nickered in the corral, and a cricket chirped near the end of the porch. At least she and the children weren't by themselves.

It only felt like it.

Her memory teased her with Cade's smile, his touch, his wooing words. Though he talked of marriage, he had never said that he loved her. But he had called her the other half of his soul. Wasn't that the same thing?

Had Cade started home? Was he alone beside a campfire on the open prairie, looking up at the stars and thinking of her? Did he miss their time together in the evenings? The teasing and flirting or the occasional misunderstanding, smoothed over with a hug and a kiss. Oh, those kisses! Did he long for her as much as she longed for him?

Or was he sitting on a rancher's front porch telling tales and listening to yarns, thoughts of her far from his mind and conversation? Being away from her, perhaps with the rancher's pretty daughter making eyes at him, had he suddenly realized how foolish he had been? That there were many others—brighter, prettier and wealthier—who would jump at the chance to become his wife?

On that gloomy thought, she went inside, locking the door behind her. She crossed the room to close the front curtains, but a movement near a mesquite about fifty yards away drew her gaze. Peering out the window from the dark room, she watched as a man dismounted, leaving his horse hidden in the shadow of the tree. Crouching low, he hurried across the open prairie toward the house.

Jessie raced across the room, grabbing the shotgun from the wall rack, checking to make certain it was loaded. When she returned to the window, she spied the man near Cade's house. He paused for a second, glancing around, then moved stealthily up the front porch steps and disappeared in the darkness.

Chapter Twelve

Jessie eased open her front door, moving across the porch and down the steps. She hurried across the yard as quietly as she could, thankful when she reached the shadow of Cade's house. Tiptoeing alongside the building, she stopped at the corner of the porch and listened.

A board creaked. Then another, along with the faint tap of boot heels as the man walked across the porch. When the sound stopped, Jessie pulled one hammer back, raised the gun to her shoulder and stepped out from behind the wall. "Hold it right there and put your hands up."

The man threw up his hands. "Jess, don't shoot! It's me."

"Quint!" Staring at the shadowy form of her brother, Jessie lowered the gun.

"Hi, little sister." Though he moved near the railing, he stayed in the darkness.

"What are you doing sneaking around Cade's house?" Jessie asked softly. Pointing the shotgun away from the porch and toward the ground, she eased the hammer forward so it wouldn't fire. She laid it on the end of the porch, then raced around to the front and up the steps.

He gave her a big hug, then draped one arm around her

shoulders. "I needed to talk to him but can't let anyone else know I'm here. Except you."

"Why?"

"It's a long story. Is he in town?"

"He went to Fort Concho to talk to the commissioners about improving the road. He planned to be back by Saturday. Maybe even tomorrow."

"Then you'll have to give him a message for me. But first, tell me about you and the kids. I heard that you were working as Cade's housekeeper—and that you're a widow. What happened?" he asked gently.

"The mayor caught Neil in bed with his wife. Shot him on the spot."

Quint groaned softly, hugging her again. "Sis, I'm sorry. I should have done something about him years ago. Or convinced you to leave him."

"You tried." She pulled away and looked up at him. "Cade said you suspected Neil was running around. But you never said anything to me."

"I wasn't positive. Just heard lots of rumors. I didn't want to hurt you if it wasn't true. Reckon I should have said something anyway. Or beat him to a pulp for good measure."

"That wouldn't have helped. And I would have had to listen to him moan and groan for who knows how long. Let's go over to my house and visit a while."

"Better not. I can't let the kids know I'm here. Ellie would spill the beans for sure. Are they doin' all right?"

"They are now. It was real hard on Brad, though. Not that he misses his father. But there was so much talk. Ellie doesn't know what really happened. I told her he was killed in an accident." Jessie sat down on the porch, resting her feet on the top step. Quint joined her, stretching his long legs out in front of him. She was itching to find out what he was up to, but she knew he would tell her in his own good time.

"I don't suppose the sheriff did anything about the murder?"

"Of course not. He was more concerned about his own hide than his cousin. The mayor said Neil shot first, and the sheriff backed him up. I didn't try to fight them on it."

"It wouldn't have done any good. Not in that town." He pulled off his hat and laid it beside him. "And I don't suppose you wanted to wait around for me. Who helped you come out here?"

"Nobody."

He stared at her and clenched his jaw.

Poor Quint, she thought, hiding a smile. *He can't even yell at me.*

"You came by yourself?" he asked hoarsely.

"Brad and Ellie were with me."

"Jessie…"

She thought for a minute he might lose control and yell anyway. "I didn't have any money to pay anyone. And I wouldn't have known who to ask or trust anyway."

"Valentine made it?"

"All the way," Jessie said proudly. "We couldn't go very far at a time. Whenever I could, I let her rest every couple of days. You probably won't recognize her. Cade's been fattening her up. She follows him around like a puppy." She laid her hand on his forearm. "But what are you doing here at this time of night? Where have you been?"

"We'll get to that in a minute. How's he treating you?"

Jessie sighed at his stubbornness. "Good."

"How good?" he asked in a protective-big-brother tone.

"He's paying me more than he should and spoiling the kids rotten. They adore him. It took Brad a while to warm up to him, but Cade's teaching him how to ride and rope. He reads to us every evening after dinner.''

"I heard he's interested in you.'' He hesitated. "Real interested.''

Judging from the edge in his voice, Quint had heard some of the kind of talk Jessie had been worried about— speculation that she was more than Cade's housekeeper.

"He is. But he hasn't made any improper demands.'' She smiled slightly. "He even promised Brad that he wouldn't. He says he wants to marry me.''

"Do you want to marry him?''

"Sometimes I do.'' She glanced at her brother and shrugged. "This week, most of the time. I sure miss him.''

"You haven't known him very long.''

"No, but I know him better than I did Neil when we got married, and he courted me for six months.'' She sighed. "At least I thought that's what he was doing. I've often wondered if he married me simply because he couldn't seduce me.''

"Cade's not anything like Neil.''

"No, he's not. He's a fine, decent and honorable man.'' And he lights a fire in me I didn't know existed, she thought.

"He'd be a good provider, and you wouldn't ever have to worry about him running around on you.'' Quint looked at her and grinned. "As we say out here in the wild West, he's a good man to ride the rivers with.''

"A man you can trust.''

He nodded. "With my life.''

"Then why did you get mad and punch him? Make him fire you?''

Quint shifted, glancing at her warily.

She'd seen that look before and knew she wasn't going to like what he had to say.

"I needed to make it look like we had a fallin'-out. You remember Jack Shepherd?"

"Yes. You worked for him for a while right after you left home."

"Rustlers hit his herd a while back. Jack had been out on the range for a few days, checking his cattle, and tried to stop them. Years ago he probably could have done it, but he's an old man now. Doesn't see as good as he used to, or move as fast. They almost killed him."

"Shot him?"

"No. They roped him and dragged him. Broke several ribs, his leg and knocked him unconscious. He had a bump on the back of his head the size of a goose egg. He was unconscious for over a week, and the doctor didn't know if he would make it or not."

When he turned toward her, and Jessie saw the determination in his expression, she knew he was trying somehow to right the wrong done to his old friend. "What are you doing about it?" she asked, her heart pounding.

"I joined up with the rustlers."

"Quint! You could go to prison!"

"No, the sheriff and I planned it. He agreed it's the only way to capture them. Somebody has to stop them. Word got around quick enough about my fight with Cade, so even when I pretended to look for a job at a couple of ranches, no one would hire me. Didn't want a troublemaker.

"I hung around town for about a week. One night at the Diamond Saloon, one of the rustlers struck up a conversation. Asked me if I wanted a job. I had an idea who he was, but couldn't be sure until he took me to meet the number two man. They didn't take me to their main camp. A couple of the men stayed with me away from their hideout and watched me like a hawk. Said I had to prove myself." He took a deep breath, exhaling slowly.

"You stole some cattle?" she whispered.

He nodded. "The first time, we took twenty head from a big ranch in the northern part of the county. A couple of nights ago we took five more from Jack Shepherd." His voice was thick with anger and disgust.

"Oh, Quint." Jessie caught his hand, holding it tight.

"His operation is real small now. The last couple of years, he mostly ran it by himself. They knew he was still laid up and wouldn't be out lookin' for them."

"So no one was guarding the herd."

"It's open range. You can't guard a herd unless you've rounded them all up. Then you need a whole crew to keep watch and hold the cattle together."

"You did what the outlaws wanted. Do you know where their camp is now?"

"Yes. They took me there after we stole Jack's cattle. Tell Cade to let the sheriff know it's in a box canyon east of the headwaters of Mustang Creek."

"Why don't you just go tell the sheriff? You found the camp. He can arrest them now."

"Not yet. I don't know who is running the operation. I think it's somebody from town, but I'm not sure. I got a glimpse of him last night at their hideout, but wasn't close enough to recognize him. He was wearing a suit, though, so he's either a rancher or a businessman of some kind. I asked one of the men who he was, but he just called him the boss. I didn't think I'd better pry too much or they'd get suspicious. I don't think any of them would cross him, either. The guy I talked to seemed real afraid of him."

"How did you get away from them tonight?"

"A couple of them were going to visit one of the parlor houses. They're careful about riding into town one or two at a time so no one will realize they're all together." He grinned at her. "I told them I was going to see a lady friend at another place."

"I don't suppose you could tell them you were coming to see me."

"No. Some of the men were in town last weekend and heard you were working out here. They saw you with Cade." He rubbed the back of his neck and rotated his shoulders. "They knew about our fight and that he'd fired me, so I let them think I didn't care that you were here. Said I didn't want to see you. That if you were involved with Cade, then you deserved each other." He chuckled softly. "I meant it, but not the way they thought."

Quintin picked up his hat. "I'd better get going. Tell Cade to pass on the information to the sheriff."

"That the hideout is in a box canyon east of the head of Mustang Creek. Do they have the cattle there, too?"

"They're holding about thirty head there right now. They've sold the others somehow, but I don't know who the buyer is. Tell Cade that as soon as I know who their leader is, I'll signal him. I couldn't get away before this to leave him the sign and meet like we'd planned."

Jessie's heart froze. Cade had known all along what Quint was doing but pretended he didn't. The man she'd considered honest and trustworthy had lied to her.

She prayed that she'd misunderstood Quint. "Cade knows about all this?" she asked quietly, trying hard to keep her voice steady.

Quint glanced at her and cleared his throat. "Yes, but he didn't like it, not one bit."

"Well, he did a fine job of stopping you from being an idiot."

"He tried to talk me out of it." He paused, facing his sister. "This is something I have to do, Jessie. Jack saved my hide more times than I can count. He took a green, scared kid and made a man out of me. I owe him.''

"You don't owe him your life." She fought back tears of fear and anger. "If the rustlers find out what you're doing, they'll shoot you without a second thought. And if they don't, some rancher is liable to kill you. I admire what you're trying to do, Quint. But it's too dangerous. There has to be some other way.''

"There isn't. The sheriff is good at his job, Jessie, but the rustlers are always one step ahead of him. Someone in town is tipping them off. Cade and Ty are the only other people he trusts." Quint stood and put on his hat. "We'll get this taken care of soon."

Jessie rose, barely resisting the urge to double up her fists and pound on him as she had done when they were little. Or maybe hog-tie him and lock him in the house until he got some sense. Instead, she gave him a fierce hug. "Please be careful."

"Always am."

She all but snorted. "And I can rope a cow with my eyes shut.''

"I didn't know you could rope one with your eyes open." When she glared at him, he just grinned. "Hold off on gettin' hitched. I want to be at the wedding."

Pain and anger washed through her. "There won't be a wedding. I won't make the same mistake twice."

"Give him a chance, Jess."

"He had his chance. Lying is never right." She brushed past her brother, going around to pick up her shotgun. "I don't want anything to do with a man I can't trust."

Chapter Thirteen

Cade arrived home midafternoon on Friday. He slowed Mischief as they approached the house to keep from sending a cloud of dust through the open windows. Smiling in anticipation, he watched to see if Jessie and the kids came out to meet him. Ellie would probably squeal and throw herself into his arms for a big bear hug. Brad would grin and maybe sidle up to him for at least a one-armed hug.

Then he'd pull Jessie into an embrace for his welcome-home kiss. He'd have to be careful and control himself in front of the children. Later, when they were alone, he'd show her how much he missed her. Unfortunately, even then, he would have to keep a tight rein on his desire.

The yard between his house and Jessie's came into view, revealing her old wagon sitting close to her back porch. Though Valentine was nowhere in sight, the wagon held at least half of their things. "What the...?"

He stopped Mischief near the wagon and dismounted, letting the reins trail along the ground. He barely noticed, and didn't care, when the horse turned and moseyed toward the barn. Storming up the steps, Cade came to an abrupt halt when Ellie ran out to meet him. Instead of a squeal of delight, her little face was a picture of unhappiness. Big tears welled up in her eyes and rolled down her cheeks. Her lips quivered and a sob broke from her throat. He dropped to one knee and gathered her in his arms.

Lifting her gently, he stood, cradling her against his chest. "Shh, honey, don't cry." She tightened her arms around his neck, and for a minute, he could barely breathe. Tugging gently at one tiny arm, he eased the pressure on his windpipe. "What's wrong? Why are you leaving?"

She shook her head and tried to burrow closer. "I dunno," she mumbled.

Brad stepped out the back door, his face filled with sadness, disappointment in his eyes. "You lied to Mama."

His heart pounding, Cade glanced behind the boy at Jessie, who stood in the kitchen. He dragged his gaze away and looked back at Brad. If they knew about Quint, he had either accomplished his job or been hurt. Or maybe killed. Fear settled in a cold lump in his belly. "What about?"

"She won't say." Anger flashed in the boy's eyes. "But you hurt her, and you promised you wouldn't."

Cade's chest tightened with pain. "No, son," he said softly, "I promised I'd *try* not to hurt her. Sometimes, there isn't any way to avoid it."

"Telling me the truth would have taken care of it," said Jessie stiffly, stopping in the doorway. "Brad, go fetch Valentine. And take Ellie with you."

Ellie raised her head and frowned at Jessie. "I wanna stay with Cade."

"Do what your mother tells you, honey," Cade said softly. "Go with Brad down to the barn." He leaned down, setting her feet on the porch. When she tried to hang on to him, he shook his head. "Don't, Ellie. Go with your brother. Jessie and I need to talk."

She reluctantly loosened her grip and stepped back, sticking out her bottom lip. Brad put his hand on her shoulder and maneuvered her down the steps and toward the barn.

Cade straightened, pinning Jessie with his gaze. "What's this all about?"

"Quint came to see you last night."

"Is he all right?"

"Oh, he's fine, except for being an outlaw and a cattle rustler. He may get his head shot off any second. Or lynched by some angry rancher." She moved toward him, spitting fire. "But that's old news to you."

Cade shoved his hat back and rubbed his hand over his face. "I wanted to tell you about it. But I was afraid it would make you worry."

"That's another lie, Cade McKinnon." She poked him in the chest with her index finger. "I never expected you to be so good at it."

"But it's the truth."

"You don't think I've worried since I got here? About Quint, about providing for my family, about us?"

"Well, yes. But I've tried to reassure you as much as I could by giving you a job. You would have fretted more if you'd known what he was doing."

"Maybe." She spun around, going back into the house. He followed. "But you had no right to keep it from me."

"I was trying to protect you. And Quint. Only the sheriff, Ty and I knew what he was doing. It was safer to keep it that way."

She stopped, staring at him incredulously. "You thought I might tell someone and put him in danger?"

He cringed inwardly. Coming from her, it sounded like a lame excuse. "I know you wouldn't do anything intentionally to put him in danger, but you might accidentally let something slip. Or the kids might have overheard something and told someone."

She rolled her eyes.

He had a flash of inspiration. "Since you didn't know, if someone asked about him, you didn't have to lie. You could honestly tell them you didn't know where he was, that maybe he'd gone to East Texas to see you. It made it easier for you, too, all those times you asked other folks in town if they'd seen him."

Crossing her arms, she studied him, her expression shuttered. Cade didn't like that. He usually could read her emotions and most of the time had a good idea of what was going through her head.

"Let me get this straight," she said. "You only wanted to keep me from worrying too much and to keep me from having to lie about what he was doing."

Cade crossed his arms, too, standing with his legs widespread and firmly planted in a show of strength. "That's right. If one of the rustlers had questioned you about Quint, he might have picked up on a lie. I doubt you'd be very good at it."

"Unlike you."

"I didn't like lying to you, Jessie. Despite what you think, it doesn't come easy for me. I'd planned to tell you about Quint after I heard from him and knew what the situation was." He took off his hat and tossed it on the table, rubbing the back of his neck. "You were so worn-out when you arrived, I decided not to say anything. I figured the best thing I could do for you and him was to keep you safe, to look after you."

She lifted one eyebrow.

"I was sure I'd probably talk to him within a few days, and once he learned you were here, he'd forget about his cockeyed plan to join up with the rustlers. But as weeks passed with no word from him, I got more worried about him and grew more uneasy about keeping it from you. I'd made up my mind to tell you this week, even if I hadn't heard from him, but I had to go to Fort Concho. I didn't want to dump it on you and leave. I was going to tell you tonight.'' He reached out to touch her, but she stepped away.

"That's convenient. You can try to justify it all day, Cade, but it still comes down to the fact that you deceived me." She moved around to the other side of the table, gripping the back of a chair. "And you manipulated me into staying here."

Cade frowned. "I offered you a job and a place to stay. You didn't have to take it."

"I was broke and exhausted, and you used Quint's absence to keep me here. The sheriff played right into your hands with his story about me being safer out here than in town. Willow Grove is no more dangerous than any other town."

"Quint is my friend. I owed it to him to take care of you."

"I'm sure that was part of it. But you wanted me," she said softly. "I saw it in your eyes that first night."

"Yes, I did. Still do. But I never forced my attentions on you. I never even tried to seduce you." He raked his fingers through his hair, wondering if they'd be having this conversation if he hadn't been so noble. When she lifted that delicate eyebrow again, silently challenging his honesty and honor, his temper flared.

Cade moved swiftly, circling the table before she could react, and stopped inches away. "If I had, I would have succeeded and you know it. You want me, too, Jessie, and you can't deny it."

Her eyes widened, but she stood her ground. "I don't deny it. But you used that to your advantage, too. I stayed with Neil because he knew which strings to pull. He used my honor, my belief that marriage vows were sacred, and threats against the children to keep me there. You used desire, tenderness, protection and the promise of security. Much more enticing than my husband's tactics, but a method of controlling me just the same.''

"I never tried to control you." *That's exactly what you've done.* He clenched his jaw at the chiding voice of conscience.

"Perhaps not intentionally." She squared her shoulders and stood a little straighter. "But you lied to me about Quint.''

"It was necessary," he said stubbornly.

"I can't accept that. I don't want anything to do with a man who isn't honest with me, Cade. How will I ever be able to trust you? To believe anything you tell me? I won't live like that again. I can't.''

She sighed heavily and walked over to the rocking chair and sat down. "Quint gave me a message for you. The rustlers' hideout is in a box canyon east of the headwaters of Mustang Creek." She looked up at him with sorrow-filled eyes. "He had to go with them a couple of times to prove himself before they would take him to their main camp. The last time, they stole five more of Jack Shepherd's cattle.''

Cade uttered a mild oath under his breath. "That must have about killed him.''

"It did.''

"Why didn't he go to the sheriff with the information? He could lead us right to the camp.''

"The rustlers are working for someone who doesn't ride with them. Quint thinks it's a rancher or someone from town, but he isn't sure. The man came out to the camp a few nights ago, but he couldn't get a good look at him. All he could tell was that he wore a suit. He asked one of the other men who he was, but he simply called him 'the boss' and seemed afraid of him. He said as soon as he finds out, he'll contact you.''

"I'll ride to town and let the sheriff know. Maybe he has some idea who the leader might be." Hearing the rattle of a harness, Cade glanced out the window to see Brad and Ellie approaching the wagon. "Jessie, stay here."

When she looked up, the pain in her eyes tore at his heart. "No."

Simple. Final. Shattering hopes and dreams.

"Fine." He spat the word, striking out at the hurt with anger. Glancing around, he focused on the trunk she had dragged halfway to the door. "I'll help you load up." Turning swiftly, he picked up the heavy trunk. Shaking his head, he carried it outside. How had she expected to get it into the wagon?

As he stepped off the porch, Brad took one look at him and started hitching Valentine to the wagon. With a resigned sigh, Ellie slowly walked up the steps and disappeared into the house.

Cade set the trunk in the wagon bed, shoving it to the front, and rearranged a few boxes. Not that they needed it. But the physical exertion made him feel better. Jessie came out with an armload of bedding. He glanced up and moved out of her way. "What else?"

"Just the rocking chair."

He nodded and went to get it, along with his hat. Loading the rocker in the wagon, he tried to stoke his anger, but sadness—heavy and almost unbearable—smothered it. "I need to change horses, then I'll ride to town with you."

"There's no need."

His anger sparked again at her stubbornness. "Yes, there is. I'm not going to let you drive in there alone."

"We came halfway across Texas alone," she snapped.

Resting his hands on his hips, he gave her a look that made men quake.

She didn't even flinch.

"You're in my territory, now. And I intend to protect you, whether you want it or not. Despite your opinion, it can be dangerous in Willow Grove. Some of the men coming into town are rough and mean. If they know they will have to answer to me or Ty, they might think twice about dragging you down some alley."

Her eyes widened, and she drew in a quick breath.

For a heartbeat, he was distracted by her slightly parted lips. "The sheriff wasn't lying. He does a good job, but his jurisdiction covers several counties. We haven't been able to keep a decent town marshal. The one we have now is good at chasing stray dogs and hauling tame drunks to jail, but that's about it. If you needed help, he'd likely run away and hide."

He couldn't keep from touching her. When he lightly caressed her cheek and she didn't jerk away, hope surged through him. "You'll have to be on guard all the time, Jessie. You'd be a whole lot safer out here."

She shook her head. "I'll take my chances in town."

"Stubborn woman." He gritted his teeth to keep from saying more and took a moment to calm down. "I'll see you settled at the hotel and pay for a room as long as you need it. But that won't be long. There are probably a dozen men around, businessmen and ranchers, who will jump at the chance to have you work for them. And I guarantee every one of them will have something besides cooking and cleaning on his mind." The thought of another man lusting after her made his blood boil.

Grabbing her shoulders to hold her still, he surprised her

with a hard, quick, possessive kiss. He released her and took a step back to keep from hauling her into his arms. "If any man so much as touches you—whether you want him to or not—I swear I'll beat him to a pulp."

Chapter Fourteen

Jessie didn't want Cade to pay for a hotel room, but he wouldn't back down. To keep from making a scene in the lobby under the curious eyes of the desk clerk and half a dozen guests, she agreed to it. Before they left the ranch, he paid her wages for the week he had been gone. Adding it to what she had already earned would feed them for a while and eased the pressure of having to take the first job that came along.

The next morning, she left the children in the room, with strict orders not to leave, intending to ask Ty if she could return her new dress and get her money back. She had seen others return things a time or two, and since it had never been worn, she doubted he would refuse.

She had barely reached the foot of the stairs when a man approached her from across the hotel lobby. In his early forties, he was well dressed and reasonably good-looking. He quickly removed his Stetson, holding the brim in both hands, and nodded politely. "Mrs. Monroe?"

"Yes."

"I'm Jim Peters, one of the owners of the Lazy Z ranch about twenty miles north of town. I understand you're no longer working for Cade?"

"That's right."

"I'm in need of a housekeeper, ma'am." His gaze swept over her in an appreciative, nonthreatening way. "My partners are from England and will be coming to visit in about a month. It would be mighty nice to have good meals and a clean house all the time, but especially while they're here. They're both lords of the realm," he added with a grin. "Used to having things comfortable." He took a small step closer. "And having someone as pretty as you around would be a downright pleasure."

He seemed nice and respectful, but she wasn't about to go to work twenty miles from town for a total stranger. At least with Cade, she had known a great deal about him through Quint. "Thank you for the offer, Mr. Peters, but I'm hoping to find a job here in town so my children can attend school."

He shrugged, offering her a smile tinged with disappointment. "It's good for a mother to think of her young'uns. But if you don't find anything to your liking, you send word out to the Lazy Z."

"I will." Jessie started toward the front door but only made it halfway across the hotel lobby before she was stopped by the owner of the restaurant where they had eaten numerous times.

"Mrs. Monroe, I understand you're looking for work."

Jessie wondered how word had gotten around so quickly. "Yes, sir, I am."

"I hear you're a fine cook. I could use you over at my place. We have more business than my wife can keep up with."

Jessie smiled at the older man. "Thank you. But I'd like to try to find a housekeeping position where I can watch over my children, too."

"Let me know if you change your mind. Can't promise I'll still need you, though."

"I understand. Give my best to your wife." She made it to the boardwalk before she was stopped again. Jessie didn't know the man, though she had seen him around town. He was tall, blond and attractive, dressed in an expensive light blue tailor-made suit that matched his eyes.

He doffed his hat, holding it casually in one hand, and smiled. "Mrs. Jessie Monroe?" When she nodded, his smile widened. "I'm Tate Doolin, attorney-at-law." He motioned toward an office near the hotel. "My office is right here. I'm also a rancher, though I prefer to live here in town. I moved into my new home this past week, and I'm looking for a housekeeper. I understand you have experience in that area."

"Yes, I do. I recently worked for Cade McKinnon. For the past three years, I was employed by the mayor of Riverbend and his wife."

"Excellent. Would you care to step inside for a few minutes so we can discuss the possibility of you working for me?"

"That would be fine." Jessie felt a twinge of uneasiness, though she couldn't find any particular reason for it. He seemed every inch a gentleman. Refined and polished. Perhaps a bit too polished. Still, he was charming, carrying on a relaxed conversation as they covered the short distance to the door.

Inside, he nodded to his clerk. "Good morning, Henry. I'll be in my office with Mrs. Monroe. See that we aren't disturbed."

Jessie frowned, watching the exchange. The clerk took his orders amicably, then nodded at her with a polite smile. "I only have a few minutes," she said. "My children are waiting for me at the hotel."

"Then I must be mindful of the time," said Doolin, showing her into his office. He followed and started to shut the door, pausing before closing it completely. "I'll leave it open if you would be more comfortable, though I personally don't care for others to hear my business dealings. Henry would never say anything, but people come in and out all the time."

"I suppose it's all right. I won't be here very long."

"Good." He closed the door, flashed her another smile and offered her a chair. When she sat down, he walked around to his chair behind the large desk. "I'll come right to the point, Mrs. Monroe. I intend to pursue a life in politics. Once I'm well established here, I plan to run for state office. Since you have worked as a mayor's housekeeper, I believe you would be a great asset."

"Riverbend is not much larger than Willow Grove," said Jessie with a trace of amusement.

"But I suspect the mayor and his wife gave the most ostentatious dinners and parties in town." Humor lit his eyes. "Or did that honor fall to the banker and his wife?"

Jessie laughed. "They certainly tried to outdo each other." She considered the question for a moment. "But generally, the mayor topped them."

"You topped them," he said quietly. "If the food and other preparations are poorly done, no party is a success, no matter who gives it." Studying her thoughtfully, he stood, moving slowly around his desk, then around her. Jessie felt his scrutiny, even when he was behind her. When he stepped back in front of her, his gaze slid slowly down her body and back up again, lingering on her bosom, finally returning to her face.

At the open lust in his eyes, Jessie's skin crawled. She stood quickly, but he moved just as swiftly, blocking her way.

"I offended you."

She forced herself to look up at him. "Yes, you did."

"I apologize. You are much more beautiful than I'd expected. It would be a pity to hide you away in the kitchen. I would much prefer to have you grace my table, help me entertain my guests." Even though her dress had a high collar, his gaze dipped lower again, as if he were picturing her in something low-cut—or perhaps in nothing at all. She had seen that look many times in the past and had a good idea he would also want her in his bed. "I could hire someone else to do the labor. As housekeeper, you would only have to supervise them. Then you would be free to act as my hostess."

"I doubt that would go over well in Willow Grove."

"It isn't as unusual as you think. I'm sure you are well aware that there is a shortage of women here. Two of my rancher clients have housekeepers who fill just that role."

"And what other role would you expect me to play?"

"Expect? None. Hope?" His hot gaze swept over her again. "That is another matter entirely."

"Good day, Mr. Doolin. I'm not interested in your offer. No part of it." Jessie sidled between him and the chair, hurrying toward the door.

As her fingers closed over the knob, his hand flattened against the wood by her head, holding the door shut. She felt his chest brush against her back, the warmth of his breath on the side of her neck. Though he made no effort to press his body against hers, she was trapped. Heart thudding painfully, she strove not to show her panic. "Open the door."

"Not just yet. And don't do anything foolish like screaming. Henry will attest that you came in here willingly and had no problem with me shutting the door. If you make a scene, your reputation will suffer. Many already believe you were more than merely McKinnon's housekeeper.''

He trailed the tip of his finger down the side of her neck, along her collarbone and back up again. "I assure you that I can please you as well as he can.''

Never! Jessie tried to twist away from his touch but was blocked by his other arm.

"Since you aren't wearing mourning clothes, I assume your husband has been dead for quite some time. If McKinnon wasn't your lover, then you've been without a man too long." His fingers moved beneath her chin in a light caress.

Jessie shivered. He was right about one thing—if she made a scene, it would be all over town in a matter of minutes. Quite possibly, she would receive more condemnation than him. If Cade beat Doolin to a pulp as he'd promised, that would only fuel speculation, either about her and Cade or her and Doolin. Probably both. It wouldn't help her keep her good name—or try to establish one—but right then, she would gladly suffer the repercussions to see this vile man get his due.

Doolin shifted minutely closer. "See, you already tremble with desire.''

"No!" she whispered, jerking her head away.

Seconds later, his hand slid around her waist. He leaned closer, holding her against him. "Then I've frightened you. Good. You have no idea of the potential perils awaiting you, my dear. Keep my offer in mind. You would be well compensated, both financially and in other ways. Being under my protection would be to your advantage.''

Did every man within a hundred miles think she would so easily bow to their wishes? "Release me." Anger made her voice steady and strong.

"Ah, the lady does not surrender meekly. I like that.''

He lifted his hand and moved back slightly, brushing his knuckles along the nape of her neck.

So much for not making a scene, but she didn't care. Jessie jabbed her elbow in his stomach as hard as she could.

"Oof!"

She kicked back, catching him in the shin with her heel.

"Ow!" He stumbled backward, gasping for breath, trying to rub his leg.

If she hadn't been furious, she might have laughed. "Stay away from me, Doolin. If you don't, I'll make sure the whole town knows what kind of man you really are."

"And ruin your reputation? I doubt it," he wheezed.

"You aren't important in this town yet. Otherwise, I would have known your name and all about you. Your reputation is also at stake. An attorney with political ambitions has more to lose than a lowly housekeeper." Throwing some of his own words back at him, she added, "It would be to your advantage to keep that in mind."

To Jessie's surprise, he leaned against the desk, pulled in a deep breath and smiled. "Yes, I expect it would. It seems I listened to the wrong gossip. It would be best if we forgot all about this."

"I have a very long memory." Opening the door, she walked out of the lawyer's office, head held high. She managed a civilized nod to the clerk, fighting the urge to run from the building. Once outside, she took a deep breath of fresh air and hurried to McKinnon Brothers, praying Cade wouldn't be there. He would take one look at her and know something was wrong.

Inside the store, she waved to Lydia, who was helping a customer, then pretended to look at some lace handkerchiefs. She reached for one and noticed her hand was shaking, realizing a moment later that her whole body quaked like a leaf in the wind. Gripping the counter, she took a slow, deep breath, telling herself to calm down. Unfortunately, telling and doing were two completely different things.

Suddenly Ty was at her side. "Jessie, are you all right?"

She looked up into his concerned eyes. "I need a pistol. A small one."

Frowning, he took hold of her elbow in a firm but gentle grip. "Come with me."

For once, Jessie did as commanded, blindly moving across the store, letting him lead the way to his office in back. He guided her into a chair by the desk and shut the door. A flash of fear shot through her. *Don't be silly. Ty is a friend.*

But he caught her panicked glance at the closed door. "Do you want me to open it?"

"No." She gave him a wobbly smile. "I know you aren't going to do anything."

He smiled and sat down, drawing his chair closer. "And get a thrashing from my brother? No, thanks." His expression sobered. "What happened?"

"A big reminder that I need to be more cautious."

"Did someone try to hurt you?"

"No. But he made it clear that he wasn't just looking for a housekeeper."

Ty's jaw tightened. "And not from across the room."

Jessie nodded. "An elbow to his stomach and a kick to his shin solved the problem."

"No wonder you made it halfway across Texas alone."

"I had my shotgun on the trip. That works a lot better than elbows and heels."

He sat back in the chair. "I expect he got the message. But you should carry a gun, especially since you know how to use one. I have a two-shot derringer that will fit in your handbag or skirt pocket."

She toyed with the handle on her bag. "I need to return the dress I bought on Wednesday so I can pay for it."

"I'll give you the derringer."

"I can't let you do that."

"Yes, you can. I won't take your money for it, Jessie. Keep the dress."

"Even if you won't let me buy the gun, I need the money. I don't know how soon I'll find a job."

"You already have a job. Go back to the ranch before Cade goads all the ranch hands into quitting."

"I can't. He lied to me."

"He thought he was doing the right thing. Even if I did tell him he wasn't."

"At least one of you has some sense," she mumbled.

Ty leaned forward again, resting his hand on her forearm. "Who scared you, Jessie?"

"I don't want to say."

"Because Cade will whip the living daylights out of him?"

"Yes. I was partly at fault, too. I should have been more careful and not let him close the door. I don't want to stir up trouble, Ty. I don't think he will bother me again, but someone else might. I'd feel better having a gun, and I can't very well carry my shotgun around."

He straightened with a grin. "You could, but it might be a little awkward. Especially if it falls over when you prop it up against the pew during church. I can see the newspaper headlines—Man Shot While Taking Church Offering."

Jessie laughed, finally relaxing. "Please don't tell Cade about this."

"Only if you promise to let one of us know if the man tries anything again. And let us take care of it."

"I will."

"Come on out and I'll get you the derringer. When we're done, check with Lydia. She might know of someone who is looking for a housekeeper. Someone who won't maul you every chance he gets." He stood and opened the door, waiting as she exited the room. "I can't imagine you having trouble finding a job. I figured half the town would be waiting in the hotel lobby this morning."

"Only two in the lobby. One more outside. But none of the positions were suitable. It make take a while before I find the right place."

"The right place is with Cade."

"It will never happen." She marched across the store, with Ty at her side, and diverted the conversation to the upcoming Fourth of July festivities.

Half an hour later, Jessie approached the home of Mrs. Nola Simpson, an older widow she had talked to a few times at church. Lydia said she was looking for a housekeeper. She knocked on the door and waited, silently asking the Lord for one more favor. It was a nice home, with gingerbread trim, honeysuckle trailing along the white picket fence, and a shady, inviting porch that wrapped around the house.

Mrs. Simpson opened the door with a warm smile. "Why, Mrs. Monroe, how nice of you to stop by." She opened the door wide, motioning Jessie inside.

"Actually, ma'am, it's not a social call." Jessie stepped into the foyer, waiting until the tiny lady shut the door. "I understand you're looking for a housekeeper."

"Why, yes, I am. Come in here where we can sit." She led the way into the front parlor, her cane tapping on the wooden floor, and nodded at red upholstered chair in the corner. "You sit there, and I'll take this one. Won't get a kink in my neck looking at you that way." Once they were seated, she rested the cane against the side of the chair and pinned Jessie with a keen look. "Are you looking for a job?"

"Yes, ma'am."

"Have a spat with Cade?"

Jessie's cheeks grew warm. "We had a disagreement."

"Land's sake, child, kiss the man and make up. He dotes on you."

Jessie's face flamed. "He's a fine man, but I'd rather not work for him."

Mrs. Simpson shrugged. "I expect he can get a bit bossy. He reminds me of my husband, God rest his soul. The dear man thought he knew what was best for everyone around him and did everything he could to make it happen. He had a good heart and always meant well, but sometimes he was just plain wrong. Didn't like hearing it, either," she said with a chuckle. "But you'll learn to handle that. Easier to do as a wife than a housekeeper."

Jessie changed the topic, relating her previous work experience. "If possible, I'd like to keep the children here during the day. When school starts, it would just be Ellie. They're good and would stay out of your way. They play outside most of the time when the weather is nice."

"They won't bother me. I enjoy children. But have you already rented a house? I was hoping to find someone who could live here with me. My balance isn't what it used to be, and I've fallen a couple of times. Cracked my head against the kitchen table the last time. I'd feel better if you stayed here. I have plenty of room for the children, too."

Jessie almost jumped up and hugged the older woman. "That would be perfect. When would you like for me to start?"

"Right now, if you want. I have a pot of soup simmering on the stove, so we won't have to fuss with meals today."

She tipped her head, her silver hair glinting in a ray of sunlight. "I can't pay more than twenty dollars a month, plus room and board. But I'm not stingy with the food."

"That will be fine." Jessie stood. "Now, if you'll excuse me, I'll go tell the kids. Do you have a place I can store some things? I don't have a lot, but I can't very well leave it in the wagon at the wagon yard."

"I have a storeroom out back that has some space. There's also a small pen for your horse. I had it put up when I built the house." Mrs. Simpson laughed and reached for her cane before standing. "Had the fool notion to get a cow. Took me about three days to figure out that I'd be better off buying my milk and butter from the grocer."

Jessie smiled, letting her new employer lead the way to the door. "It certainly is a lot less work."

"More economical, too, even for a small family, if you count the cost of the cow and feed. Your horse can graze on the lots behind the house. The owner lives back East, and nobody uses them. Don't have a place to keep your wagon inside, but you can put it behind the storeroom if you want."

Jessie laughed as she opened the screen door and stepped onto the porch. "The only place that poor wagon was stored undercover was in Cade's buggy shed."

Mrs. Simpson's eyes softened, her expression gentle. "You stay here until he persuades you to marry him."

"I'd be here forever."

"Maybe a month if you're real stubborn." The old lady grinned, delight easing the lines time had etched in her face. "Dear, when you forget that you're mad at him and you mention his name, your whole face lights up. That kind of love won't be denied, not if he feels the same way. Now hurry along and get your things. I can't wait for the excitement to begin.''

"What excitement?" Jessie frowned warily.

"Why, when he comes calling, of course.''

"I don't think that will happen, Mrs. Simpson."

"I've known Cade McKinnon for years, long before I moved to Willow Grove. I've never seen him taken with a woman the way he is with you. He will come courtin', just you wait and see.''

Bemused, Jessie walked down the steps and across the yard to the front gate. *I won't have anything to do with him if he comes to see me.*

Closing the gate behind her, she sighed softly. Now if she could only quit wishing with all her heart that he would.

Chapter Fifteen

Cade stared at the column of figures in the ledger, the numerals blurring. He'd added them three times and come up with three different totals. Throwing his pencil on the desk, he closed his burning eyes and rotated his tired shoulders. Jessie had been gone four days. He doubted he'd slept more than four hours the whole time. "Blasted woman. If I don't sleep tonight, Asa might as well shoot me."

Pushing the chair back from his desk, he wandered out to the back porch. They'd had a thunderstorm earlier in the afternoon, bringing some needed rain and cooling the air. The remnants of clouds hovered in the sky, now painted a brilliant pink and gold.

"It's a beautiful sunset, darlin'. Does watching it all by your lonesome make you feel as sad as it does me?" He hoped so. He hoped it reminded her of the times he had slipped his arms around her waist, and she had leaned back against his chest so they could enjoy God's splendor together. He had planned to share a lifetime of sunsets and sunrises, of hot summer nights and frosty winter mornings.

He glanced over at her house, then walked down the steps and across the yard. Would he ever be able to look at it without thinking of her? Opening the door, he looked around at all the new furniture. How could he hire someone else and let them use the things he had bought for Jessie? His gaze fell on the pretty silk screen, folded carefully and leaning against the wall beside the bathtub. He should have insisted she take it.

He went into her bedroom, relieved that she had taken the china washbowl and basin. He hadn't seen it in the wagon and had worried that she might not have wanted the gift he had specifically bought for her. Maybe it would remind her that he wasn't as much of a villain as she thought.

Stretching out on the bed, he closed his eyes and breathed in the subtle hint of lavender that clung to the mattress. "Jessie, I'm sorry I wasn't honest with you," he whispered. "I should have told you about Quint the day you got here. But I didn't want you to leave."

He closed his eyes. It was just tiredness that made them sting. Not heartache and self-reproach. She was right. He had used Quint's absence to manipulate her into staying at the ranch. Even that first night, he couldn't bear the thought of not seeing her sweet face the next morning. Being without her was even worse than he had thought it would be.

"Lord, I just wanted to love her, have her love me." He yawned and rolled over on his side. "If I could start over, I'd do it different. Tell her the truth." He yawned again and curled one arm beneath his head. "And tell her I love her. Never even said the words. A woman needs to know how her man feels about her." *Her man.* "Always will be," he mumbled, drifting off to sleep.

When Cade woke up, it took him a few minutes to realize where he was. Judging from the position of the moon in the western sky, he had slept most of the night—right where he was supposed to be, in Jessie's bed. What a shame she wasn't there, too.

"So what are you going to do about it?" he muttered, his voice still raspy from sleep. A good night's rest had cleared his mind and put things in perspective. "You too proud to eat a little crow?"

Nope. I'd crawl on my hands and knees down Main Street to get her back.

"Hope it doesn't come to that." Smiling, Cade rubbed his face and stretched. His fingers touched something tucked between the mattress and the headboard. Pulling it out, he squinted in the moonlight but couldn't quite tell what it was. Maybe a scarf of some kind, though he had never seen Jessie wear one.

Taking it with him, he rolled off the bed and went into the kitchen, picking up the screen that had shielded the bathtub from view. He'd rather burn it than let any other woman use it. "I'll put this away for safekeeping."

He closed the door and strolled back to his house. Once inside, he set the screen in the corner of the kitchen. Laying the cloth on the table, he lit a lamp and instantly recognized the blanket for Ellie's doll. "Poor kid. She's probably real upset because she lost it." A slow smile touched his face. "Guess I'll just have to return it."

Anticipation made his footsteps lighter as he brewed a pot of coffee and hustled about frying up bacon and scrambled eggs for breakfast. In his early days as a Texas Ranger, he had quickly learned never to go into battle unprepared. Though the situation with Jessie held the potential for great reward, it was also fraught with danger—it might be his last chance to win her heart.

He studied the problem as he ate, plotting out his strategy. By the time he sipped the last drop of coffee, he had a plan in place, as well as a backup. If neither of those worked, he would think of something else. It all came down to an accepted fact. No matter how hard he had to work, or how long it took, Cade McKinnon got what he wanted.

And he wanted Jessie Monroe.

That evening Jessie sat on the front porch swing, enjoying the cool breeze that sprang up at sunset. Mrs. Simpson had taken up her regular position in a rocking chair on the other side of the steps. Brad and Ellie were pitching horseshoes at the side edge of the yard.

The scent of honeysuckle on the fence mingled with the fragrance of climbing roses from the trellis at the end of the porch. A dog barked in the distance, and a buggy creaked as a couple drove slowly by, more interested in each other than where the horse was taking them. Another couple called a greeting and waved as they walked past, out for their evening stroll around the block.

It was the kind of evening Jessie had often dreamed about in Riverbend. Quiet and peaceful, her family living in a pretty, comfortable home in a nice part of town, with no fear of a drunken husband and father stumbling in to shatter their happiness.

But she wasn't happy. She had come to realize over the past few days that she had never truly known loneliness until Cade was no longer a part of her life. How she missed him! The chasm in her heart grew bigger every day. She looked up, gazing at the darkening blue of the sky. A streak of pink slowly widened, mingling with another swath of purple.

A squeak drew her gaze to the gate, and she forgot how to breathe. Cade stood there, resting his hand on the open gate, watching her, waiting for an invitation to come farther. Merciful heavens, he was beautiful. Dressed in his black suit, crisp white shirt and best Stetson, he looked like a man on his way to church. Then she spotted the flowers in his hand. Or one who had come courting. Jessie tried to drum up her anger and tell him to go away, but nothing could get past the lump in her throat.

"Cade!" Ellie's delighted cry jerked her attention away from him for a second. Her daughter raced across the yard toward him. He dropped to one knee just in time to catch her as she flung herself into his arms. He gave her a big hug and a kiss on the cheek.

The tender scene tugged at Jessie's heart. That's how it should be when a father came home. The lump in her throat grew bigger.

Cade stood and pulled Ellie's doll blanket from his coat pocket. "I found this at your house last night. Figured I ought to bring it to you."

When he handed it to Ellie, she held it close to her face. "Thank you! Dolly has been so sad without it."

"And Ellie, too, I bet."

She nodded, her curls bouncing. "But I feel better now. It's nice here. But not as nice as your house."

Cade rested his hand on her head. "I'm glad you have a good place to stay." He looked at Jessie, still waiting.

"For Pete's sake, Cade, come on up to the porch," said Mrs. Simpson. She threw Jessie a shrewd glance. "She won't shoot you. Left the shotgun in the house."

The derringer, too, only the older lady didn't know about it.

Cade grinned and walked up to the porch, escorted by a beaming Ellie. He handed a pot of pink geraniums to Mrs. Simpson. "These are for you, Nola." He leaned over, dropping a kiss on her cheek. "For being such a sweetheart, now and always."

"Why, thank you." Smiling, she admired the flowers. "Geraniums. The symbol of true friendship. You been reading up on the language of flowers, boy?"

"Yes, ma'am. *Colliers Cyclopedia* has a whole section on it."

She winked at him. "But I'm not the one you're supposed to bring flowers to."

He winked back. "I have that covered." He reached inside his coat and pulled out a small bouquet. The red roses caught Jessie's eye. Beautiful and perfect, the first flowers a man had ever brought her. She swallowed hard, wondered how in the world he'd kept from crushing them when he hugged Ellie. Not a single petal was bent or smashed.

"These are for you, darlin'." He handed them to her with a tender smile. His eyes begged her not to refuse his gift.

She took them and quickly glanced away, thanking him politely. *Don't fall for his charm and sweet talk.* Oh, but how she wanted to. She wanted to throw herself into his arms and thank him appropriately, not politely.

"And these are for the kids." He handed Ellie a bag of striped stick candy and held out a bag of jelly beans to Brad. When the boy didn't reach for it, Cade said quietly, "Please take it, son. It's a peace offering."

Brad glanced at his mother. When she nodded, he took the candy. He looked back up at Cade, his expression painfully serious. "Why are you here?"

"I've come courtin' your mama." His gaze settled on Jessie. "To try to win the heart of the woman I love."

Tears sprang to Jessie's eyes as joy and pain battled in her heart. He loved her! But was it enough to help her move past the fear of betrayal? She looked down, lowering her lashes to hide her soul from him, and noticed the other things in the bouquet. Her heartbeat jumped to triple time. The language of flowers…

Roses for love. Forget-me-nots, true love. Double red pinks, pure and ardent love. Intermingled throughout were

sprigs of dark green ivy, most faithful of all. Fidelity. He
knew that was as important to her as love. Tucked in beneath a rose was a tiny four-leaf clover, be mine. She
wasn't positive about the piece of foliage on the other side,
but she thought it was an olive branch. Peace.

"I brought the candy to you young'uns because I love
you and miss you." His tone shifted, shaded with amusement. "And I brought the flowers to Mrs. Simpson because
I figured I'd better sweeten up the chaperone."

"You scamp." Nola laughed and held out her hand for
Cade to help her up. "I'll take these inside. Have the perfect spot for them on the back porch." She picked up her
cane and paused, looking at Jessie's bouquet. "Where did
you get such beautiful flowers anyway?"

"Fort Worth."

Nola's eyebrows shot up. Jessie stared at him. She didn't
realize her mouth had dropped open until he leaned over
and gently pushed up on her chin with his finger. "Careful,
darlin', or you'll catch flies."

She snapped her mouth shut. Then had to ask. "How?"

"Well, they just fly right inside. They like sugar, you
know."

She narrowed her eyes. "I meant the roses. How did you
get them here?"

"I know a man who has a big garden full of all sorts of
flowers and plants. So I sent him a telegram at the crack
of dawn this morning, asking to buy some roses and the
other flowers and have them sent out on the train. Suggested he pack the box in ice and sawdust to keep them
from wilting, which he did. They've been sitting in water
over at Ty's house since the train arrived this afternoon."

He grinned, much too satisfied with himself, though in
truth, she couldn't blame him. It was quite a feat.

"Well, I declare," said Nola. "I've never heard of such a thing. Someone should start up a business doing that."

Cade laughed. "Ty is already considering it."

"Brad, bring your mother's flowers inside," said Nola. "You and Ellie can help me find a vase."

Jessie held the flowers out to Brad. When he winked at her, she almost dropped them. Obviously, her son had accepted Cade's peace offering, probably not so much the candy but his reason for being there. But, she reminded herself sternly, Brad didn't know why she had left. He didn't know how Cade had deceived her. Somehow, that didn't seem as awful as it had a quarter hour earlier.

Cade opened the screen door for Nola, glancing at the white wooden porch swing. "I don't remember you having a swing."

"Didn't until yesterday." The old lady grinned impishly. "Since Jessie moved in, I thought I might have a use for it. It holds two, you know."

Cade smiled, first at her, then at Jessie. "So I noticed. Thanks."

"Oh, you're welcome, dear. I'll try to keep the children occupied for a while."

"You do that." He held the screen door open until they went inside, then turned to Jessie. "May I sit down?"

"I suppose."

He took off his hat, hanging it on a little post at the top of the rocking chair. When he sat down, the swing swayed precariously for a moment, but he quickly steadied it. He sat wedged against the end, leaving a little space between them, and kept his arms at his sides. "How are you?"

"Fine," she said brightly. "Nola is easy to work for."

"She's a jewel, all right. Does she still make her special chowchow?"

"Yes, we had some yesterday at dinner."

"Maybe she'll give you the recipe. That one is worth passing on."

"She already did. I copied it onto an empty page at the back of one of my cookbooks."

He nodded, then sat quietly watching the empty street. Jessie glanced at him, noting that his face seemed leaner, a few of the creases deeper. In five days could a man lose enough weight to be noticeable? "How are you?"

Turning to her, he smiled. "A whole lot better now. I've been crankier than a mountain lion with a sore paw, snarlin' at everybody. Couldn't eat. Couldn't sleep. Couldn't do anything right. I was about ready to go on a shootin' spree, and I didn't care who got in my sights."

"What changed?" She looked down, clasping her hands in her lap to keep from touching him.

"I fell asleep in your bed last night."

"My bed?" she whispered, her mind bombarding her with erotic images of the two of them. Heat warmed her face.

And he noticed, of course.

He traced the line of her jaw with his knuckle, then lowered his hand, resting it on his thigh. "I went over to your house to see if you'd forgotten anything. Or maybe left something I wanted you to take."

"The washbasin and pitcher."

He nodded. "I'm glad you didn't leave it behind."

"I thought about it. But I couldn't."

"I was so tired, I stretched out on the bed." He shrugged and looked out across the yard. "The mattress smells like lavender. Made me feel closer to you. I fell asleep and slept almost the whole night. First time I'd gotten more than an hour's rest at a time since you left. When I woke up in the wee hours of the morning, things were a whole lot clearer." He paused, as if carefully choosing his words.

"I should have been honest with you about Quint from the beginning. I made up all kinds of excuses not to tell you. They sounded right, but they weren't. Guess in the back of my mind, I knew it all along, but didn't want to admit it." He took a deep breath, releasing it slowly. "I was afraid that if you moved to town, we wouldn't get to know each other the way we needed to."

"You mean you wouldn't be able to flirt as much." She dropped her voice to almost a whisper. "Or kiss me whenever you wanted to."

"Honey, I didn't kiss you nearly as often as I wanted to." He smiled wryly. "If I had, we wouldn't have accomplished anything else." His smile faded, but he didn't look away. "I was afraid I'd lose you before I had a chance to prove myself to you. I knew that as soon as you moved to town, men would be after you like ants at a picnic."

Considering the surprising number of gentlemen who had stopped by in the past two days, it was a good analogy. A smile tugged at her lips. "Sometimes marching two by two."

"You actually had two here at the same time?"

Laughter bubbled up and, without thinking, she leaned toward him to share the joke. "It was so funny. One was a cowboy. I can't remember his name. The other one was Mr. Brooks, the tailor."

"That pipsqueak?" Cade laughed with her.

"They arrived from opposite directions and pushed through the gate at the same time. It's a wonder they didn't break it off the hinges. Then they stood there in the yard arguing until Nola hollered at them to go away, that I wouldn't be interested in fools like them anyway."

"Where were you?" He smiled and shifted, draping his arm across the back of the seat. The swing dipped, tipping her lightly against him. His hand curled around her shoulder, holding her there.

Not that she could have moved even if she'd wanted to. Her heart pounded; her breathing was shallow; and her body was as limp as a wet dishrag. "Peeking through the lace curtains in the parlor."

"How many have there been?"

"Nine, counting those who came calling and two of the three who offered me a job the first morning in town."

His fingers tightened minutely. "Why not count the third one?"

"Because he's married, and I would have been working at the restaurant with his wife."

His hand relaxed and he took a deep breath, aware that he would have no competition from the restaurant owner. He had none from anyone else, either, but she wasn't sure she wanted to admit it just yet.

"Did you talk to any of them?"

"All except the ones last night. Even Ellie giggled at them."

"Did you sit out here in the swing with anyone?" He pressed a little closer, murmuring in her ear, his fingers sliding from her shoulder to the side of her neck. "In the dark?"

Jessie glanced around, surprised to see that night had fallen. No light shone from the house. Nola must have taken the children into the kitchen or the back parlor. It was very dark in their corner of the porch, hiding them from prying eyes. She kept her head forward, facing the quiet, empty street, shivering from the teasing warmth of his breath on her ear. "No. I just thanked them for their interest and sent them on their way."

"Good." He paused so long she thought he wasn't going to say anything else. "Forgive me, Jessie. I took advantage of your loneliness and hurt to keep you with me. It was wrong. I was wrong. I promise I'll never lie to you again. I give you my word on it.''

His word was his bond. She knew it. Everyone who had ever dealt with him, likely anyone who had even heard of him, knew it.

He cupped her face in his hand, gently turning it toward him. ''I'm so very sorry I hurt you. Will you forgive me?''

In all the years she had been married, Neil had never once apologized, never asked for her forgiveness, no matter how many times nor how badly he had hurt her.

She smoothed the troubled frown from his brow and brushed her lips across his. ''Yes.''

He kissed her with aching tenderness, making the promise again through his touch. Then he deepened the kiss, promising passion and fulfillment. Someday, but not here and now. And certainly not on Nola Simpson's front porch.

He slowly pulled away and came back for a few nibbling kisses. ''It's probably a good thing you moved to town,'' he murmured. ''If we were at the ranch, I'd have you half-undressed five minutes after the kids were asleep.''

Jessie fanned her face with her hand, making him laugh. She flipped the ends of his string tie. ''Did you have a meeting today?''

''The most important one of my life.'' He kissed the tip of her nose. ''With you.''

''You're saying you got all gussied up just to come see me?''

''Yes, ma'am. I wanted to make a good impression.''

She laughed softly, pleased to her toenails. ''Well, you did. But don't forget, I've also seen you covered in dust and sweat.''

''And smelling like I'd wrestled a longhorn.''

"You had." Jessie laughed again, remembering the day he came home with cow manure smeared all over his pants.

"But I left the mud and muck out on the back porch."

After sending her and the children over to her house while he changed. She'd had a bit of trouble with her imagination that night. Why thinking about him changing clothes on the back porch was different than his changing in his room every day was a mystery, but it had fueled her dreams for a week.

"And I appreciated it, too. I had to soak those pants for two days to get the smell out."

"Would have ruined supper." His stomach rumbled and he chuckled. "Which I missed tonight. You have anything a poor, starving cowpoke could eat?"

"Well, I don't know. Are you willing to work for it?"

A slow, seductive smile lit the darkness. "Depends on what kind of work you have in mind."

"Not that kind. Would you tell the children a story? They've really missed that. So have I."

"Piece of cake."

"Yes, you may have some cake."

He gave her a squeeze and hopped up, making the swing move crazily. "Good. But that's not what I meant."

"I know. Come, noble bard, tell us a tale." She let him pull her up off the swing.

"I like the noble part, but I'm not so sure about being called a bard." He pretended to use the window as a mirror. "I don't look a thing like Shakespeare."

"Thankfully. You're much more handsome."

He put his arm around her waist and opened the screen door. "Lady, you just earned yourself two stories. Too bad we aren't already married and at home. I'd make it a bedtime one."

''Cade!'' She shushed him as heat swept through her. ''Behave yourself.''

''Yes, ma'am.'' He leaned down and whispered in her ear, ''For now. But one of these days—hopefully real soon—I'll show you just how bad I can be.''

Oh, my! Suddenly the cool evening breeze turned sultry. *This is how it should be when a husband comes home.*

Chapter Sixteen

Cade went back to town on Saturday, had dinner at Nola's that night and drove them all to church Sunday in a surrey he rented at the livery stable.

Lost in thought on the way home, he almost missed Quint's signal, a blue bandanna tied to a mesquite limb about two miles from the ranch road. Cade stopped Mischief in the shade of the tree and glanced around in a casual way, carefully looking for anyone who might be watching. He took a drink from his canteen, then hung the strap back over the saddle horn. Reaching down, as if he were checking the stirrup, he pulled the bandanna loose from the low limb, wadding it up in his hand.

He nudged the horse to a walk, staying on the road until it curved around a small hill. Stuffing the handkerchief into his shirt pocket, he veered off the road and down a draw that led to a dry creek bed. He kept moving until he heard a whistle mimicking the call of a bobwhite, a quail found throughout the area. When he halted, Quint stepped out from behind a large rock.

Cade dismounted quickly, shaking Quint's hand and slapping him on the back. "You ornery scoundrel, you're a sight for sore eyes."

Quint grinned. "That's good to hear. After I got Jessie all riled up, I was afraid you might try to shoot me."

"Can't blame you for my failings. I should have told her right at the start."

Quint leaned against the rock, giving Cade the impression it was the first time he had relaxed in weeks. "Why didn't you?"

"I wanted her to stay, so I could look after her." He smiled ruefully. "And look at her. I didn't want to upset her any more than she was. Didn't think she'd be too happy about your plan."

"You figured that one right. If she'd kept her shotgun instead of setting it down on the end of the porch, she might have conked me with it."

"Her shotgun?" Cade frowned, realizing he hadn't asked Jessie exactly what had happened the night Quint came to the house.

"She saw me sneaking up to your place and cornered me on the front porch. It was dark, and I kept low when I ran across the yard, so she didn't recognize me."

Cade closed his eyes briefly, muttering under his breath. "And she went out there to keep you from breaking into the house. Blast that woman, she's going to make me old before my time."

"So you're still speaking?"

"We are now." Cade grinned and stepped back, mindful of who he was talking to. "Kissin', too."

"That better be all," growled Quint, only half in jest. "She's my baby sister."

"And I'm treating her like it. Would even if she wasn't your kin. She's a fine woman."

Quint smiled and plucked a dried blade of grass from a crevice in the rock. "Yeah, she is. Are you going to be my brother-in-law?"

"That's my intention. I haven't officially asked her yet. Figured I needed to court her right and proper for a while. She's working for Nola Simpson, and they're living at her place."

"That's what I heard. Should make courtin' her easy. Mrs. Simpson has a soft spot for you."

"She's a good friend and tickled to death to see romance bloom right in front of her." Cade's thoughts and expression sobered. "I've never been so miserable in my life as I was when Jessie moved to town, mad at me and wishing I was roastin' somewhere besides Texas. I was scared to death somebody would come along and attract her interest before she forgave me."

"How long was that?"

"Five miserable days."

Quint chuckled and tossed the grass into the wind. "And how many would-be suitors called at her door?"

"Seven. Two others offered her a job, but she didn't think that was all they had in mind. Judging by the disappointed faces when we walked into church on Sunday, there were a dozen more who hadn't worked up the gumption yet to make their move."

"I bet there were a few females who weren't happy to see you with her."

"A few. The die-hards that held on to a glimmer of hope even when I ignored them."

Quint winced and laughed. "You got a mean streak I didn't know about."

"Only when it comes to women more interested in how much money I make than me." Cade looked around. Though they were secluded, he didn't think it would be smart to keep talking to Quint for too long. "So did you have another reason for meeting me, other than Jessie?"

"The leader of the rustlers is Tate Doolin."

"The lawyer?" Cade stared at him. "Are you sure?"

"Shook hands with him yesterday at the camp."

Cade whistled softly. "I never even suspected him. He has a reputation for dealing fair and square. He's picked up several big ranchers as clients, along with probably a third of the businessmen in town."

"You included?"

"No. We're still with Joe Bynum. He's a good man. Never gave us any reason to think about switching to someone else." Cade glanced down and scuffed a dirt clod with his boot, shaking his head in bemusement. "Tate Doolin. He's another one the ladies go all dewy-eyed over."

"Not all of them."

At the hard edge in Quint's voice, Cade looked up quickly. "Jessie?"

Quint nodded. "Doolin said he'd offered her a job as his housekeeper, but she wasn't interested. Said it was a pity, too, because he liked her fire as well as her beauty."

"What the devil did he do?"

"I don't know. I had to keep my temper and act like I didn't care. Figure she's safer that way. He made it plain he wasn't just interested in her cooking, but she's not high enough up on the social ladder for him to be thinking about marriage. He's the one who told me about her working for Mrs. Simpson."

"So he's keeping an eye on her. Jessie said three men offered her a job, but the only one she mentioned specifically was the restaurant owner. Guess she didn't think she'd better give me any information on the other two."

"She likes to handle her own business."

"And I admire her for it, but it also annoys the heck out of me. Too bad Sheriff Procter is out of town, or I'd ask him to haul Doolin to jail pronto. I don't trust his deputy to handle the arrests. The sheriff won't be back until Tuesday night, in time to ride herd on the Independence Day celebration.''

"Procter needs to be in charge. They're planning to go after your herd Wednesday night. Another one, too, though I don't know which one. I'm out here on a scouting mission to see where your cattle are grazing. I hate for you to lose any, but the only time the gang is together is right after the raids. You'll have a better chance of capturing them if you show up at the canyon early Thursday morning. Might even catch Doolin. According to the men, now that he trusts me, he'll probably be out early to inspect the new cattle. That was his routine before I came along. He keeps the best ones for his ranch, as long as he can easily change the brand, and sells the rest to somebody in Colorado.''

"I'll talk to the sheriff. How many men are there?''

"Ten besides me.''

"That's a big operation,'' said Cade with a frown. "It doesn't take eleven men to steal a dozen head of cattle.''

"There were only five when I joined up. The rest of them came from New Mexico. He's been running the same operation out there, then herding them here with a phony bill of sale. They brought a hundred head in last week. Some of the men work at the ranch, then join us for the raids. Now, they're hitting two herds at a time.''

"Maybe Doolin's getting greedy.''

"Or anxious to wind down the operation. I overheard him tell the range boss that he didn't want to push his luck.''

"He's already out of luck.''

"Maybe not totally. The men are afraid of him. Don't know if it's true, but a couple of the New Mexico bunch were talking about how Doolin killed a man for questioning an order. Just pulled out his pistol and shot him. Could be something he told them to say to keep the others in line.

Still, if we don't catch him at the camp, I'm not sure any of them will testify against him.''

"You will.''

"Which means it will come down to my word against his.''

"You've been here longer. Folks know you better. When the sheriff testifies that you joined the rustlers to help capture them, and that he's been working with you all along, they'll be even more inclined to believe you over him. Just don't go getting' yourself killed.'' Cade gripped Quint's shoulder. "Promise me you'll get out of that camp before we move on.''

"I will if I can.''

"We won't attack unless you're out of there. I'm not about to risk losing you now.''

Quint grinned. "Jessie would never forgive you.''

"I'd never forgive me.''

Quint's smile faded. "I'll get out somehow. If I can't testify, they might all go free. The stealing is bad enough, but I'm afraid it's just a matter of time before they kill somebody. Most of them aren't too bad, but some are two shades meaner than the devil himself.''

"Doolin included?''

"Maybe. I need to be extra careful. Won't be able to get in touch with you.''

"I'd better spend the next few days in town and keep an eye on Jessie, too.''

Quint shook his head. "Don't do anything out of the ordinary or Doolin might get suspicious. He seems to know what everyone in the county is up to.''

"Probably has people spying for him that don't even realize it.''

"Or he's cozy with the town gossips.''

Cade grimaced. "And we have more than enough of those. They aren't always right, though."

"I expect that in his profession—the lawyer one—he's learned to sift information to sort out the truth."

"Well, let's hope he's not so good at it that he figures out what you're doing." Cade pulled the bandanna out of his pocket and handed it to his friend, his heart heavy. He would be very glad when this was over and justice served. "Watch your back."

"Always."

Chapter Seventeen

Cade knocked on Ty's door at seven the next morning. He'd barely slept for imagining all the things Doolin might have said—or done—to Jessie. He couldn't worry about it anymore. He had to know.

Ty opened the door with a puzzled expression and a cup of coffee in hand. He took one look at Cade's scowl and stepped back to let him in. "What's wrong?"

Cade shoved the door closed. "I think Tate Doolin said or did something to Jessie."

"So he's the one."

"What do you mean?" Cade's anger rose a notch, now encompassing his brother. If he knew something about it and hadn't told him...

Ty started toward the kitchen, lifting his cup. "I need a refill."

Steaming, Cade followed. "Tyler, what are you talking about?"

"The morning after she moved to town, she came into the store." He poured his coffee, then took another mug from the shelf and filled it for Cade. "She was shaking like a leaf. When I asked her what was wrong, she said she needed a pistol. A small one."

"Oh, God..." Cade closed his eyes. *Please, don't let Doolin have harmed her.* "Was she hurt?"

"Not that I could see. And she said she wasn't." Ty's voice gentled. "You know I would have told you if she had been."

"You didn't bother to tell me about this," Cade snapped.

"She made me promise not to." And Ty kept his promises. "She was upset, but not disheveled or anything. I tried to find out what had happened, but all she would say was that she'd been given a big reminder to be more cautious. Jessie blamed herself in part because she had let him close the door." Ty took a sip of coffee, then smiled. "She also jabbed him in the stomach with her elbow and kicked him in the shin."

"Which means he had her cornered." Cade hit the table with the side of his fist. "I'm going to break his nose...and half a dozen other bones while I'm at it."

"That's why she refused to say who it was. She was afraid you'd find out and beat the daylights out of him."

"I want to. But I can't." Cade slumped in his chair. "Not yet anyway. Maybe after he's arrested, Procter will give me some time with him."

"You know he won't." Ty frowned and set his cup on the table. "Are you going to try to get him arrested for what he did to Jessie?"

Distracted by the thought of what he'd like to do to the man, it took Cade a moment to answer. He looked back at his brother and shook his head. "No. It would only embarrass her. I saw Quint yesterday. Doolin is the head of the rustling operation."

Ty's jaw dropped. "He's positive?"

"Talked to him at the camp. He concluded from a comment Doolin made about Jessie that he had tried something."

"You think he was baiting Quint, testing his loyalty?"

"Probably. That's what Quint thought." He related the rest of what Jessie's brother told him about the rustlers.

"So we have to just sit tight and hope we capture them on Thursday morning." Ty rubbed his forehead. "I guess it's all we can do. And you can't do anything to tip off Doolin that we might be on to him."

"I know." Cade grimaced. "But I can talk to Jessie and warn her to steer clear of him."

"I don't think you have to worry about that. She seemed to think he wouldn't bother her again, but she's too smart to risk it. I gave her a two-shot derringer just in case some other idiot tries anything."

"Good. Quint thought I shouldn't hang around town too much or Doolin might grow suspicious. Though maybe he'll just think I'm courting her. You'll keep watch over Jessie when I'm not around?"

"I have been."

"Thanks. Can I use your buggy this morning?"

"Of course. Want a horse to go with it?"

Cade chuckled and shoved the chair back. "Don't want you pullin' it. You'd be too nosy."

Ty gave him a knowing grin. "Don't forget she has a derringer in her purse."

"That's to protect her from advances she doesn't want."

Ty laughed. "It's a nice morning, still cool enough to sit in the shade a spell."

"If I can find any shade. In case you haven't noticed, trees are sparse in these parts."

"There's some pecan trees out on Rabbit Hollow Creek."

"How do you know? You been seeing somebody you haven't told me about?"

"I rode there a while back just to get out of town. Went by myself."

Cade merely nodded. Every so often Ty went off to be alone, sometimes camping out on the range for a few days. He figured it was when the memories of Amanda weighed heavy on his mind.

"There are two good-sized trees right on the creek bank. They ought to keep you from gettin' sunburned. Want to borrow a quilt?"

Judging by the mischievous gleam in his brother's eyes, he wasn't thinking about a sunburned nose. "No, thanks. And don't go giving me ideas. I have enough of those already."

"Go for a buggy ride?" Jessie stared at Cade, pausing as she dried a plate. "It's not even eight in the morning."

"Perfect time to go. If we wait until later, it will be too hot."

He sat at the table, Ellie in his lap. He smiled, but Jessie sensed a tenseness in him, different from the undercurrent of sexual awareness that was always between them. Something was wrong. She looked at Nola. "Do you mind if I go?"

"Not a bit. Brad can walk Ellie over to Sarah's at nine and go get her before noon if you're not back." When Brad nodded, she winked at him. "I expect you and Will have something planned for the morning, too. And there's not a bit of housework that can't wait."

Jessie put the plate in the cupboard and draped the dish towel over a thin rod near the window. "Then I think a morning drive would be nice." She untied her apron and hung it on a peg on the coatrack.

"Can I go?" asked Ellie, looking up at Cade.

"Not this time, sweetheart. Besides, Sarah will be disappointed if you don't go over to play."

She pursed her lips in a pout for about ten seconds before shrugging. "Okay."

Cade lifted Ellie down and joined Jessie by the door. She put on her old wide-brimmed hat and looked up to find him smiling. "I want to keep the sun off my face." She glanced at his everyday clothes. As good as he looked in a suit, she liked him this way better. "And you didn't dress up."

"Nope. Already did that on Sunday, and that's enough. I didn't figure you'd mind."

She smiled, fighting a sudden urge to stand on tiptoe and kiss him. "Not a bit." She turned to her family and Nola. "We'll be back in time for me to fix dinner."

"And if you aren't, I'll start something. Enjoy your morning."

As they walked out to the street, Cade settled his hand at the small of her back, sending little shards of awareness darting through her. When he helped her into the buggy, he seemed to do so with even more gentleness and care than usual.

Jessie started to worry. He walked around the buggy and climbed in, picking up the reins. "What's wrong?" she asked quietly.

He flashed her a smile. "I'm fighting a battle."

"Oh?"

He flicked the reins, and the horse moved forward at a walk. "The gentleman in me is trying to keep the rascal from kissing you and giving all the old biddies peeking out their windows something to talk about."

She chuckled wryly. "Well, I appreciate the gentleman's efforts. At least for now."

"So I can untie the rascal later?" He sent her a heated glance.

"Maybe one hand."

He laughed and nodded a greeting to one of the neighbors walking in the opposite direction toward downtown.

"Where are we going?"

"Ty said there are some nice shady pecan trees out on Rabbit Hollow Creek. It's about three miles north of town. I thought you might like to see some new scenery."

"Is it different than out toward the ranch?"

"Not much," he said with a smile.

Other than Cade occasionally pointing out a house and telling her who lived there, they rode along in comfortable silence. Eventually he turned off the road, simply driving across the range near a creek bank.

"Rabbit Hollow?" she asked, grabbing hold of his arm when they hit a bump.

"Sorry." When he glanced down at her hands on his arm and how their bodies were now touching from shoulder to thigh, a hint of a smile lifted his lips. "On second thought, I'm not sorry at all. Not if it keeps you this close to me. And, yes, this is Rabbit Hollow. We should spot the trees shortly."

They hit a few more bumps, but even if they hadn't, she didn't intend to move. It felt too good to touch him. The top half of the pecan trees came into view, surprising her at how large they were. Cade guided the horse down a mild slope to the creek, stopping where she could graze and drink from the two-yard-wide stream of water flowing lazily along. He handed the reins to Jessie and hopped down, lifting a heavy iron weight from beneath the seat. Setting it on the ground near the horse's head, he tied a rope from a ring in the top of it to the harness to keep her from running away if she were spooked.

Then he came around to Jessie's side of the buggy. She looped the reins over the rail in front of her and stood.

When she leaned toward him, resting her hands on his shoulders, he put his hands around her waist and picked her up, slowly sliding her body down the length of his. She shivered in anticipation, but instead of kissing her, he plucked the hat off her head and tossed it onto the floorboard of the buggy. His followed, and he led her across the grassy bank into the shade.

If he didn't kiss her in the next thirty seconds, she would be forced to take the initiative, brazen or not.

Cupping her face in both hands, he said quietly, "I love you."

Tenderness, desire and love filled his eyes, along with something else—a hint of sorrow? She cradled his cheek with one hand. "I love you, too."

He kissed her gently, but it wasn't enough. He raised his head, lowering his hands to the small of her back. She slid her hands across his shoulders and around his neck.

"My sweet, beautiful Jessie. Mine," he whispered against her lips, then crushed her to him, deepening the kiss, devouring her mouth with a hunger that surprised her. No, not just hunger. Desperation. *Something is wrong.* His hands roamed over her, touching her in ways he never had before, and the thought vanished in a tide of sensation.

She fumbled with the button at his collar, freeing it and the next two, slipping her hand beneath the cloth, caressing the tight muscles, tangling her fingers in the coarse hair.

Gasping, he carefully lowered her to the grassy slope, following her down, lying on his side next to her, one leg thrown across hers. He captured her mouth again, giving and taking, whispering words of love between kisses. She felt his fingers work the buttons loose at her collar, and the cool morning air whispered across her throat. Then heat, scorching, wonderful heat as he touched her skin with his lips, teased it with his tongue.

He moved slightly and mumbled incoherently. Then, with a muttered grumble, he abandoned her and raised up on one elbow. Scowling, he reached beneath him with his other hand and pulled out a fist-sized, sharp-edged rock and tossed it over his shoulder.

He trailed his fingertips along her cheek, and a troubled frown settled between his brows. "I think I've just been reminded that I didn't come out here to ravish you."

"That's not exactly what was happening," she said with smile. He sat up with a heavy sigh, facing the creek. The gentleman was back in control. She sat up, too. "I liked the rascal better."

He glanced at her with a smile, but a frown quickly replaced it. "What did Doolin do to you?"

She caught her breath. Had someone seen her come out of Doolin's office? Had Ty been asking questions? "How do you know about Doolin?"

"Blast it, Jessie. What did he do to you?"

"He offered me a job as his housekeeper—and his hostess."

Cade lifted an eyebrow. "Hostess?"

"He decided he should hire someone else to do the labor, and I would supervise. Then I would be free to grace his table and entertain his guests, act as his hostess."

Cade's frown deepened, and he searched her face. "That's all he wanted?"

"No. He wanted me to be his mistress. He didn't use the actual word, but that's what he meant. I refused and headed for the door, but he held it shut."

"He was behind you?"

She nodded.

"Did he touch you?" His voice was hard.

"On the neck. Lightly. Put one hand around my waist. Nothing else. By then I didn't care if the whole town heard a ruckus and came running or if my reputation was ruined. I jabbed him in the stomach with my elbow and kicked him in the shin. I made it very clear to him that I wasn't interested and that if he bothered me again, I would make sure the everyone knew what kind of man he was. He got the message, said he'd made a mistake and apologized. I don't think he will bother me any more."

"But you went straight to the store and got a derringer."

"He frightened me and made me realize how vulnerable I am without protection. You were right. There are rough men in Willow Grove, but you can't necessarily tell it just by their appearance. You were also right that I need to be on guard all the time when I'm out and about. I should have listened to you."

"You should have listened to me and never moved to town." He raked his fingers through his hair, shoving back a strand that had fallen over his forehead. "Why didn't you tell me?"

"Because I was afraid you'd beat him to a pulp. He deserves it, but it would only fuel more gossip. And I didn't think it would help my reputation any."

He sighed wearily and caught her hand. "No, it wouldn't. And I can't beat him up, though right this minute, there's nothing I'd like more." A smile touched his mouth and he lifted her hand, kissing her fingers. "Well, there is one thing I'd like more, but it doesn't have anything to do with him. And it's not right until my ring is on your finger."

"You could still kiss me."

"Yes, ma'am. I could." He released her hand and put his arm across her back, supporting her, and leaned down. "And will."

He kept his passion carefully in check this time, but love flowed between them, pure, sweet and precious.

When he finally ended the kiss, she leaned her head against his shoulder. "How did you find out about Doolin?"

"Quint."

She straightened, looking up at him. "I don't understand."

"I saw Quint yesterday on the way home from town. Doolin is the head of the rustlers."

Jessie stared at him until the words soaked in. "He has an evil streak—but rustling cattle? He wants to run for state office someday."

"Well, he won't get to. Quint met him at the camp the other day. Doolin keeps some of the stolen cattle at his ranch and sells off the rest to someone in Colorado. He's been running the same operation in New Mexico, but that crew has moved in here, too. They're planning to hit my herd and someone else's on Wednesday night. He said we'll have a good chance to capture most of them if we surprise them at the camp early Thursday morning."

"What about Doolin?"

"He might be there, too. Now that he trusts Quint, he may go back to his old routine of inspecting the cattle each morning after a raid. Doolin mentioned that he'd tried to hire you as his housekeeper, but you refused. Said he liked your fire as well as your beauty. He made it clear that he had things beside housekeeping in mind. Quint pretended that he didn't care. Figured it would be safer for you. I think Doolin was giving Quint a warning, using a potential threat against you to keep him in line until they're through with the rustling. Quint thinks Doolin is about to put an end to it."

"But you and the sheriff are going to do it for him."

"Along with Ty and Quint, maybe a few others. Until

Doolin is behind bars, you need to be extra careful, sweetheart.''

"Do you think we should move back to the ranch?"

"I'd like nothing better. But if you moved back so soon after Quint found out about Doolin, he might get suspicious. It's not likely, but we can't take the chance. Supposedly, Doolin has already shot one man in cold blood for disagreeing with him."

A cold shiver raced down her spine, and Cade put his arm around her again.

"Quint didn't even think I should come to town again so soon, but I couldn't stay away from you. I had to be sure Doolin hadn't hurt you. And I needed to warn you about him." He kissed the tip of her nose. "If I make a big show of courtin' my woman, maybe he will think that's all I'm up to."

"So this is merely for show?"

He nodded, sliding his other hand around her waist, and began nibbling on her earlobe. "Showing you how much I love you."

Chapter Eighteen

"Aren't you going to race, Cade?" asked Brad, moving to stand in front of Jessie as everyone lined up on Main Street to watch the annual Fourth of July horse race.

"No, son, I learned a long time ago that racing is for lighter men. Works a horse too hard to carry my weight and try to run full speed."

Brad considered the statement for so long Cade wondered if he'd just lowered himself in the boy's eyes. When he looked up with a slight frown, he was certain of it.

"So you never could win?" asked Brad.

"No. Though I never came in last, either."

"Wouldn't be any fun if there was no chance to win. And it would be real bad to push the horse too hard. It might hurt him, right?"

"Right."

"Then it's good you don't."

Cade felt a swell of pride at the boy's wisdom. He glanced at Jessie, meeting her pleased smile with one of his own. Resting one hand on Brad's shoulder, he said, "I'm glad you think so."

The boy glanced up with a grin that made Cade want to give him a hug, but he saved it for later. Though Brad smiled and laughed a whole lot more than he had when they first arrived, Cade figured such a display of affection in public would embarrass him.

"Here they come!" someone shouted.

"Buster's in the lead," yelled Brad, jumping up and down, cheering for one of the younger men from the McKinnon Ranch. Ellie joined him, bouncing like a Mexican jumping bean. Cade and Jessie laughed at the kids and hollered their encouragement to the young wrangler, clapping and cheering wildly when he won.

After all the racers had crossed the finish line, they made their way through the crowd to congratulate him. "Best riding I've ever seen," said Cade with a grin, shaking the man's hand. "Next time a cow breaks from the herd, I'll know who to send after it."

Buster laughed, rubbing his horse's nose. "It was more Big Red than me. He couldn't stand to let any of those other horses beat him. Did you bet on me, boss?" he asked, his eyes twinkling.

"Nope. You know I'm not a bettin' man, but I expect you'll collect a tidy sum besides the twenty dollars for winning. Everybody figured Melrose and Lightning were a cinch to win."

"It was close." The cowboy turned to the man who had come in second place, offering him his hand.

Melrose hesitated, then shook it, finally smiling at the younger man. "You won fair and square. I didn't know Big Red could run like that."

"Neither did I. It's the first real race we've ever been in."

"Let's get together and talk. I might be interested in sponsoring you two on the racing circuit."

Buster's eyes widened, and he glanced uneasily at Cade. "I don't know, Mr. Melrose. I've already got a job."

"It wouldn't hurt to listen to his offer," said Cade. "But come talk to me before you agree to anything."

"Yes, sir. I will."

They moved away so the young man could enjoy the limelight and headed back toward the picnic area by the creek on the outskirts of town.

"Are you going to advise him to go?" asked Jessie, smiling when he offered her his arm. He smiled back when she curled her fingers around it.

"Depends on what Melrose has in mind, and what Buster wants to do. The racing circuit can be hard on a man and a horse. Mostly, I want to make sure he understands the risks and that it might not be glory and good money. And to let him know that he'd have a job to return to if he does go. He's a good hand."

"And you're a good man."

"Darlin', if you keep lookin' at me like that, I'm going to kiss you right here."

Roses bloomed in her cheeks and she ducked her head. He glanced around to see if anyone was within hearing distance. Leaning a little closer, he said, "I love you, Jessie Monroe. I'll shout it to the world if you want me to."

She laughed softly. "I don't think that's necessary."

Maybe not. But before the day was over, he intended for every man there—especially Doolin—to know that she was his.

They reached the picnic area beneath the large grove of giant weeping willows that gave the town its name. The fragrance of roasting meat filled the air, although the breeze thankfully blew the smoke away from them. Cade and the other ranchers had dug the large barbecue pits that now held meat from four beeves cooking over a thick bed of coals. He had also helped to fill the pits with mesquite branches and start the fires.

On the flattest spot in the shade, wide boards from the lumberyard sat on top of sawhorses to form two forty-foot-long tables for the rest of the food. The ladies had covered them with a variety of colored and patterned tablecloths. The wood practically groaned under the large assortment of food—ears of corn, fresh fruit, salads of all kinds, pickles, fancy yeast rolls, and more desserts than a man could sample in a month.

Large metal washtubs filled with bottles of ginger ale and lemonade were nestled in the shallow water at the edge of the stream. Some families brought their own large covered jars of tea or lemonade and set them in the water to cool near where they spread a blanket or quilt.

Since the celebration included women and children, the city council had decreed there would be no liquor allowed at the picnic. The saloons were still open, however, and only a few blocks away, so the men who associated alcohol with a good time wouldn't die of thirst. The past two Independence Day celebrations had been relatively free of problems, but if anything happened, the sheriff and his deputy were on hand to take care of it.

The city council had erected an elevated platform at one end of the grove where various officials could expound upon matters political and patriotic. McKinnon Brothers had provided the wide bunting of red, white and blue draped along the front of it.

Cade spotted Ty walking over to a large iron triangle tied to a tree branch. "Looks like it's about chow time. Brad, Ellie, come here, please." The children hurried to join him and Jessie as their friends scurried to meet up with their parents.

Ty hit the inside sections of the triangle with a short iron bar, the clanging ring calling everyone to the table in the

traditional cowboy manner. He kept it up until most of the
people had gathered around, empty plates in hand.

"Ladies and gentlemen, youngsters and scalawags, it is
my honor to welcome you to the third annual Fourth of
July picnic of Willow Grove." The crowed cheered, and
he paused for a minute. "Normally, this honor goes to the
mayor, but he yelled so much during the horse race that
he's lost his voice." Scattered cheering again sounded
through the park. Ty laughed and held up his hands. "He
assures me that he just needs to rest it for a little while so
he can deliver his speech later on." Good-natured groaning
brought laughter.

"Our fair ladies have forbidden us to start with the desserts." More groans, especially from the cowboys. "And
they said we have to eat at least one vegetable. There are
a lot to choose from, though, so I'm sure you can find
something to your liking. They tell me that we should start
with the beef—Rob is already slicing it up—then form a
line on each side of the tables. You men with long arms
might have to help the little ones—or the ladies—if they
spot something they want on the other side of the table."

A ripple of laughter went through the crowd, and Cade
smiled, proud of his brother. If anyone had told him twenty
years earlier that one day he and Ty would be prosperous
and leaders in the community, he would have scoffed.
They'd come a long way from those frightened orphans
who tearfully walked away from their mother's grave to try
to make it in the world on their own. He glanced at Jessie,
love filling him body and soul. *You've been good to me,
Lord.* Turning his gaze back to his brother, he silently
prayed that God would bring someone into Ty's life to fill
the void left by his beloved Amanda.

"We want to thank the ranchers who supplied the beef
and dug the barbecue pits, and their range cooks, who have

tended to the cooking.'' Most of the men involved merely nodded at the applause, but a few doffed their hats and bowed to the crowd, evoking more laughter.

"We also want to give our lovely ladies a round of applause for all their hard work in providing everything else we have to eat. I don't think anyone will go away hungry.'' More applause and loud cheers from the men as the ladies preened. "After Reverend Peterson asks the blessing, we can all eat.''

The reverend cleared his throat and waited a moment for the men to remove their hats. "Please bow your heads.''

Cade slipped his hand around Jessie's. The minister thanked the good Lord for the town, for Texas and for the blessings of living in a free country, along with a blessing for the food and the hands that prepared it. Cade added silent thanks for his family—Jessie and the kids and Ty. "Amen.''

"Come get your plates, then line up with us,'' Jessie told the youngsters. She selected her food, along with Ellie's, while Cade helped Brad when he wanted something he couldn't reach. Their plates were full before they were halfway down the table, so they headed back to the spot they had picked out earlier. Ty and Nola were right behind them. Cade had hauled a rocking chair along for Nola. The rest of them sat down on a couple of quilts spread out on the ground. Asa and Lydia were nearby, but they were so wrapped up in each other they might as well have been alone.

Ty eyed Cade's heaping plate and chuckled. "I think you'd better move back to the ranch, Jessie. The poor man is starving.''

"I doubt that. He's been eating at our place more than at home,'' said Nola, grinning affectionately at both men. She nodded at Ty's equally full dish of food. "Looks to me like Mr. Boswell needs to enlarge his servings at the restaurant.''

Ty laughed, set the plate on the quilt and picked up an ear of corn. ''They're big enough. I just wanted to sample everything.''

''Impossible.'' Jessie watched the line of people moving along the tables. There was still plenty of food for everyone. ''I've never seen anything like this.''

''Didn't you have a Fourth of July picnic in Riverbend?'' asked Cade around a bite of beef.

''Yes. But everyone brought their own food. They didn't barbecue or have a big potluck. Of course, there weren't very many single men there, either.''

''With all the ranches out here, the cowboys make up half the population. Probably two-thirds of it, if you're only counting adults.''

''At least,'' said Ty. ''It's not just the cowboys. More than half the men in town are single. Which means you ladies won't get to sit down once the music starts.''

Nola laughed. ''I will. These old legs don't move like they used to.''

''I'll be brokenhearted if you don't dance at least once with me.'' Ty gave her a rakish smile. ''We'll pick a slow one.''

Nola waved her hand at him and laughed, soft color touching her cheeks. ''Save that charm for the younger women, boy. I intend to watch and enjoy the music.''

Ty put his hand over his heart. ''I've been spurned. Jessie, will you save a dance for me?''

''Of—''

''She will not,'' Cade interrupted. ''I'm claiming them all.'' He grinned at Jessie. Judging from her expression, she couldn't decide whether to be put out at him or flattered.

"You do, and there's liable to be a lynching." Ty's tone grew serious. "It's up to you, Jessie, of course. But we're mighty short on females. One dance with a pretty woman like you will go a long way to brightening a lonely man's days for a long time."

Cade knew his brother was right, but he didn't want to share her with anyone. Still, he remembered how a woman's smile stayed with a man when he was out on the range for months at a time. "I reckon I could settle for every other one. I won't like it, but I can live with it."

Jessie laughed and caught Ellie's glass of lemonade as it tipped. "Better to live with it than be strung up."

They polished off their food and went back for dessert. When they were done with that, Jessie and Cade rinsed their dishes in the stream and packed them away. Ellie and Brad went off to play with some friends, following Jessie's admonition to stay where she could see them.

She and Cade leaned back against the tree, stretching their legs out in front of them on the quilt. Ty sprawled on the one next to them. "Time for a nap."

"You're going to miss the mayor's speech." Cade nodded toward the platform where the gentleman hovered near the steps, talking to another alderman.

"That's the whole idea." Ty grinned and settled his hat over his eyes. He tipped up the brim with one finger, meeting Cade's gaze. "Next year, I plan to be the one making the speech."

"You're going to run for mayor?" That was the first Cade had heard of it.

"Yep." Ty raised up, leaning on one elbow and spoke quietly. "Jacob has shown up drunk at three of the last four city council meetings. He finally admitted last night that his missus didn't go to her sister's for a visit. She's left him. He plans to resign tomorrow and move back to Atlanta, too. See if he can't patch things up with her.''

"Is that the real reason he didn't give the welcome speech? Is he drunk?'' asked Jessie, glancing anxiously toward the man.

"No. He wasn't drinking last night. He'd decided what he had to do and that lifted a load off his shoulders. Sweeny has been ridin' herd on him since breakfast this morning, though, to make sure he's all right. It would be a real shame if he made a fool of himself in front of everybody. He's a good man and has done a lot for this town. I'd just as soon folks in general don't learn about how he's been this past month.

"The council has already agreed to appoint me as interim mayor. Then I'll run for the office in the fall, along with anyone else who wants to try for it.''

"You'll be a shoe-in,'' said Nola. "Though Tate Doolin might run against you. He tries too hard to be friendly to everybody, just a bit too slick for my tastes. Bound to have political ambitions.''

Cade and Jessie exchanged a glance, both trying hard not to let their feelings about the man show.

Ty carefully ignored them and teased Nola. "Are you saying I'm slick? I'm a politician.''

"No, you don't strike me that way. Course, I've known you since you were too young to shave, so reckon that clouds my judgment a mite. You're smooth and charming, but honest as the day is long. Everybody knows it.''

"Doolin has a reputation for honesty,'' said Cade.

"I'm not saying I ever heard anything against him, but he makes me uneasy. Can't tell you why, he just does. Just don't feel like I can trust him.''

"I've never known your intuition to be wrong,'' said Ty, finally glancing at Jessie.

"There's been a time or two," said the older woman. "But a time or two in almost seventy years doesn't count for much," she added with a laugh.

No it didn't. And this time she was right on the money.

Chapter Nineteen

Jessie had the best Fourth of July of her life. The children spent the afternoon playing with their new friends and even entered a few of the games. Ellie won third place in the race where each contestant carried an egg on a serving spoon. They didn't discover until the race was over that the kids her age were given a boiled egg instead of a raw one like the older children. Brad and his friend Will came in second in the three-legged race and were as proud as if they had won.

Cade stayed by her side the whole day. After the speeches, they strolled around the picnic grounds, visiting with friends and neighbors. It seemed as if Cade knew everyone. He always introduced her to those she didn't know and made an effort to include her in the conversation. He treated her with the utmost courtesy, even on the numerous occasions when he rested his hand at her waist. Secretly she was thrilled by his possessive manner and amused by a few men's annoyed expressions.

When some of the men tried to draw him away to a discussion of cattle and politics, he politely refused, telling them outright that he wanted to spend the day with her.

Later, when the musician for the evening mounted the

stage and began to tune his fiddle, Cade broke into a grin. ''Finally. Now, I have a legitimate excuse to hold you in my arms.''

''You're only allowed to put one arm around me.'' When he pretended to pout, she laughed. ''You get to hold my hand, too.''

''Not quite as good as wrapping both arms around you, but it will do.'' He held her gaze, his voice dropping low. ''For now.''

She took a quick breath, wishing they were back out on Rabbit Hollow Creek beneath the pecan trees. Not that she wanted to make love with him. *Stop lying to yourself.* But she wouldn't. She couldn't. But, oh, how she wanted to. *Someday.* She forced herself to look away, only to be drawn back again. *Soon.*

Desire flared in his eyes, accompanied by a flash of something else. Triumph? Perhaps. But joy and understanding lingered there, too.

''How do you do that?'' she whispered.

''What?'' A small frown creased his brow.

The music began and she slipped her hand into his. ''Know what I'm thinking.''

A slow grin replaced the frown. ''Because most of the time I'm thinking it, too.'' He guided her onto the smoothly graded, hard-packed dirt dance floor. ''And because you live in my heart,'' he murmured against her ear as he put his arm around her. ''How can I not know when you're such a part of me?''

A sweet, tender ache filled her heart, bringing both a smile and tears to her eyes. ''Hush, or you'll make me cry.''

''Mercy, woman. Don't do that, or half the men here will pounce on me. I'm liable to be tarred and feathered.''

''Heaven forbid. I certainly don't want that.'' Was there

anything this man did poorly? He spun her around in a waltz, smoothly moving through the steps and the crowd. "You dance pretty well for a cowboy." Or anybody else.

"Courtesy of Mrs. Nola Simpson. She gave dancing lessons to those of us who needed it. Along with a lot of other instruction on how to be gentlemen. Didn't want her cowboys to be slouches when it came to the social niceties."

"She taught you well. No wonder she's such a good friend."

He drew her a little closer to avoid colliding with another couple, then kept her there. "I doubt we'd be where we are today without her. Ty and I were just youngsters when we hired on with her husband. She not only taught us how to behave but also talked him into giving us two days a week for schooling. He indulged her because she'd been a schoolteacher when he married her. Figured it would help keep her on the ranch if she could do the job she was trained for and loved."

"She would have stayed no matter what. The way she talks about him, she thought he hung the moon."

"They had a good marriage. Not without an argument on occasion, though." He looked down at her, his eyes twinkling. "He said it kept things interesting."

"I had enough fights with Neil to last a lifetime." A twinge of her old fear pricked her.

"We're bound to have some, honey. Two people can't always agree on everything." His fingers tightened slightly at her waist. "But I promise our quarrels will never be like what you went through with him." The music ended and he escorted her toward Ty, who had claimed the second dance.

"I know. But I still get scared sometimes."

"Don't be. Please."

Ty glanced from one to the other. "You two are lookin' mighty serious all of a sudden."

"Tell her I'm a saint," said Cade.

"Nope. You're not." Ty offered Jessie his arm, and they headed onto the dance floor. "A man needs a little bit of deviltry in him to be fun." Taking her hand and resting his other one at her waist, he smiled in reassurance. "He's no saint, Jessie, but he is the best man I've ever known."

She returned his smile. "You're prejudiced."

"Yes, ma'am."

The music began—a polka—and there was no time, or breath, for any more talk. Just as the dance ended, Jessie caught sight of Cade talking to the fiddler. Grinning, the man glanced in her direction and nodded. Cade hurried out to meet them, she suspected before some other man intercepted them. "What was that all about?"

"What?" He gave her the wide-eyed innocent look that meant he was up to mischief.

"You were talking to the fiddler."

"He's an old friend."

"He looked at me."

"Darlin', most of the men here have been staring at you all day." He held out his hand, and she placed hers in it.

"But he looked at me after you said something to him."

"Oh, that. We were just discussing the music. Asked him to make every other one slow, starting with this one."

Jessie laughed and glanced at Ty, shaking her head. "He got more than his fair share of deviltry."

"You two been talkin' about me?" asked Cade.

"You told me to." Ty mimicked his innocent expression, then grinned, surprising Jessie with his next words. "Don't look toward Doolin. He watched you two almost the whole time during that first dance."

Cade's hand tightened on hers, but he faked a smile. "Angry?"

"If he was, he didn't show it. But toward the end of the song, he was smiling."

"Like he was going to get even for losing Jessie?"

"Something like that. Sheriff Procter said four of Doolin's men left town in the last hour."

"Probably heading for my place." Cade tugged gently on her hand. "So we need to enjoy the evening and make him believe that we haven't given the rustlers a second thought."

This time when the music started, he pulled her closer than was proper. Not enough to cause a scandal, but they probably provoked a few murmurs of disapproval—or approval, given Nola and her cronies' smiling faces.

The evening continued with Cade claiming her for the slower dances and reluctantly relinquishing her hand to various men for the others. After a few of Cade's brisk, "This one is mine," the others accepted the pattern he had established. No one seemed to consider that they should ask her opinion about it. She didn't quite know what to think of that at first, then decided that it was more of an indication of Cade's standing among the men than disregard for her feelings. Since she always asked the men to return her to him, maybe her feelings were obvious.

When it was dark, the fiddler took a break. Jessie and Cade joined Nola and the children to watch the fireworks display provided by the county commissioners. Brad and Ellie were already half-asleep on the quilt, worn-out from their hard play. But they perked up when the first Roman candle lit the night sky.

The display lasted less than ten minutes but captured the spirit of freedom they all treasured. Yet mingled with the excitement and cheer were painful and bitter memories of a war that had pitted neighbor against neighbor, brother against brother. The eighteen years since the end of the War Between the States had healed some wounds, but not all.

She had learned soon after arriving in West Texas, however, that for the most part, folks didn't discuss the war or their loyalties. People had come from both the North and South, hoping to start a new life and tame a frontier together. They were united in a common goal, a new beginning.

For that matter, it was considered impolite—and sometimes downright dangerous—to question people about their past. Cade said he didn't doubt that many of the county's most upright citizens had had some kind of run-in with the law in other states.

"Cade, are you going to take me and these youngsters home in the wagon or make us walk?" Nola stood up from her rocker, tapping her cane on the ground.

"You probably ought to walk. It would be good for you." Cade grinned, offering Nola his arm to help steady her. "But since Ellie would probably sleepwalk right into the creek, we'll take you home."

"I'm not gonna go into the creek." Ellie shot him a perturbed glance, then looked sleepily up at Jessie. "What's sleepwalk mean?"

"It's when someone is sound asleep, gets up and walks around in their sleep. I've heard of it, but I've never known anyone who actually did it." She folded up the quilt. "Come on, honey, let's go."

"Doesn't sound like any fun if you don't know where you're going." Ellie walked between her and Brad to the wagon. When they stopped, she leaned against Jessie's side, watching Cade lift Nola up to the seat. He headed back for her rocking chair.

"I don't think so, either. Seems to me a body could get into all kinds of trouble," said Nola.

"Like fall in the creek," said Brad, yawning. "Wouldn't have minded this afternoon after the three-legged race. I was hot."

"It's nice now, though." Jessie stepped back, drawing Ellie with her as Cade opened the back end of the wagon bed and slid the rocker into it. She laid the folded quilt down on the other side, and Cade lifted the kids up. Then he picked her up and sat her beside them. When she curled her legs up beside her, he closed the tailgate.

"I'll try not to hit too many bumps."

"It isn't far. We'll be fine."

When they arrived at the house, Jessie and Nola took the children inside while Cade unhitched the horse. He led her out back to the small pen holding Valentine. After feeding his horse, he gave Valentine a little extra, too, and took the time to rub her neck. "One of these days, ol' girl, you'll be livin' back at the ranch where you belong. You talk to your mistress and tell her to accept when I officially propose."

Valentine snorted and nodded her head as if she understood, making Cade laugh. "Yeah, I know you get lonesome. But you and Whiskey can visit all night tonight. She'll catch you up on all the ranch gossip."

He went inside and gave the kids a good-night hug, helping Jessie tuck them into bed. Standing in the doorway while she sat on the edge of the bed, they listened to their bedtime prayers. Contentment filled him, along with a restless impatience to have this family—his family—living in his house again.

When they went downstairs, they met Nola heading for her bedroom. "You two go on back to the dance. The kids will be here to take care of me. And I can take care of them if they need anything. Neither one of them ever gets up at night anyway.''

"Thanks." Cade grabbed Jessie's hand, practically dragging her out the door. "We won't be too late," he called over his shoulder.

"I'm not all that interested in going back to the dance," said Jessie. But she slipped her arm around his and walked along with him, happy as you please.

"Neither am I. But if I don't get you alone real soon, I'm going to raise a ruckus."

"I think we are alone. Everyone else is still at the party."

"Maybe. But I swear I just saw the corner of a curtain lift across the street."

"Mrs. Smith. I forgot about her. She left the picnic right after we ate. We'll just have to settle for walking a bit, I guess."

Cade was glad to hear disappointment in her voice. "We could walk down to Ty's house. He's not home yet. Won't be for a while, either."

"Hmm. This sounds planned to me."

"Now, would I do that?"

"Yes." She laughed, hugging his arm. "I like a man who doesn't leave things to chance."

He shrugged. "Sometimes that's the best way, but not when I want to kiss my woman without nosy neighbors watching."

They weren't walking fast, but it didn't take long to reach Ty's house. Except for the times Cade had brought Jessie and the children to town, he always stayed there. Actually, it belonged to both of them, just as the ranch house did. But Cade planned to build another house in town when he and Jessie got married, though he hadn't mentioned it to her yet.

He carefully looked around as they approached the

house. The full moon made walking easy, but it didn't particularly help them be discreet. No one lived right next to Ty, mainly because they owned two lots on each side of the house. As best he could tell, the neighbors across the street were still at the celebration. He expected as much, since they had no children and were usually the last to head for home. Two new houses were being built on the block, but they weren't finished yet.

They strolled leisurely up the porch steps, but the instant they were inside, Cade shut the door and pulled her into his arms for a long, passionate kiss. Stopping to catch his breath, he leaned against the door, holding her close. "I've been starving for that all day."

"Me, too. Though it's been a wonderful day." She leaned back, looking up at him. "We've never had such a nice Fourth of July."

"I'm glad you enjoyed it. It's the best one I've ever had, too." He cupped her face with his hand. "I love you, Jessie."

She smiled tenderly. "I love you, too. I didn't think I'd ever say that to another man. But I've realized that I never really loved Neil. I cared for him in the beginning, but it wasn't love. Not like this." She stood on tiptoe and tugged his head down toward hers.

She didn't have to encourage him, but he let her take the lead, delighting in her sweetness. Then she sighed softly, tightened her arms around his neck and deepened the kiss.

He thought they might both go up in smoke. Holding on to his control by a thread, he gave in to his need to caress her, at least as much as he could and still keep her clothes buttoned and the hem of her skirt where it belonged. If he dared touch skin that he didn't see every day, he'd be hauling her into the bedroom with no turning back.

After several minutes of exquisite torture, she drew back,

resting her forehead against his chin. It took her another minute to speak. "We better stop."

"Not if I lock the door. We could make sure everybody saw us leaving together in the morning. Then I'd have to do the honorable thing and marry you tomorrow."

She shook her head and smiled. "I don't want a shotgun wedding. Besides, this is Ty's house."

"He's smart. He'd figure out he wasn't welcome and go stay at the hotel."

"Probably couldn't get a room."

"True." He loosened his embrace, resting his hands lightly on her back. "And I did make that promise to Brad." He smiled ruefully. "Foolish me."

"Noble you."

His smile widened into a grin. "Well, now, since I'm so noble, and such a good kisser, maybe you should marry me."

"Maybe I should." She grinned and smoothed his collar.

His heart leaped. "Is that a yes?"

"Was that a proposal?"

"Yes, ma'am."

"Then it was a yes."

When he took a deep breath to cut loose with a rebel yell, she clamped her hand over his mouth. "Don't you dare holler. You'll stir up every dog in town and have everybody who's still awake running up here to see what's wrong."

He smiled against her palm. "Yeth, um."

"Promise to be quiet?" She tipped her head and narrowed her eyes.

He nodded, and she moved her hand away. "Maybe I should just kiss you instead."

"Good choice."

Quick as a wink, he scooped her up in his arms, making

her squeal in surprise. "Shh, or you'll wake everybody up."

"Cade..." Her voice held a note of warning as she glanced toward the bedroom.

"Don't worry, darlin'. I'm just going over here to the couch. Tired of standing." When he reached it, he turned around and plopped down, snuggling her on his lap. He looked from one end of the couch to the other. "And this thing isn't big enough to get comfortable." He could have sworn she blushed, though it was hard to tell in only the moonlight. "I do believe there are distinct advantages to falling in love with a widow woman."

"Oh?" She relaxed, leaning comfortably against his chest, his arm supporting her back.

"A spinster would be screaming her head off by now."

Jessie laughed and smoothed a lock of hair back from his forehead. "A young woman might. A spinster would probably rip your clothes off."

Cade leaned his head against the back of the couch and laughed. "You mean I've misjudged all those old maids and missed no tellin' how many opportunities over the years?"

"You may have misjudged the ladies, but you wouldn't have taken the opportunities if you'd had them. You're too good a man."

"Darlin', your opinion of me may be a bit high. I was young once and sowed a few wild oats."

"Any of them I need to worry about?"

"Such as having a young'un show up on your doorstep? No. I made it a point to check back and make sure. All that happened years ago." He brushed a tender kiss across her lips. "And I never met a woman I wanted to spend my life with until you."

Unfastening the button on his shirt pocket, he pulled out

a small bundle of velvet. He unfolded it, revealing an engagement ring. Taking her right hand, he slipped it on the third finger. "I've been carrying this around, waiting for the best time to give it to you." He looked at her face, concerned to see tears slipping down her cheeks. "I sure hope those are happy tears."

She nodded and sniffed. "They are." She wiggled her finger, trying to catch the ring in the moonlight. Throwing her arms around his neck, she hugged him fiercely and gave him a kiss that would have sent him to his knees if he hadn't been sitting down.

Several minutes later, he asked softly, "Do you want me to light a lamp so you can see it better?"

"Yes, please."

He lifted her off his lap, chuckling as she grabbed his shoulder for balance when she stood. "Been nippin' the bottle, darlin'?"

"Giddy with love." She smiled and stepped aside so he could stand. "Maybe we'd better go into the kitchen so nobody can see us."

"Coward." He grinned and led the way, lighting the lamp that sat on the kitchen table. At her soft gasp, he turned—and felt about ten feet tall.

She gazed at the ring, a half-carat diamond surrounded by small rubies, and her eyes misted again. "Cade, I've never seen anything so beautiful."

"I thought it was the prettiest one they had in the store." Frowning, he moved it up and down on her finger. "It's a little big. You should go by the store tomorrow and have Mr. Jones size it for you. He said it wouldn't take too long to do it."

"I don't deserve this," she whispered, laying the side of her face against his chest.

"Yes, you do. You deserve everything I can give you

and more." He embraced her carefully. "Maybe I should buy one for every finger. Toes, too."

"I wouldn't be able to lift my hands or wear shoes." The hint of laughter in her voice eased his worry. "And unlike my children, I don't like to run around outside without shoes."

"So when are you going to put me out of my misery, woman? Tomorrow?" He kissed her forehead.

"You'll be busy catching outlaws tomorrow."

"And maybe the next day, too. How about Saturday?"

She shook her head, her hair tickling his chin. "Not a good day."

"Who says?"

"Everybody." She eased out of his hold. "Don't you know the poem about choosing the right day for a wedding?"

"Can't say that I do," he said with a grin. "Nola didn't teach poetry when she was drilling etiquette into our heads and dancing into our boots."

> "Monday for wealth,
> Tuesday for health,
> Wednesday the best day of all;
> Thursday for losses,
> Friday for crosses,
> And Saturday no luck at all."

She paused, then looked up, sadness lurking in her eyes. "Neil and I were married on a Saturday. And it certainly lived up to its reputation."

"I'm not a superstitious man, but how about next Wednesday, since that's the best day of all? I think I can stand to wait that long, but not a minute longer."

"I don't really want to wait long, either. But if we get

married on Monday, everyone will think I'm marrying you for your wealth.''

He laughed, pulling her back into his arms. ''Just tell them I'm marrying you for yours.''

''That would give them a good laugh.''

''Don't know why it should.'' He bent down, hovering just above her mouth. ''You're my greatest treasure.''

Chapter Twenty

Lying on his stomach, Cade peered over the rim of the cliff in the early light of dawn, studying the outlaw hideout below. Sheriff Procter and his deputy, Dwight Jacobs, were next to him, with Ty and Asa farther east, watching the entrance to the box canyon. There were no buildings, not even a dugout. A makeshift brush corral held approximately thirty head of cattle. The horses were confined in a rope corral, the kind more often seen in the Northwest than the Southwest. They did have a chuck wagon for the cooking supplies and bedrolls.

"There's Quint," whispered the sheriff.

Cade nodded, watching his friend through a spyglass as he sat up and stretched his arms over his head. He wondered if Quint had actually slept or merely pretended to for a couple of hours. Quint picked up the gun and holster lying beside him, stood and strapped the firearm on.

Cade scanned the rest of the men. Three were still asleep. One was cooking breakfast. Three others stood on one side of the campfire, drinking coffee. "I only count eight, including Quint. Should be eleven."

"Could be guarding the entrance," said Procter.

"Maybe."

Quint tossed his war-bag, a sack that held some of his personal belongings and also served as a pillow, onto the bedding and rolled it up. Tying it securely, he set it in the bed of the chuck wagon and chatted with the cook for a minute. Then he picked up a cup and joined the others at the fire, pouring himself some coffee.

"No sign of Doolin," said Cade.

"Probably too early for him. He was at the dance until the fiddler called it a night at two."

"And made sure plenty of folks knew he was there, right?"

The sheriff nodded, and Cade turned his full attention back to the camp. They were too high up to hear more than a quiet hum as the men talked, except when the cook called them to breakfast. Even those who were sleeping quickly roused and hurried over to pick up plates and silverware and get their grub. Quint ate quickly and set his plate in the dishpan by the chuck wagon.

When he picked up his rifle and headed toward the canyon entrance, Cade grinned. "Looks like Quint has guard duty this morning."

"Best news I've heard all morning."

They waited until another man returned to camp, eagerly filling his breakfast plate. "That leaves two unaccounted for." Cade skimmed the scene with his spyglass again. "Nobody seems in any hurry to join Quint and replace another guard."

"The other two must not be here. Likely went back to the ranch last night."

Sheriff Procter scooted backward down the slope, motioning to his deputy, who followed. "You stay here and back us up." Cade glanced back to see him smile at the middle-aged man's relieved expression. With a wife and four kids, he probably would have rather stayed at home.

"If shooting starts, feel free to pick off as many as you can."

"Yes, sir," said the deputy. "I'm better with my rifle than a pistol anyway."

Procter nodded and motioned for Cade to join him. Crouching low until they were certain they couldn't be spotted, they quietly covered the ground to where Ty and Asa were. Asa stayed at the canyon edge, on the lookout while Ty came down.

"There was only one guard, and Quint took over for him a few minutes ago."

"Good. That man is back at camp," said the sheriff. "Cade, go talk to Quint. See if he knows whether or not Doolin is coming out here this morning."

Cade walked as quietly as he could through the brush-covered hillside, stopping when he could see Quint. Using the bobwhite's call, he got Quint's attention. Quint looked in his direction and nodded. Cade moved closer, keeping to the brush. He stopped when he got close enough to talk but still remain hidden.

"Is Doolin coming out?"

"No. Had to meet with an important client this morning."

"What about the other two men?"

"They left after we brought the cattle in. They might have gone back to the ranch. One of them is the horse wrangler, so he spends time at both places."

"Are you ready to ride?"

"Did you bring an extra horse?"

Cade smiled, glad he had planned for the possibility they might need one. "I did."

"Then I'm ready. The sooner we move, the better."

"Be right back."

Cade quickly returned to the others. "Doolin isn't coming out this morning."

"Then let's make real sure nobody gets away to warn him." The sheriff signaled Asa, waiting a minute until he reached them. "We'll go in slow and quiet."

They checked their pistols and rifles one last time, then mounted up. Cade led the horse for Quint as they moved single file through the rugged terrain.

Quint was perched on top of a rock, surveying the countryside when they arrived. "Figured I'd better look like I was doing my job in case anybody wandered out to check on me. Keep an eye open for the other two, and for Doolin, in case he changed his mind."

"Don't think we're going to be that lucky." Sheriff Procter studied the entrance to the canyon while Quint swung into the saddle. "Looks about three horses wide. Plenty of room to maneuver. Cade, Ty, take the lead with me. When we get to the bend, speed up. Try to catch them off guard."

Tensing, Cade looked his brother, and they started into the canyon. As Texas Rangers, they'd ridden into similar situations many times, but never without fear and a silent plea heavenward for their safety.

Going at a walk, it took them almost ten minutes to reach the bend. The sheriff nodded, and they spurred the horses to a quick walk, then a gallop. Reaching the wide clearing at the end of the canyon, they fanned out in a shallow semicircle, rifles aimed at the outlaws.

The rustlers scrambled, trying to find cover, some of them opening fire but missing in their haste. Cade took one down. Ty another, and Quint a third. One dove beneath the wagon and covered his head with his hands. Another ran for the horses, firing toward the posse without aiming, throwing down his pistol when he ran out of bullets. Asa fired at the ground in front of him, and he dropped to his knees, hands in the air.

A shot whizzed by Cade's head. He whirled toward the left side of the clearing, but Jacobs spotted the man before he did, wounding him in the shoulder. The last two, hiding behind the chuck wagon, threw out their pistols. A rifle followed. "Don't shoot! We give up."

"Hands up high. Walk out slow and easy," ordered the sheriff. Cade and Ty kept their guns leveled at them when they stepped into the open. "You under the wagon, come out, too."

The youngster wiggled backward and stood, slowly facing them, hanging his head. Cade recognized him as a young cowboy from an outfit in the next county. He couldn't have been more than seventeen.

"Sam, what are you doin' with this bunch?" asked the sheriff.

"I got in too deep in a poker game." Sam motioned toward one of the men standing by the wagon. "Rawlins said I could join up and work it off, or he'd use me for target practice. He would've, too."

Cade studied the man he indicated, noted the pure meanness in his eyes and decided the boy was right. Even now, the man was trying to figure out a way to escape.

Then the outlaw's gaze shifted to Quint, his expression changing to hatred. "You'll pay for this, Webb," he snarled.

"No, you will," Quint said quietly. "For rustling and for trying to kill my friend." He glanced at the sheriff. "He bragged about roping Jack Shepherd and dragging him, leaving him for dead."

"The ol' coot shouldn't have interfered. Deserved to be buzzard bait."

"You'd better be thankful he didn't die," said Procter.

"Or you'd be tried for murder instead of attempted murder."

"All you got is Webb's say-so."

Ty and Asa dismounted, checking on those who were wounded.

"I expect some of the men who were there will testify against you, unless they want to be tried for attempted murder, too."

"Not this one," said Asa, kneeling beside the man Cade had shot. "He's dead."

Cade hated killing a man, even one shooting at him, but sometimes it couldn't be helped.

"These two will be all right once we get them to the doctor's," Asa added.

Gun drawn, Ty walked over to where the man Jacobs had shot was sitting on the ground, holding one hand pressed against the opposite shoulder. "This one will make it, but we'd better tend to his shoulder so he doesn't bleed to death."

"I have some bandages in my saddle bag." Procter motioned toward the other wounded outlaws. "Bring him over here, and y'all can patch them up. Cade, if you'll tie up the ones who aren't hurt, I'll make sure nobody gets frisky."

Ty, Asa and Quint bandaged wounds as best they could, mostly in an effort to stem the bleeding. Afterward, they securely tied each man's hands. Quint cleaned out the chuck wagon, tossing the sacks of flour, sugar and potatoes on the ground, along with the bedrolls that had already been stored for the day. As an added precaution, he removed all the knives, forks and cooking utensils from the chuck-box. Though it opened on the outside at the back of the wagon, he wasn't going to take any chances of Rawlins or one of the others somehow getting into it and finding something they could use for weapons.

They helped the injured men into the wagon. Once they were in place, they tied the feet of the two who had shoulder wounds. The third had been shot in the leg, so they didn't figure he would try to run away.

Cade had already hog-tied the others. Ty helped him get them into the wagon, while Asa and Cade laid the dead man over a horse and tied him in place.

On the way to town, Quint told them that Rawlins had been in charge at the camp. "He and Doolin go way back. Nobody crossed him. The dead man is another one the others feared, along with Hobson, one of the men who left last night. He got real surly on occasion, though I'm not sure he would hurt somebody just out of meanness like the other two."

When they were about a quarter mile from town, the sheriff halted, glancing at Jacobs, Ty and Asa. "You three keep the prisoners here for a spell. When we have Doolin in jail, I'll send Cade back for you."

"Yes, sir," said the deputy. Ty and Asa nodded their agreement.

The lawman looked at the prisoners, waiting until each one met his eye. "These men are deputized and under orders to shoot to kill if you try anything."

"Ain't afraid of no storekeeper," said Rawlins, glaring at Ty.

"You'd better be." Quint shifted in the saddle, glancing from Ty to Cade. "Seein' as how he was a Texas Ranger. His brother, too."

A spark of fear shot through Rawlins's eyes before his bravado took control again. "I don't care what he used to be."

Ty grinned amiably. "Doesn't matter. I'm armed. You're trussed up like a Christmas turkey."

Cade and Quint rode into town with the sheriff, tying their horses to the hitching post near Doolin's office. It was a quarter past nine, so most stores were open but not doing much business yet. The few folks who were out and about watched curiously as they entered Doolin's office.

Henry, the attorney's assistant, stood when they walked in. "Good morning, Sheriff Procter." He nodded politely at Cade and Quint. "Gentlemen. How can I help you?"

"Is Doolin here?" asked the sheriff.

"Yes, sir, he's in with a client." He edged around the end of his desk. "But I'll tell him you're here."

"No need. I'll tell him myself." The sheriff moved toward the inner office door. Cade was right behind him, pulling his Colt Peacemaker from the holster. Quint stood to the side, so Doolin wouldn't see him when the door opened.

"But you can't just barge in." Henry fidgeted but didn't get in their way.

"I can and I will." Procter opened the door and walked into Doolin's office, nodding to the rancher sitting in front of the desk. "Mornin', Mr. Clark."

The man returned the greeting, frowning when he saw Cade take up a position behind the sheriff, obviously protecting his back.

Doolin stood and straightened his suit jacket, smoothing the lapels. He glanced at Cade, his eyes narrowing briefly, then turned his attention to the lawman. "It's customary to knock when you enter, Sheriff."

"This isn't a social call. Tate Doolin, you're under arrest for cattle theft."

Clark stood, stepping back out of the way. Cade glanced at him and decided he just didn't want to get caught in the middle of anything. The rancher had always been Procter's staunch ally.

Doolin smiled, though his stance remained tense. "What happened, Procter? Did one of McKinnon's cows wander into my herd? That's hardly grounds for an arrest."

"Try thirty head in a pen, driven there by your men on your orders," said Cade.

"Some of my men are involved in rustling? What shocking news! I've tried to be careful who I hire. But I live in town. I don't know what they do at night."

Quint stepped into the room. "You know exactly what they do at night, especially when they go on a raid. You planned them all." He glanced at Clark. "Including the one on your herd a couple of weeks ago."

Doolin's face grew a shade lighter. "This man is lying. He's trying to blame this on me because I made inappropriate advances toward his sister." His gaze shifted to Cade. "A regrettable mistake for which I apologized."

"I didn't know you'd met my sister until you mentioned it to me last week at the rustler's camp."

"There! He just admitted he's one of the outlaws. How can you believe him?"

"Easy." Sheriff Procter seemed relaxed, but Cade knew he was ready for any move Doolin made. "He was working for me the whole time. I expect some of the rustlers will testify against you, too. Why should they go to jail without you? We arrested most of them this morning. We'll have the others soon enough.

"Now, I'm through jawin'. Do I have to put handcuffs on you, Doolin? Or are you coming peacefully? It's up to you. I don't mind making a big show of hauling you off to jail."

"This is an outrage!" shouted Doolin.

"The outrage is the crimes you and your gang have committed against the good citizens of this area."

"I'm innocent until proven guilty." Doolin assumed a haughty air. "I expect to be treated as such."

"You'll get the same treatment as any prisoner. Turn around and put your hands behind you."

When Doolin glared at the sheriff and didn't move, Procter grabbed his shoulder and spun him around. Jerking first one hand, then the other into a tight hold, he clasped the handcuffs around his wrists.

"I'd be happy to teach the prisoner a little respect for your authority, Sheriff," drawled Cade.

Procter turned the attorney back around and glanced at Cade. "Seein' as how he insulted your betrothed, I'll keep it in mind. If he gives me any trouble, you can pay him a visit." He gave Doolin a little shove toward the door.

Cade stepped aside, coldly meeting Doolin's gaze, taking satisfaction in the fear he saw there.

Chapter Twenty-One

"What was it like, Uncle Quint? Pretending to be an outlaw, I mean?" Brad sat beside his uncle on the sofa, as close as he could without being in his lap. His friend, Will, had taken up a position on the floor on the other side of Quint, practically worshiping at his feet. To the boys—and the whole town—Quint was a hero.

Some of his glory had spread to Cade, Ty and Asa for their part in the actual capture of the rustlers, but Quint received most of the adulation and acclaim. Which didn't sit too well with him. Naturally a bit shy, he was more comfortable staying in the background, letting people like Cade and Ty entertain folks.

"I bet it was exciting," said Will.

"Sometimes." Quint shifted, draping an arm around Brad's shoulders. "But in a scary way."

"Aw, Uncle Quint, nothin' scares you."

Quint laughed and glanced across the room to where Jessie and Cade sat wedged together on another couch in Nola's family parlor. They weren't forced to sit so close. There were plenty of chairs in the room, a couple of them empty. But she couldn't help herself. She needed to touch him, to feel the solid firmness of his body next to hers, to know that he had returned safely.

Ellie seemed to need reassurance, too. She had shadowed Cade from the minute they walked in the door, sitting on his lap at every opportunity.

"Well, Brad, I hate to disappoint you, but I was frightened just about every minute I spent with those outlaws. I think I would have been even if I'd truly been part of the gang. There were a couple of mean hombres who would have shot any of us if we'd looked at them cross-eyed. It might have taken a bit more to rile a few others, but I was never sure about them.

"Some of the men weren't all that bad. They had probably been drawn into it by the excitement and appeal of earning money without having to work very often or too hard. I swear there were at least two who had never taken into account what would happen if they were caught. Dim-witted as possums."

The boys exchanged a grin. "That's pretty dumb," said Brad.

Quint nodded. "Then there was young Sam. He's only seventeen. Shouldn't have been in the saloon or a poker game in the first place. He got deep into debt playing with Rawlins, the man in charge at the camp. When he couldn't pay, Rawlins gave him the option of joining the rustlers and working off what he owed him, or getting shot."

"That's not much of an option." Brad frowned thoughtfully. "What will happen to him?"

"I don't know. He'll probably go to the pen like the rest of them. But I hope not. Maybe he'll get a shorter sentence." He paused and blew out a deep breath. "And there was always the worry that I might accidentally give myself away. If I had, they would have killed me quicker than a roadrunner on a rattler. Add the fact that a rancher might shoot me while we were stealin' his cattle, and I had plenty to be afraid of.''

As he stretched his legs out in front of him, careful not to bump Will, a lump rose in Jessie's throat. How easily she could have lost him!

He looked up, meeting her gaze. ''Of course, my biggest concern was that I might die from Billy Bob's cookin'. I never met anybody who could ruin a can of beans like he could.''

Jessie managed a smile while everyone else laughed. Cade squeezed her fingers, and she glanced up, seeing the understanding in his eyes. How like him.

''Mr. Webb, nobody can ruin a can of beans,'' said Will.

''Billy Bob could. He'd open up enough for everybody and heat them in a kettle, but he hated just plain old beans. He kept trying to make them taste better by adding things. Stirred up some strange concoction of vinegar and molasses, heavy on the vinegar. Made everybody gag and cough for five minutes. Same thing with the ground cayenne pepper. Used a whole pound bag. When the first couple of fellers took a bite, they tried to yell but flames shot out instead of sound.''

Even Ellie giggled at that one.

''But the last straw was when Sam caught him emptying a bottle of Warner's Kidney Cure into the pot.'' He paused while the others laughed and hooted. ''I thought for a minute the kid might wring his neck himself. After that, Billy Bob was banned from cooking. We each heated up our own beans over the fire. Turned out that Sam could make decent biscuits, and one of the other men fried the salt pork without burning it, most of the time anyway.''

He smiled at Jessie. ''Doesn't compare with that fine dinner you fixed, though.'' Quint stretched his arms above his head. "It's mighty good to be back with civilized folks."

After the initial hoopla over their arrival with the prisoners, he had slipped away to the local bathhouse for a much-needed soak. He told Jessie he had kept a clean set of clothes tucked away in his saddlebag for the day he could celebrate the outlaws' capture. Then he stopped by the barber's for a shave and haircut before coming to Nola's to eat and relax.

"Are you going to take the sheriff up on his offer?" asked Asa, reaching over the arm of his chair to take Lydia's hand. He flashed her a smile before turning his attention back to Quint.

"I'm considering it."

Jessie tensed, not liking the fact that once again she had been left in the dark about something concerning her brother. "What offer?"

"Uh-oh," muttered Asa. "Looks like I opened my mouth when I shouldn't have."

"It's all right." Quint looked at his sister. "I just haven't had a chance to talk to Jess about it. Sheriff Procter offered me a job as his deputy. Seems Jacobs resigned after we got back this morning."

Jessie bit her tongue to keep from saying the first thing that popped into her mind, an emphatic no. She had made her own choices, both good and bad. She had to allow him to do the same, without interference from her, even when they frightened her. He held strong convictions about right and wrong and had the determination to follow them through. He also had a keen sense of justice and compassion for those who had been hurt.

"Well, if you were the deputy, you wouldn't be able to join up with any outlaws to try and catch them. You'd make a good lawman," she said quietly. Surprise flickered across

Quint's face, followed by relief. She knew she had said the right thing.

"Yes, you would," added Ty. "You handled yourself well today. And the rest of the time, too, or the ending would have been different."

Cade slipped his arm around Jessie's shoulders. "You have my blessing, too. Though you still have a job at the ranch if you want it. Brad tried to get me to hire him instead, but I told him he had to grow a little taller."

Brad giggled, then looked up at his uncle, something akin to awe in his eyes. "Are you really going to be a deputy?"

"I'm considering it. It's always good to sleep on big decisions."

"Wouldn't a mattress feel better?" asked Ellie, her expression concerned.

The adults laughed, causing her to frown. "Well, wouldn't it?"

"Yes, sweetheart, it would. And I do plan to sleep on a mattress over at the hotel. What I meant was that I wanted to think about whether or not to take the job and wait until at least tomorrow to give the sheriff my decision."

"Oh." She wiggled down from Cade's lap, then turned and looked up at Jessie. "Dolly's hungry. Can we have some cookies?"

"Yes, you may. Brad, would you help your sister, please? You and Will may have a couple of cookies apiece, too. Take them out on the back porch so you don't have to worry about the crumbs."

"We'll be right back, Uncle Quint," called Brad as the children raced off to the kitchen.

Cade nudged her with his elbow. "Do the rest of us get cookies, too?"

Jessie laughed. "Your stomach is a bottomless pit. Come on into the kitchen. You can help me fix a plate."

A mischievous sparkle lit his eyes as he stood and pulled her up beside him, filling her with anticipation. "Yes, ma'am. I'm a good helper."

"None for us, thank you," said Lydia. "I need to go on home."

"I wouldn't mind taking a few with me." Asa winked at Jessie as he stood.

"Me, too." Ty led the way into the kitchen. "I need to wander over to the store."

Jessie looked back at Nola, who shook her head. "None for me, dear. I'm ready for a nap. There's been too much excitement today for this ol' lady."

Ty stuck his head back around the doorway. "Nola, you're just hittin' your prime."

"Land's sake, boy, I hit my prime thirty years ago." She smiled sweetly at him. "Nice of you to fib about it though. I'm proud of you boys. All of you."

"Thank you, ma'am." Ty came back into the room, two cookies in his hand. He grinned at Jessie. "Brad's handing them out."

He leaned down and kissed Nola on the forehead. "Thank you for dinner."

"Thank Jessie. She cooked it."

"But you paid for it." He winked at her and turned to Jessie. "Thanks for the meal, soon-to-be sister-in-law."

Jessie laughed. "Glad you enjoyed it. You're welcome to come to dinner anytime. Just give me a little warning so I can cook enough."

"Watch it, darlin', or I'll get jealous." Cade slid his arm around her waist and pulled her against his side.

"Looks to me like we're all in the way." Asa strolled

back into the family parlor and took a bite of shortbread. "Cade, are you going back to the ranch today?"

"I should. First thing tomorrow, we'll need to move those thirty head back to our range. I'll see you in a little while."

Asa nodded and held out his hand to Lydia. "You might beat me home, but if you do, I'll be along directly."

Quint stood and yawned. "I'll go now, too. I didn't sleep a wink last night and not much the night before. Come to think of it, I haven't had a good night's sleep since I left the ranch."

"You're liable to be mobbed before you get to the hotel." Jessie pulled free from Cade and hugged her brother.

"I'll use the back stairs. The clerk gave me my room key so I won't even have to stop by the front desk." He gave Jessie a squeeze. "I'll go tell the kids adios and be on my way."

When Quint went out the back door, Cade looked around, smiled and pulled her into his arms. "Finally."

His kiss was slow and gentle, filling her soul with sweetness and gratitude that he had come home safely. She laid her cheek against his chest. "I hope we never have another day like this one."

"Me, too." He sighed heavily. "I killed a man this morning."

She looked up at him, her heart aching at the deep regret in his eyes. "You didn't have a choice."

"I still don't like being the one to send a man to meet his maker. Never have, not even when he's trying to kill me. But maybe, by stopping the rustling, we kept some innocent from being murdered."

Jessie hugged him tightly. "From what Quint says, they were bound to kill someone sooner or later."

"Even if they didn't, they were about to drive a few of

the smaller ranchers out of business. Conveniently, the ones who owned land near Doolin. We should have thought of that sooner.''

''Why would you? Everyone thought he was an upstanding citizen.''

''Everyone except you.'' He cradled her head against his chest. ''You knew better. I still see red when I think about him touching you.''

She tiptoed her fingers up his chest and around his neck. ''Don't trouble yourself over it. The only touch I think about is yours.''

''I'm glad.'' His eyes grew dark as he pressed her even closer. ''But if you keep talking like that, I won't be able to wait a whole six days for the wedding.''

He glanced out the window, smiling when all three kids ran by, playing chase with Will's dog. Moving his hands to her waist, he picked her up and sidestepped away from the window until they were out of sight of the children.

Nibbling on her earlobe, he whispered ways he planned to love her on their wedding night, promises that sent heat and longing spiraling from head to toe. He caressed her with gentle urgency, stoking her anticipation and need, then kissed her with a slow thoroughness that left her clinging to him simply to stand up.

''Did you order a wedding dress?'' he whispered.

''Hmm?'' She stared up at him, blinking a couple of times to bring her eyes into focus. It took a little longer for her brain to function and note his smug smile. But it didn't annoy her. He should be pleased with himself. Neil certainly had never turned her to mindless mush. ''What did you ask me?''

''If you ordered a new dress for the wedding. I want you to have the seamstress make you something special. Don't worry about the expense.''

"With everything else that went on today, I haven't even thought about it." She tilted her hand, admiring her lovely engagement ring. "I suppose I should have a new dress for my wedding. But I'm too practical to get something that I'll only wear once."

"Buy whatever you want. And if you pack it away and never wear it again, I won't complain. I just want you to have something beautiful for your wedding."

She caressed his cheek and stretched up to kiss him lightly. "I wore my two-year-old Sunday dress for my last wedding."

"Your first wedding. This will be your last wedding."

Jessie smiled. "Yes, sir. But I don't know if the dress-maker can sew one up in such a short time."

"Tell her I'll pay her double if it's ready by Tuesday afternoon. That should encourage her to do the impossible."

"Only you can do the impossible."

He raised an eyebrow. "Oh?"

"You made me love again."

Grinning, Cade took a deep breath and flexed his muscles—popping a button off his shirt.

Jessie collapsed against him with a peal of laughter. Life was good.

But soon it would be wonderful.

Chapter Twenty-Two

On Saturday, Jessie woke up at dawn, despite going to bed at one in the morning. Nola and the children had been up until almost eleven, playing dominoes with her and Quint. After they went to bed, she sat up talking with her brother.

He told her some of what had gone on in the outlaw camp, but they didn't dwell on it. She shared a little more about Neil's death and their journey to West Texas, but like Quint, her thoughts were more on the future.

She had ordered a powder-blue silk gown from the dressmaker on Friday. The woman assured her it would be ready by Tuesday afternoon. They had looked through the pattern books together, picking a pretty but simple design that wouldn't require a lot of detail work. Later she found a pair of white shoes at the store to go with the dress.

It was customary to have weddings at home, and Nola had offered hers for the ceremony. They invited only family, close friends and the men who worked on the ranch; otherwise probably everyone in town and half the county would want to attend. She was glad they were keeping it small; otherwise, she would have been much more nervous.

Quint had decided against taking the deputy sheriff's job.

He said chasing longhorns and playing mumblety-peg was as much excitement as he wanted for a long time. Jessie was relieved, even though she knew he would make a good peace officer.

Pushing aside the temptation to go back to sleep, she climbed out of bed, washed up a bit and dressed in one of her old everyday dresses. She wanted to give the house a thorough going-over. They would be busy Monday with the trial, possibly Tuesday, too. She didn't want to be doing much other than tidying up on her wedding day.

Jessie quietly went downstairs, stopping by the front window to breathe the lovely fragrance of honeysuckle and roses. Cade had already promised to order her some rose-bushes to plant at the ranch house, and the new home he was going to build in town.

It was still hard for her to comprehend having two houses, but she could see the merit in the plan. The only thing she didn't like about it was that she and the children would likely wind up living in town during school, and Cade would have to be at the ranch at least part of that time. Many ranching families did it, but being away from him was not appealing. No doubt she would dislike it even more after she spent one night in his arms.

A little shiver of anticipation danced along her skin, prompting her to turn to the tasks at hand lest she grow all hot and bothered first thing in the morning. Giggling softly, she went through the back door and across the yard to the outhouse.

Returning to the house, she had one foot on the first porch step when she sensed someone behind her. Before she could turn, a large hand clamped down on her mouth, and a man held the tip of a knife close to her side. He was about Cade's height, with a slighter build, but strong. She couldn't see his face, but he wore a suit and smelled clean, with a hint of cologne.

"Don't make a sound or we'll hurt you, then the old lady and the kids. Understand?"

Heart pounding, she nodded, barely moving her head, wishing desperately that her derringer was in her skirt pocket instead of in her purse upstairs.

"Ira, go put that letter on the kitchen table," he said quietly. He pulled her to one side and back a couple of steps so another man could go past. This one was skinny, only a few inches taller than her, with worry in his eyes but determination in the set of his jaw.

He eased open the screen door and slipped inside the kitchen, laying an envelope on the table. Turning toward the porch, he paused and cocked his head. A second later he darted across the room. Pressing back against the wall by the doorway of the hall leading to Nola's bedroom, he drew his pistol.

Jessie stared through the screen and the soft morning shadows in the kitchen, hoping desperately that he had only heard the house creak and not the tap of Nola's cane on the floor. When she glimpsed Nola's cheerful yellow wrapper, her heart leaped to her throat.

Pulling at the hand covering her mouth and trying to cry out, Jessie did her best to warn her friend.

"Be still!"

She jabbed her left elbow into his stomach. He was tougher than Doolin, her blow merely prompting a muffled curse. As Nola stepped into the kitchen, Jessie kicked backward, but he dodged. Her heel glanced off his boot, and she felt the knife cut her side.

Ignoring the pain, she struggled harder. The man inside raised the gun and brought the handle down on Nola's head. She crumpled to the floor. Jessie moaned softly and closed her eyes. Guilt and fear overwhelmed her, and she stood still, no longer fighting her captor, holding on to his arm for support.

He swore softly as the other man barreled out of the house, catching the screen door just before it slammed shut. "Go see if she's still breathing. And check for a cut on her head, see if it's bleeding."

Ira dashed back into the house, bent over Nola, then rushed back out to the porch. He was white as a sheet. His hand trembled when he wiped his face. "She's just out cold. Getting a goose egg, but there's no blood."

Thank you, God. Jessie felt the man holding her relax slightly.

"Good. Go tie her up."

"What'll I use, Mr. Starr?"

"There's some rope on the end of the porch."

Jessie glanced at the long, heavy cord that had become one of Brad's favorite toys. He roped chairs and stumps and Ellie if she stood still long enough. He used it to learn knots or as a leash for Will's dog on those rare occasions the animal agreed to it. Just yesterday, he had hog-tied one of the neighborhood boys when he was the outlaw and Brad was the new deputy.

Now it would be used to bind the hands and feet of the dear woman who was like a grandmother to him. Why couldn't she have stayed in bed another hour like she usually did? Jessie whimpered in anguish, and the pressure of the man's fingers eased against her mouth.

"If you'll stay quiet, I'll move my hand. If you make any noise and those kids come down here, it'll be your fault they get hurt."

Jessie nodded. He lifted his hand from her mouth, and she dragged in a deep breath. Instinctively she took a step towards the kitchen, and he grabbed her around the waist, holding her back. "Stay still," he ordered curtly. "Ira, cut off a piece of rope and tie Mrs. Monroe's hands first."

When the other man approached with the rope, Starr eased back, keeping the knife close to her side but not touching her. "Put your hands behind your back."

She obeyed, a strange calm creeping over her mind and body as she felt the cord wrapped around her wrists and tied securely. Nola was stronger than she looked. *She'll be all right. She has to be.*

Was Doolin behind this? Did he think Cade would help him escape? Or maybe it was a way to try to keep Quint from testifying against him. But if he went free, would the sheriff simply turn around and arrest him for kidnapping?

"Use a cup towel or something to gag the old woman. Make sure her nose is clear so she can breathe." Starr gripped Jessie's arm. "We're leavin'. You can catch up to us like we planned. Remember to ride out slow."

Ira nodded and whispered, "The old lady ain't gonna die, is she?"

"Probably not. It takes more than that to kill somebody, unless she's already sick or something."

Which she wasn't. Jessie prayed desperately that he was right.

He half dragged her across the backyard. Pulling against him caused the cut on her side to ache. When she felt a wider area of her dress grow warm and sticky, she realized her resistance was only making it bleed more. She gave up trying to slow him down. Walking around behind the storeroom, she was surprised to find a horse and buggy waiting. It wasn't nice enough to be Doolin's, but she doubted he would use his own personal conveyance to have someone kidnapped.

Hurrying, the man put his hands around her waist and lifted her into the buggy. Jessie gasped in pain. When he released her, he stared at the blood on his hand for a second, then looked at her side, swearing again.

"Cursing isn't going to help it." Wincing, she eased back against the seat.

He glared at her, then bent closer to inspect the cut through the tear in her dress. "It doesn't look too bad. Should scab over pretty quick." He straightened and walked around to the other side of the buggy, disappearing briefly as the top of the buggy hid him from her view.

He ducked to keep from hitting his head when he climbed in. He took up more space than she had expected. His shoulder and thigh touched hers even with her wedged against the side of the buggy. Would she be able to protect herself against him? He was much larger and stronger than her husband had been. And with her hands tied... Swift, sudden fear took hold. The thudding of her heart and blood rushing through her ears overshadowed the songs of the birds and the creak of the buggy when it moved.

Don't give in to it! Keep your wits.

Breathing deeply, she told herself to focus on what was happening now, not imagine what might happen. "Everyone in town knows I'm engaged to Cade McKinnon. They're going to wonder why I'm with you." At the slight quiver in her voice, she caught her lip between her teeth.

He guided the horse down the overgrown path called an alley and turned on the next street. "Probably won't be anybody out this early anyway. If we do run into someone, you just nod polite-like. Keep your head back, and they likely won't even see you."

He withdrew a Colt .45 from the holster on his right thigh and stuck it beside him on the left side against the buggy. "Don't give me a reason to hurt anyone."

"I won't." She cleared her throat. "Why are you doing this?"

He hesitated for a moment. "I have my reasons."

"Money?"

"Partly."

Jessie studied his profile. He was a handsome man, though a day's worth of stubble darkened his face. He was dressed in a clean white shirt, black suit, cream-colored Stetson and black cowboy boots. Just like any of the ranchers who came to town on business or attended church on Sunday. But she doubted he'd ever been to church. He didn't strike her as a rancher, either.

His calm air of self-assurance reminded her of Cade, a man in control of himself and the situation. But there was a hardness about him, an alertness that told her he lived with danger. Right in the middle of it. He was no rustler. If he were, he would be their leader, not Doolin.

"Does it have to do with Doolin?"

"Let's wait until we're out of town to have a chat." Though the words were polite, it was an order.

Jessie kept quiet, searching both sides of the streets and the houses they passed, hoping someone would notice her in the buggy. He made several turns, finally onto the street Jessie recognized as the same road Cade had taken out of town when they drove to Rabbit Hollow Creek. They soon lost sight of the last building, and he urged the horse to a quicker pace. She hadn't seen another soul.

"Did Doolin hire you to kidnap me? To somehow keep him from going to prison?"

"That's right." A faint smile touched his mouth. "I'm supposed to tidy things up."

Lord, have mercy, he's a gunslinger. Jessie had never seen one, but that's what he had to be. Not the kind out to make a name for himself, either. He had too much cool confidence for that. Was he going to kill Quint? Use her as bait? "What do you mean?"

"Everyone besides your brother is too afraid of Doolin to testify against him. If they help put him in Huntsville—which is where they're bound to go since they were caught with the cattle—he'll make sure they're dead within six months.

"If Webb says he made a mistake, that Doolin wasn't involved, then he'll go free. We'll let you go, too, but by the time you wander back to town, we'll be almost to Mexico. There won't be any evidence to tie Doolin to your kidnapping or to the rustlers. Nor anyone who can prove he was involved with either one."

"Cade and Quint will look for me. The sheriff, too."

"More than likely."

She took a deep breath. "Are you going to kill my brother?"

"Don't plan to. Of course, if he starts shooting at me, that changes things." His nonchalant answer made Jessie's skin crawl. "But they won't find us. We have a good hiding spot all picked out." His gaze swept over her, and Jessie held her breath. "Has a dugout with a bed. I even brought some clean sheets."

She swallowed hard, looking away. It wouldn't be wise to make him angry, though she wanted to tell him he could burn the sheets. And the bed. Especially the bed.

Neither of them said anything for a while. Jessie noted that they passed the place where Cade had turned to go to the creek. She tried to keep track of the landmarks. "What happens if Quint testifies against Doolin?"

He looked at her, the cold hardness in his eyes making her shiver. "I'm supposed to kill you."

About two hours later, she shivered again. This time it wasn't from fear but from being chilled, too chilled for a summer morning. "I'm feeling light-headed. You'd better take a look at that cut."

He glanced at her, his eyes narrowing, and he drew the horse to a halt. Climbing out of the buggy, he slid his gun back into the holster. She noticed he wore one on the left side, too. He walked to the back of the vehicle and stopped for a minute, digging through the small boot. When he came around to her side, he unscrewed the lid of a canteen and held it up to her mouth. "Have some water."

Jessie welcomed the cool water, and took a long drink. When he lowered the canteen, she tried to dry her chin on her shoulder.

He wiped away the last bit of water with his hand, his touch surprisingly gentle, and studied her face. "Can you stand up?"

"I think so. I'm a little weak."

"I can't see good enough where you are. And you'll be warmer in the sunshine." He hooked the canteen strap over his shoulder. Taking hold of both arms, he pulled her forward on the seat, then gripped her left arm as she stepped from the buggy. The horse moved restlessly, rolling the vehicle forward, then back. "Sit over here." He helped her to a spot in the grass a couple of yards away, holding on to her until after she sat down.

He knelt beside her and laid the canteen on the ground. Studying her side, he took the knife out of its sheath. "It bled more than I thought it would. I need a better look at the wound. I'm going to cut the cloth a little more. Don't move."

Jessie held her breath as he pulled the blood-matted material away from her skin, making her flinch. He carefully eased the tip of the knife through the rip, cutting it further. Peeling the cloth back, he took a clean white handkerchief from his pocket and poured water on it from the canteen. After gently washing the injury, he examined it more closely.

"It's not deep, but longer than I thought, a little over an inch. We've been traveling fast. I expect all the bouncing on the road is making it bleed." He straightened, meeting her gaze. "I'll have to cut a strip off your skirt for a bandage. Don't have anything else."

"Go ahead. It's ruined anyway."

"Not much of a loss," he muttered, lifting the hem of her skirt and easily making a cut with the knife. No wonder it had sliced her. "You'd think a rich man like McKinnon would dress his woman better."

"I was going to clean house today."

"So you're practical as well as pretty." He put the knife away and ripped a long strip from the hem of her dress until he reached the part she was sitting on. "Bend your knees."

She hesitated, and he frowned at her. "Now. I don't have time for nonsense."

Then she ought to delay him as long as she could, but judging from the angry flash in his eyes, that wouldn't be a good idea. She bent her knees, resting the soles of her shoes on the ground. When he reached behind her legs for the strip of cloth, the back of his hand brushed her calf. She clenched her jaw, and he drew a sharp breath.

He ripped the material, the side of his hand touching her leg a couple of times, once on the calf and once on the thigh. She couldn't tell if he did it on purpose or if it was merely due to lack of space. She swung her knees away from him. The instant his hand was out from under her legs, she straightened them, flattening them against the ground. "No nonsense, remember?"

"I heard you had grit," he said with a smile. He tore the cloth loose, cutting off a short, crooked piece to make a straight edge. Next, he cut off about a foot of it, folding it into a thick pad. His mouth twisted thoughtfully, and he laid the bandage on her lap. Using the little piece with the ragged edge to blot the wound, he leaned closer, passing the long strip of cloth around her, with the ends meeting about six inches in front of the cut. "Lie down on your left side so the bandage will stay in place while I tie this."

"If you freed my hands, I could hold it in place."

"You could. But you'd probably do something foolish like try to get away. And you might get hurt." He nodded toward her side. "I don't like to see women hurt."

"Then why did you hold a knife against me?" She glared at him, biting back a sudden swell of angry words.

He sighed heavily. "Just lie down and cooperate before someone comes along and things get more complicated." Gripping her arm, he pulled her down, not giving her any choice. He placed the bandage over the wound and brought the strip of material over it, tying it in place. "Too tight?"

"It's all right."

"Good." He pulled her up to a sitting position. "Are you still cold?"

"Yes, but not as bad as before."

He removed his jacket and draped it around her shoulders.

Jessie didn't know what to think about him. One minute she felt threatened, the next protected. Maybe he was trying to confuse her. If so, he was doing a good job of it.

He picked up the canteen, holding it by the strap and helped her up. He didn't seem to notice the bloody handkerchief lying in the grass. Or the little scrap of her dress near it, the one he had used to blot the wound. She quickly looked away. Cade had told enough tales about tracking outlaws that she knew anything out of the ordinary would catch his attention. She only hoped he could recognize that little piece of cloth as part of her dress.

Starr helped her into the buggy, surprising her again

when he leaned inside and straightened the back of the coat when it bunched up against the seat. He pulled the lapels together and buttoned it. "Let me know if you get too warm."

She nodded, bemused by his kindness.

Not long after they started up again, Ira joined them. Starr slowed the horse to a walk as the other man rode along beside them. "How did it go?"

"I tied her hands and feet so she couldn't get up. She was starting to come around about the time I left."

Thank goodness, thought Jessie.

"Did you ride out to the west and work your way around to this road like we planned?"

Ira's eyes widened. "I was so scared, I plumb forgot. But I did ride out slow. Don't think nobody noticed me."

Starr scowled at him. "You'd better hope not. Get moving. The sooner we're off the road, the better."

"Yes, sir." Ira urged the horse to a gallop, quickly leaving them behind.

Starr snapped the reins and leaned back in the seat with a faint, satisfied smile.

But why?

Chapter Twenty-Three

Cade pulled up a chair beside Nola's bed and took her hand. He stared down at the thin, wrinkled fingers, realizing for the first time how fragile she had become. The doctor had assured him she would be fine after a few days' rest, but he silently vowed to find the men who had hurt her.

And who had taken Jessie. Anguish tightened his chest until he could barely breathe. *Please God, keep her safe. Don't let them hurt her. Help her not to be afraid.*

He took a deep breath, fighting back his own fear. He didn't have time for it. Anger and determination had to carry him through. If they harmed a hair on her head, he'd kill them.

He had been three miles from the ranch house checking a sick cow when Ty reached him. Brad had found Nola and taken the note to Quint, who was staying in town until after the trial. While Ty came after Cade, Quint and Sheriff Procter questioned the neighbors to see if anyone had noticed Jessie and the kidnapper leave.

They came up empty-handed.

Nola opened her eyes and looked up at Cade. "Have they found her?"

He shook his head. "They've talked to about everybody

in town. So far, folks have mentioned seeing three buggies leave town early this morning, all in different directions. We'll ride out in a few minutes, split up to cover as much territory as we can. The sheriff is organizing things right now." He patted her hand. "How do you feel?"

"Like a useless old fool. I should have sensed something was wrong. Would have when I was younger." She grimaced and scooted up on the pillow. Cade quickly put another one behind her. "Reckon I don't hear quite as well as I used to. Now I got a headache the size of Oklahoma and a pug-knot to go with it."

"I'm glad they didn't hurt you worse."

"Me, too. Though I don't think that was their intention. The man who tied me up kept apologizing under his breath, telling me how sorry he was he hurt me. Then, he'd ask God to please not let me die. His hands were shaking so hard it's a wonder I wasn't able to just slip the knot loose. I peeked up at him a couple of times without him knowing."

"Did you recognize him?"

"No. I expect he was a little younger than you. A lot smaller. Maybe five-six or so and skinny as a rail. Not anything like the man who had hold of Jessie."

"What did he look like?" Cade knew the sheriff had asked the same thing, but he hoped she might remember something new.

"I only got a glimpse of them through the back door a second before that mangy galoot hit me. He wasn't dressed like a cowboy, wore a suit. He had one hand over Jessie's mouth and the other holding a knife to her."

Even though he knew about the knife, Cade clenched his free hand into a fist.

She looked toward the window, her expression thoughtful. "Black suit. White shirt. Regular Stetson, like you wear. He was about your height, but slimmer. Not skinny at all, though. Handsome. The kind of man a woman notices, even an old one like me.''

''You think he might have been a rancher?''

''No, I didn't get that impression.'' She looked back at Cade. ''Mind you, it was only a glimpse, but they were standing in the sunlight, not in the shade of the porch so I saw him clearly. He was the complete opposite of the one who hit me. I almost feel sorry for that boy. But the man outside was the one in control. Calm, like nothing would faze him.''

''Like he had done this kind of thing before?''

''Maybe. Kidnapping a woman didn't bother him any. Or seeing an old woman smacked on the head. Professional. That's the word that comes to mind when I think of him.'' A frown darkened her face. ''I suppose that could be real bad.''

''If we don't find them, it could be. A professional will be more likely to kill Jessie if Quint testifies. On the other hand, he might be more careful with her, not as prone to accidentally harm her, or let someone else hurt her. Quint said one of the men who got away, Hobson, was mean, could get real ornery at times.''

''That doesn't sound like the one who hit me.''

''It wasn't. His description fits the other man, Ira. Quint never heard his last name. So that could mean Hobson has left or was waiting for them somewhere. If he's with them, Ira wouldn't be able to keep him in line, but this other man would.'' Cade sighed, released her hand and leaned back in the chair. ''So in that sense, I'm glad he's involved.''

''Will Quint testify?''

''He'll have to. But we're not worrying about what he says right now.'' He forced a smile. ''We intend to find Jessie before Doolin's trial starts. We've already talked to the prosecutor, and he's agreed to put everyone else ahead of Doolin if we have to.''

"Will the judge agree to that?"

"If we explain what's going on, he will. He's a good man. He'll do his best to give us as much time as we need.''

"So you're certain Doolin is behind this? Not just somebody with catawampus loyalty?"

"I'm sure he's behind it. Proving it is another matter.''

"You go find Jessie. Then we won't have to worry about Doolin anymore. Quint will send that scoundrel to Huntsville where he belongs.''

"If we can prove he ordered Jessie's kidnapping, too, he'll stay in the pen until he rots.''

Nola chuckled, then winced and touched the side of her head. "I expect if you find this Ira feller, he'll be real happy to lay as much blame as he can on him.''

Cade stood and leaned down, kissing her forehead. "We'll let you know as soon as we find her. You get plenty of rest and let Lydia take care of you.''

"I'll be out of this bed by tomorrow. Those children need me. In fact, why don't you see if they want to come sit with me a while. Tell Ellie I need some cuddle time.''

"I will. After I spend a few more minutes with them.'' Cade went into the family parlor. Lydia sat on the couch with Brad on one side and Ellie on the other. The children scrambled down and ran to meet him when he came into the room,

"Are you going to find Mama?'' Ellie looked up at him with tear-swollen eyes.

He knelt down in front of them, gathering them to him, one arm around each child. "We'll find her, sweetheart.''

"Uncle Quint told me he'd lie at the trial if he had to,'' said Brad. "But isn't that wrong? Won't he go to jail if he does?"

"He might. But you just keep praying that we find your mama before he has to deal with that."

"Are those bad men going to be mean to Mama?" asked Ellie, tears welling up in her eyes.

"I don't think they will, honey. There isn't any reason for them to. And Doolin respects your mother. If he's behind this, he would tell them to treat her well." Cade met Brad's troubled gaze. "She'll be all right, son. Jessie isn't any wilting violet. She's resourceful. You can bet she's trying to figure out how to get away from them right this minute."

"She might make it, too." Brad's expression eased slightly. "She handled a bunch of scary things when we were coming out here."

Ellie nodded her head, her curls bouncing. "Remember when she drove those nasty men off with the shotgun?"

Cade stiffened. Jessie hadn't mentioned anything like that to him. "What men?"

"Once we met some men on the road. The other time, two followed us out of a little town, but Mama sent them packing." Brad glanced at Ellie, then back at Cade. "I was wishin' mighty hard that we had another gun. But Mama stood her ground and didn't act one bit scared. She just leveled that shotgun at a gut and told them she'd kill them before she let them do anything to her or us. She spent a lot of nights sleeping sitting up against the wagon wheel, that ol' gun across her lap. Sometimes, when she got real tired, she'd let me sit up and keep guard for a couple of hours while she slept."

"Your mama is a very brave woman. And you're brave, too." Cade hugged them both at the same time. "She'll be just fine. Now, Nola wanted y'all to come in and see her." He kissed the top of Ellie's head. "Said she needs some cuddle time. But be real careful climbing up on the bed and don't bounce her around. Her head still hurts.''

"Okay." Ellie gave him a kiss, then walked slowly down the hallway.

Cade leaned the side of his head against Brad's. "I'm proud of you, son. You handled yourself well this morning, tending to Nola, then going to Quint for help."

"I wish I'd gotten up sooner. They'd been gone almost two hours before I woke up. Poor Miss Nola lay on the floor that whole time. She even knocked a chair over, but I was so asleep I didn't hear it. I sure was scared when I found her."

"I would have been, too." He still was. They all were, even though they tried not to act like it.

"I wish I could've stopped them."

"When a man's holding a knife to somebody, it's hard to do much to him without the other person being injured. You go on and see to Nola. She's feelin' poorly because she couldn't help Jessie, either. Try to cheer her up a mite."

"I'll try. But I don't feel too cheerful."

"I don't, either. But worrying doesn't help any. You keep your eyes and ears open. If you see anybody else coming around here that you don't know, raise a ruckus."

"Yes, sir." Brad turned and gave him a fierce hug. "Find my mama. Bring her back so we can all be a family."

Cade's eyes misted over. "I will, Brad. And we'll become a family next Wednesday, just like we planned. I love you, son."

"I love you, too. When you find Mama, be sure to tell her we're all right. And Miss Nola, too." His voice cracked. "She'll be worried about us."

"I'll set her mind at ease."

Brad nodded and went down the hall to Nola's room, wiping his eyes with his hand.

Cade stood, blinking back his tears, and noticed Lydia drying her eyes, too. "Thank you for staying and taking care of them."

"I'm glad to do it. Wish I could do more."

"This is the best thing you can do for any of us. I don't think they'll try anything else, but keep watch anyway."

Lydia glanced at a Winchester rifle leaning in the corner of the room. "My dad brought that over before he went to the sheriff's. I know how to use it."

"Good. I'd better go before they leave without me."

"Keep faith," she said softly.

"I will." He nodded and left quickly, riding over to the sheriff's office. About twenty men had gathered in front and were listening to Procter give instructions.

"I've already asked some of you to guard the jail and the prisoners. The rest of you stay here in town and be ready to ride if we need you, or take your turn at guard duty tonight. The only way we'll find them is to try and track them, and if too many go out at a time, it could just cover up the trail. We know he used a buggy because we found the tracks in back of the house. But there have been so many people in town the last few days and this morning, that we lost the trail after he got on the more traveled streets.

"Ty, Cade and I will each take a road. We'll take one man with us. Nolan, you've done some tracking, haven't you?"

The man nodded. "A little. Not near as much as you three, though."

"Take Asa with you. He's done a little, too, so between you, you should spot anything unusual. You take the north road." He looked at Ty and Cade. "I'll go west, Ty east and Cade south. If you find anything, one man comes back. He can send men out to bring in the rest of us. Look until dark. If you don't find anything, come back tonight, and we'll see what else we can figure out.''

Quint moved beside Cade. "I'm going with you."

"Good." He glanced up at the noonday sun. "I wish we could have started four or five hours ago."

"Four or five hours ago, we didn't know we had a problem."

They guided the horses back from the crowd and headed south. Cade understood why the sheriff had sent him that direction. It was his territory, and he knew it well. Which was what bothered him. "It doesn't make a whole lot of sense for Doolin to send them out this way. Too big a risk of running into me or somebody she knows."

"Or that we'd find them too easily. Course, he might have left it to Ira to pick a place to hole up. Ira's not real bright. And if the other man is a stranger, he wouldn't know the best way to go."

"I reckon that's possible."

But he couldn't shake the feeling that he was moving farther away from his love instead of toward her.

Chapter Twenty-Four

Starr suddenly veered off the road and headed across the prairie, making the sharp turn so quickly it threw Jessie against him. She hadn't detected any particular landmark and wondered if he did.

"Lost your way?" she mumbled against his shoulder, struggling to right herself.

"Nope." He slowed the horse slightly and pushed her back up to a sitting position. "Benefit corner." Jessie glared at him, and he shrugged, amusement lighting his dark blue eyes. "Close as I'll get."

She honestly didn't know what to make of him. He'd kidnapped her for goodness' sake. He was a gunslinger or something akin to it. He might even kill her. Yet he kept surprising her with moments of compassion or humor. Would a cold-blooded killer have a sense of humor? At least a normal one?

An hour later, he drew the buggy to a halt beside a small creek.

"We walk from here." He pointed at a narrow trail that went up a rugged hill, then got out of the buggy and tied the reins to a small mesquite. Returning to her side, he helped her from the vehicle. "Do you still need the coat?"

"No."

He unbuttoned the jacket, lifted it from her shoulders and slipped it on. Picking up the canteen, he took a long drink.

"I could use some of that." Jessie licked her dry lips. Her throat was dry, and her head ached from hunger and everything else that had happened.

"Turn around and I'll untie you."

"It's about time." She turned her back to him. He freed her hands and let her rub her wrists for a minute before giving her the canteen. After she drank her fill, she handed it back to him.

"Let me check the bandage," he said. She raised her arm, only because she couldn't see the injury well enough to take care of it herself. He touched the pad to make certain it was still in place and tugged on the knot. "Doesn't look like it bled much after we wrapped it. Feel up to a walk?"

"Do I have any choice?"

He smiled. "No. Besides, there's food at the dugout. If you're as hungry as I am, that's a good enough reason to keep moving."

"I'm starving," she admitted. She glanced at the noonday sun, wondering how long it would be before Cade found them. Would he be able to follow the buggy tracks? Or would too many other vehicles have gone over the same streets before he even knew she was missing? *This way, my love. Listen to my heart.* She sighed and shook her head at such foolishness.

"What are you thinking?" Starr motioned for her to go in front of him.

She started toward the trail. "Nothing."

"Nothing you want to share with me."

"That's right."

Suddenly his hands covered her shoulders, halting her.

His grip was firm but not painful. "I'm not going to kill you, Mrs. Monroe."

She looked over her shoulder at him. "What if my brother testifies against Doolin?"

"He won't. Not if he believes you're in danger. That's what makes this such a good plan. If everybody does what they're supposed to, no one actually gets hurt. Except for that cut on your side, and that was an accident." He released her and put his hand at the small of her back, prodding her forward. She complied, the thought of food urging her on. "I hadn't expected you to fight so hard. Though I reckon I should have," he added in a thoughtful tone.

"Why?" She lifted her skirt to keep from stepping on it. Even without the three-inch strip he had cut off, she would trip over it going uphill if she weren't careful.

"Ira said he heard you came from East Texas in a wagon. Just you and the children."

She nodded and paused to catch her breath. The hill was steeper than she'd expected.

He waited until she started walking again. "So how did you meet McKinnon?"

"I was looking for my brother, but he wasn't there. Cade hired me as his housekeeper." She heard him chuckle.

"He's smarter than I thought."

"Smart enough to catch you."

"We'll see if he still has what it takes."

Jessie spun around to face him, almost losing her footing. His hand shot out to steady her. "You know Cade?"

His expression became guarded. "I met him when he was a Ranger."

"When he arrested you?" she asked sweetly. She thought she saw his lip twitch before he frowned at her.

"Get moving. My stomach is eating a hole in itself."

"Then I should drag my feet." But she didn't. Her stomach was gnawing on itself, too.

She turned around and went up the trail. Halfway up, where the footing was particularly tricky, she stumbled, but he caught her again before she could fall. His action didn't surprise her. And that worried her, because she was beginning to trust him.

They went over the hill and down the other side, which wasn't quite as steep or as rugged. After that, the trail twisted and turned through the brush until they suddenly stepped into a clearing. A dugout had been built in the side of another hill. It was protected on both the left and right by tall cliffs.

"Who owns this?"

"Nobody. Ira said one of the early cattlemen built it when he first came out here. There were still Indians in the territory then. It was abandoned a few years ago, but the stove is good. We got the cobwebs out, but that's about all. Don't know if the roof leaks." He glanced at the bright, cloudless sky and peeled off his coat. "But I doubt we'll have to worry about that."

Ira came out the door and nodded politely. "Ma'am. I tried to clean up in there some more. It's cool inside. That's about all I can say for it." He noticed the strip of cloth at her waist and the blood on her dress. His eyes grew round and he swallowed hard. "What happened?"

"She tried to warn the old lady. Moved quicker than I anticipated, and I cut her. It's not too bad. Should heal up fine." Starr touched her back again, nudging her forward. "We need to eat. Go tend to the horse and hide the buggy."

"Yes, sir. I just carried in a fresh bucket of water from the creek."

Starr pushed the door open wider and gave Jessie a slight bow. "Your very humble abode, madam."

She stepped inside, wrinkling her nose at the musty smell but grateful to be out of the sun. Ira was right. It was cool inside. Starr followed her and suddenly the one room seemed much smaller. She glanced at the bed, which was barely big enough for one, then looked up to find him watching her. "For how long?"

"Until I say it's time to leave."

Or until I find a way to escape.

As they had expected, Quint and Cade didn't find anything to indicate Jessie and her kidnapper had gone south. They turned back toward town shortly before dusk, covering the distance at a gallop on the way back. When they arrived at the sheriff's office, Ty was right outside the door, about to enter. Asa and Nolan's horses were already tied to the hitching post out front.

Ty stepped back to the edge of the boardwalk. "Find anything?"

"No. You?" asked Cade.

"No. We followed the tracks of four different vehicles. But they all either came from ranches or went back to them. We checked each one, and everyone had a legitimate reason for traveling."

"Same with us." Cade followed Quint and Ty through the doorway. The grim expressions of the men already in the office sent a surge of dread through him. The sheriff nodded, then looked down at his desk.

There, in the middle of it, was a bloodstained handkerchief and scrap of cloth. Cade's breath caught, and his throat thickened. Picking up the small piece of cloth, anguish filled his soul. "It's Jessie's," he whispered. He met Quint's agonized gaze. "It's from her old blue dress. The one she wore the first time I saw her." He stared at the blood for a minute, then cleared his throat, looking up at Procter. "Where did you find it?"

"About twenty miles north of town."

"They were lying in the grass a couple of yards from the road," said Asa.

Dear God, what did he do to her? Cade turned away from the others, unwilling for them to see his pain. He couldn't breathe, couldn't think past the horrible image his mind conjured up—Jessie knocked to the ground, the man on top of her. Did she fight him? Or did the terrifying ghosts of her past paralyze her? He didn't know which would be better. He felt a hand on his shoulder and looked up to see the concern and understanding in Ty's eyes.

"Look at the handkerchief," his brother said quietly. "The blood has been diluted, as if the cloth was wet at the time. And the stains are streaked."

Cade dragged in a deep breath and stared dully at the handkerchief in Ty's hand.

"Like someone cleaned a wound. The piece of her dress is from the hem, and it's the right width for a small bandage. Remember when Pete got gored by that longhorn, and Nola ripped off the bottom of her skirt to bandage him up?" His voice dropped lower, to make certain the others couldn't hear. "If he's a professional like Nola thinks, he wouldn't harm her right by the road. He'd wait until they reached wherever they plan to hold her."

It wasn't much consolation, but it prodded Cade's mind to start to work again. "But she's been hurt, Ty. Kindhearted as she is, she's not foolish enough to help the kidnapper if he was wounded."

"Not unless he held a gun on her. She might not have had any choice."

Cade realized he was slumped over, leaning one hand

against the wall. He straightened and turned back to the sheriff. "What do you have in mind?"

"We get some sleep. You ride out first thing in the morning and find them. Take whoever you want. I need to stay here and guard the prisoners. I'll keep other men posted around the jail, in case this is all a ruse to break Doolin and his gang out."

"I hadn't even thought of that. I'm slipping." Cade wiped his face with his hand. "Doesn't seem like Doolin's style."

"No, but that may be why he'd think it would work. We wouldn't expect it."

"I'll take Ty, Quint and Asa with me. Even if there are a few more, we should be able to handle them. There is too much risk of Jessie being hurt if we go charging in there with a large posse. And you need plenty of men here." Cade glanced toward the door, blocking the jail cells from view. "The last thing I want is for Doolin to escape. Unless I'm around to shoot him when he does."

He wasn't a bloodthirsty man by nature. But, then, he'd never had the woman he loved threatened with murder. "We'd better go tell the children that we have an idea of their direction. We'll check back here in the morning before we leave."

"I'll be here." Procter came around his desk and put one hand on Cade's shoulder, the other on Quint's. "You'll find her. She's a strong, intelligent woman. She'll hold her own against them."

Not if he hits her, thought Cade, his heart heavy. Or even threatened to. He sent another fervent prayer heavenward for God's protection over her.

When they reached Nola's house, Ty offered to take their horses to the livery stable. "I need to check by the store."

"I'll be along after I spend some time with Brad and

Ellie. I expect Lydia has supper fixed for us. There is probably enough for you, too.''

"I'll get something to eat at the store. Give the kids a hug for me."

Cade nodded, walking slowly toward the front door, following Quint and Asa. Lydia gave Asa a welcoming kiss as the children wrapped themselves around Quint.

What if we don't find her? The burning ache in Cade's heart seared his soul. How could he live without her?

Chapter Twenty-Five

J essie watched Starr pull in another catfish from the creek. She supposed if someone saw them, they might think they were simply a couple on an outing. She sat in the shade of a mesquite while he fished, his shirtsleeves rolled up on his forearms, his hat sitting beside her on the grass in case she needed more protection from the sun. In West Texas, folks might not pay much attention to the fact that her companion wore two six-shooters.

Nor were they likely to notice that he kept one eye on her and one on the creek. Behind them someplace, Ira stood guard, both over her and their camp. But she appreciated being out in the open and not locked in the dugout. The price of that freedom? A promise to cook for them.

"What do you think? One more?" He looked at her as he knelt beside the bucket of fish and removed the hook.

"It depends on how hungry you are." They'd had cheese and crackers and shared a can of peaches when they arrived. Though she had been famished, she quickly discovered that with her nerves on edge, her stomach was, too. She ate enough to ease her hunger, but that was all she could manage.

He pondered the comment and threw the line back in the

water. "Ira has a hollow leg, so I'd better try for one more."

Right then, he didn't seem like an outlaw, though she supposed they weren't necessarily nasty all the time. He wasn't notorious. She didn't think she'd ever heard of him. "Is Starr your real name?"

"Yes." He tugged on the line, frowning when it came up empty. He pulled it in and added another worm. "I have two older brothers, Hezekiah and Erasmus. I was luckier. My parents named me Ransom."

Ransom Starr. "I've never heard of you."

"That's good." He threw the line out into the water again and sat down on the bank.

"I thought gunslingers wanted a reputation."

"You think that's what I am?"

She shrugged. "I don't know. You said you were specially hired for this job. Maybe you just go around kidnapping people."

"It pays good."

"How much? What am I worth?"

His face softened. "I expect a price far above rubies."

He knew scripture? That shattered another one of her ideas about him.

"But I'm getting five hundred for the job."

"Does that include killing me?"

"No. That's another five hundred. But like I told you earlier, you don't have to worry about that." He looked back at the fishing line just as it dipped under the water. Scrambling to his feet, he jerked the pole and pulled in another fish. He dropped it into the bucket and removed the hook, then slung the cane pole over his shoulder. "This should do it. You're cleaning them, right?"

"Wrong." She stood, dusting the grass off her skirt, then wondered why she bothered. "I cook. You clean."

"Worth a try." On the way back to the dugout, he stopped, blocking her way.

Jessie's pulse picked up as he faced her, and she suddenly felt threatened again. She caught sight of Ira up the hill behind him. Would he come to her aid if the larger man tried something?

"You're safe with me, Jessie." His gaze held hers. "That's why I took this job. To protect you."

"I don't understand."

"Cade is my friend. I haven't seen him in a long time, but I still consider him a friend."

"Then take me back to him, to my family."

"I can't. Not yet." He shifted and glanced up at Ira, who watched them closely. "I can't explain it now. Just trust me."

"I don't know if I can."

"You have to. Unless he's cornered, Ira is harmless. But there is someone else involved who isn't. He would put a bullet in your heart without batting an eye. Then he'd kill your family."

She gasped, her heart constricting in her chest. "My children?" she whispered.

"He's done it before."

"Why is he free?"

"Because they can't prove it." He glanced at Ira again, who had taken a couple of steps toward them and halted. Starr set the bucket on the ground. "Ira's getting suspicious of us talking so long. And he's more afraid of the other guy than he is of me. I'm going to act like I'm trying to kiss you. You push me away and slap me." His eyes crinkled with the hint of a smile. "But not too hard."

Jessie barely had time to consider his words before he grabbed the back of her head and leaned toward her. She shoved against his chest, knocking his hand loose from her head, and slapped him across the cheek. Hard.

He winced as his head jerked to the side. Scowling at her, he muttered a mild oath and rubbed his face.

Without a word, she stepped around him and stormed up the hill. If he got mad at her for hitting him so hard, so be it. He deserved it for terrifying her and her family and Cade. Sudden tears welled up in her eyes. *Oh, Cade, I wish you were here.*

The breeze rustled the leaves nearby. Though she knew it was only the wind, she heard his voice in her heart. *Hold on, darlin'. I won't let you down.*

The next morning, Ty fastened his gun belt at his waist. "I have an idea where they might be."

Cade looked up quickly and almost poured coffee on his hand instead of in the cup. "Where?"

"Buck Grime's old dugout. It's up in the hills near the Caprock. I found it one time when I was out camping. It's well hidden and protected. A creek fed by a spring from higher up runs nearby, so there is always water. A year or so ago, it still had a stove in it. And an outhouse." He smiled. "All the comforts of home."

Cade knew he was trying to lighten his mood. "Not even close. Can you find it again?"

Ty frowned thoughtfully. "It may take a few tries. I was wandering around the hills and came on it by chance. I didn't approach it from the road, but I have a general idea of the area. As far as I know, it would be the best place up that way to hole up."

"Then it's worth a look."

A brilliant orange and golden sunrise greeted them when they stepped out the door. Ty clamped his hand on his brother's shoulder as they walked down the porch steps. "A good day for a treasure hunt."

This time Cade smiled.

Even though Jessie had entertained a vague thought of trying to escape during the night, the howl of wolves and the scream of a mountain lion nearby quickly banished the idea. Nor did she have an opportunity, even if she'd had a plan. Starr and Ira took turns keeping watch, sitting in a chair at one end of the room. They nailed curtains of burlap bags over the two windows and kept a lantern on the table, turned low. It illuminated the room enough to alert them if she so much as wiggled. She dozed a little, irritated that both men seemed to sleep just fine when they weren't on guard duty.

She cooked a breakfast of bacon and scrambled eggs, then took the dishes to the stream to wash them. Ira had offered to do it, but she wanted the chance to study the area once again.

The hill she and Starr had walked over served as the bank along that portion of the creek. When Ira brought the buggy horse to the house, he had ridden it down the stream. There were three horses at the dugout, including Starr's big black stallion that he had evidently left there earlier. She didn't intend to go near that one, but if she could get away from him and Ira, she might be able to ride one of the others out of there. She hadn't ridden bareback since she was a child, but it wasn't an ability a person forgot.

During the early morning hours, she conceived a plan that might work. If it did, she'd have to thank Quint for sharing his story about the outlaw's cooking disasters.

"Mrs. Monroe, can I carry those back for you?" asked Ira.

"Yes, thank you. How kind of you to offer." Jessie

stacked the plates and silverware in the fry pan and handed it to him. The cups were still in the dugout in case they wanted more coffee during the morning. "You seem like such a nice man, Ira. How did you get mixed up in such sorry business?"

"I'm not quite sure, ma'am. I was working for Doolin as his horse wrangler at the ranch. One day he told me to go with Rawlins to a line camp and take care of the horses. That night Rawlins and the other men rode out. I thought they were going to town, but since I was broke till pay day, I didn't ask to go along. Next thing I knew, they were riding in with fifteen head of cattle that weren't wearin' Doolin's brand. They put them in the pen and Rawlins told me that I belonged to an outlaw gang. My job was to take care of the horses. If I didn't want to do that, Doolin had ordered him to shoot me right then and there."

"You didn't have any choice then." Jessie felt sorry for the man. "But you do now. If you'll help me get away from here, from Starr, we'll go to the sheriff. If you explain what happened, surely they wouldn't send you to prison. Doolin and Rawlins are in jail now. They can't hurt you."

He slowed his steps, glancing toward where Starr leaned against the dugout, cleaning his nails with his knife. Jessie was positive he watched every move they made. "But his partner can," Ira said.

"Who is his partner?"

"I don't think I'd better tell you. Sometimes I think he's worse than Doolin. He knows things, too, like how my ma is all crippled up and can't walk good, and that I send money to her in Fort Worth every month. He said she'd pay if I didn't help kidnap you. And he wasn't talking about money. I feel real bad about this whole thing, ma'am, but I don't rightly know what to do about it. My mama's the only kin I have." He sighed heavily. "It'll break her heart when she finds out what I've done. Will your brother testify against Doolin, with you being gone and all?''

"No, I don't think he will. My children and I are the only family he has. Just like you, he'll protect us, no matter the cost to him. Don't worry about it, Ira. It will all work out.''

"I sure hope so, ma'am.'' He went on ahead of her and set the dishes inside. When he came back out, he carried a rifle. "I think I'll go keep a lookout on the other side of the hill.''

Starr nodded and straightened, stepping away from the dugout. "Come back in a couple of hours, and we'll switch places.''

Jessie went past him into the dugout, mulling over what Ira said, putting it together with what Starr had told her. She needed something to occupy her hands while her mind sorted things out. Cooking was always her first choice, and glancing around the room, the only one. She wasn't about to try to clean up years of neglect. Rummaging through the foodstuffs the men had brought with them, she rounded up with the ingredients for biscuits. She was already mixing everything together when Starr came into the house.

"What did you learn from Ira?'' He poured himself a cup of coffee, peeked over her shoulder to see what she was doing, then sat down, stretching his legs out in front of him.

"That he was tricked into working with the rustlers. He was Doolin's horse wrangler at the ranch. Doolin sent him out with Rawlins to take care of some horses and the next thing he knew, he was an outlaw.''

"Figured it was something like that.'' He sipped the coffee, watching as she dumped the biscuit dough out on a floured plate and began to lightly knead it. "So that's the secret to good biscuits?''

"That's what my mother said. It's her recipe." She paused, looking up at him, still not quite certain she should trust him. "Ira said Doolin has a partner. Is it the man you were talking about yesterday?"

He nodded. "Henry Wyman."

Jessie stared at him. "Doolin's assistant? That meek little man?"

"He's anything but meek. I suspect he's the brains behind this whole operation." He stood and walked to the doorway, casually looking around outside. He came back to the table, standing across from her. "I'm a detective, Jessie. I've been looking for Wyman for over six months. We believe he killed a family in Denver, shot them all, even the children. He'd had some business dealings with the father that evidently didn't go the way he expected. The last day he was seen in the city was the day they died. Like I said, there's no proof he did it. But a lot of things point to him. I was hired by the man's brother to find him in the hope that we can catch him in another crime, something that would send him to jail for a very long time."

Jessie turned the dough one last time before pinching off a lump and rolling it into a biscuit. She would have preferred a nicely floured board and biscuit cutter, but this would have to do. She flattened it slightly and laid it in the greased frying pan. "Wyman hired you to kidnap me?"

"Yes."

"But how did you get involved with him?"

He smiled slowly and sat back down. "Providence, I think. I only arrived in town day before yesterday. I'd heard he was here, working in Doolin's office. I followed him to one of the saloons on the edge of town. I'm good at what I do, and maybe he got a little careless. I sat a couple of tables away with a bottle and a blonde." He wrinkled his nose. "She's homely as a horse and stank, but her company kept him from paying any attention to me.

"He was talking a little louder than he realized, which makes me think he's getting desperate. If he was merely worried about Doolin implicating him, he would have left town. I suspect he hasn't gotten all his money yet. He wanted Ira and a man named Hobson to kidnap you. I learned from Ira that Hobson was the other rustler who wasn't captured at the camp the day before. Hobson didn't want any part of it. He just up and walked out on Wyman, hightailed it out of town. But Ira was afraid of what would happen to his mother if he didn't go along with it. I was weighing the options of speaking up when Ira mentioned Cade's name. It didn't take much to sort out that you two were about to get hitched. So that made up my mind."

"How did you get Wyman to hire you?"

"Told him I'd overheard the conversation and offered my services."

"Just like that? And he hired you?"

"Pretty much. I mentioned a few shady characters that he knew, and a few he didn't, so it wouldn't seem so obvious. Reckon he took me for a gunslinger or something, too. Knew Ira couldn't handle it on his own."

"Why didn't you go to the sheriff with the information instead of actually kidnapping me?"

"That was my original intention. But it was four in the morning, and from then on, Wyman watched us every minute. Insisted on playing cards. I was afraid that if I left, he'd hire one of the hooligans in the saloon to take my place. They were a rough bunch. He stayed close by, right up until Ira left the house."

"Wyman was there?"

"Next door. Those folks were out of town, and he hid in their grape arbor, watching everything that happened.

There wasn't a chance to tell anybody anything. I didn't dare not follow through and bring you here. Actually, until the trial starts, this is probably the safest place for you. I don't think he will show his face around here.

"But if Cade is still as good as he used to be, he'll pick up the signs I left him." He pulled his watch from his vest pocket. "If he left at daylight, I expect he'll show up early this afternoon."

"Signs. The handkerchief and piece of my dress."

He grinned. "I thought you noticed those."

"But what else?"

"That quick turn off the road wasn't really for my enjoyment. The tracks should catch his eye. Especially since we dug up some grass."

"Any other clues along the way?"

"No. From there on out, he'll have to rely on instinct and luck." He walked over to where he'd hung his coat on a nail and pulled a small mirror from the pocket. "Or the old sunlight on the mirror signal from our Texas Ranger days."

Jessie shook her head in bemusement. "You worked with him."

"Rode together for four years." He set his cup on the table and turned the chair around, straddling it, resting his arms on the top of the chair back. "Now we have to figure out what to do about Ira."

"Will the sheriff arrest Wyman on what you tell him?"

"He should. I'll testify against him in court, and I expect we can find some witnesses that were in the saloon that night who saw us talking—and him giving us money. But if we can persuade Ira to tell everything he knows about him and Doolin, we'll have a stronger case. Stronger against Doolin, too."

"He's terribly afraid of Wyman. Can we convince him?"

"I think we'd do better after Cade gets here. Make him realize he doesn't have many options."

"Isn't he liable to start shooting if Cade simply rides in? Maybe we should tie him up."

"Do I detect the desire for revenge?"

"If so, you're the one who should be hog-tied." She waved away his argument. "I know you thought you had to so I wouldn't hit you over the head and escape."

"You would have if you'd had the chance."

Jessie laughed. It seemed like the first time in forever. "Yes, I would have."

"I'm not sure he'd be too cooperative if we hog-tied him."

She thought of her earlier plan to escape. "What if we only distract him for a few minutes when Cade arrives? I assume you're going to watch for him and bring him in here?"

"That was my plan. What do you have in mind?"

"A peach pie. Originally, I was going to give it to both of you, but now I think it should just be for Ira." They had stored the salt and sugar on the table in an effort to keep the ants and mice out. She tapped first one bag and then the other. "I declare, my eyesight is a bit poor in this dim light. They need to make brighter printing on these sacks. A body could get them mixed up and put in a cup of salt instead of sugar."

Starr laughed, rocking his chair onto the back legs, then down again when it squeaked in protest. "I like the way you think, Jessie. No wonder Cade wants to marry you. He always said he'd rather have an intelligent wife than a pretty one." His voice softened. "Lucky devil got both."

Jessie smiled, blushing slightly, and put the pan of biscuits in the oven. "What happens if Cade doesn't find us?"

"We tie up Ira and haul him to town. Show up at the trial, hopefully before your brother goes on the witness stand against Doolin. You can count on Wyman being there. If we do it right, the sheriff will arrest him, at least for questioning. No matter what, I don't intend to let him get away." His expression hardened, his eyes growing cold, deadly. "He won't get the chance to kill anyone else."

Chapter Twenty-Six

Squatting, Cade studied the ruts in the grass where a buggy had turned off the road. He looked over at Ty. "What do you think?"

"It's the right direction, and they were in a big hurry. But I don't see any reason for such a sharp turn. He could have slowed down and turned fifty yards farther. The prairie isn't any different there than here."

"Maybe it's a trap," said Asa, nudging back his hat. "He'll figure Quint is looking for his sister, so he makes it easy to follow them. But when we get close enough, he picks him off from a distance with a good chance of getting away. If Quint's dead, Doolin goes free."

"Makes sense," said Cade. "Quint, you'd better stay here and let us scout the area."

"No, I'm going with you. They're just as liable to shoot any of you as me. Maybe he's injured and made Jessie drive. She can handle a buggy as good as I can. It would be like her to try and give us something to follow."

Cade frowned and remounted. "I guess that's reasonable, though not as likely as Asa's theory. You won't stay here anyway."

"Got that right."

Cade and Ty led the way, keeping some space between them. Every once in a while they spotted the buggy tracks again where the grass gave way to plain dirt. Sometimes, it seemed as if the driver went out of his—or her—way to make certain the tracks were discernible. As they drew nearer to the hills, he grew more uneasy. There were dozens of places a man could hide and pick off a rider with a good rifle. They were out in the open, without even a prickly pear cactus breaking up the flat sea of grass.

Suddenly a flash on a hill about a hundred yards ahead caught his eye. "Take cover!" He turned toward an out-cropping of rock and brush about fifty yards to their left. Spurring their horses, they reached their destination without anyone shooting at them.

Dismounting quickly, they ducked down behind the rocks, searching the hillside. "What did you see?" asked Quint.

"A flash of light." Crouching low, Cade moved around the rock for a better view.

Ty moved beside him. "Rifle?"

"Maybe." He shifted so Ty could look, too, and kept watching the spot where he had seen it. "There it is again." This time, the flash was followed by another...a pause... then several more, deliberate and carefully timed. Cade turned around, keeping low, his back against the rock and looked at Ty in disbelief. "Did I see that right?"

"It's our old company signal."

They crept back around to Quint and Asa. "Somebody up there is signaling us with a mirror," said Ty.

"Catching the sunlight to let us know they're there." Quint rubbed the side of his nose. "You must have told Jessie some good tales."

"Not this good. It's a specific signal we made up in our

Ranger company," said Cade. "One man would scout ahead, then use it to tell the rest of us to join him."

"Then you have a friend up there?" asked Asa.

"Or an old one who's become an enemy." Cade stood and caught his horse's reins. "I'll ride up and see who it is. You stay here and cover me. If he starts shooting, return his fire. I'll try to stay out of the way."

"I'll go," said Ty. "Jessie would a whole lot rather have you in one piece than me."

"Probably." Cade swung up into the saddle. "But she's my woman. I'm going."

"I am, too." Quint reached for his horse.

"Not this time." Cade nodded at Ty to keep Quint there. "We need you to put Doolin in prison. Besides, if I get shot, she'll need you to take care of her."

Quint glared at him. "You just want to play the hero."

"The hero gets the girl."

"Dang it, she's my sister."

"She already thinks you're a hero. It's my turn." Cade laid his rifle across his thighs and nudged the horse to a walk.

As he neared the hillside, a man carrying a rifle stepped out from between the rocks and worked his way down toward Cade. He stopped a little above him and pulled his pocket watch from his vest and flipped it open. "You made good time. I didn't expect you for maybe another hour."

"Ransom, what the devil are you doing here?" Cade rested his hand on the rifle, his finger ready to slip onto the trigger. He knew full well that his old friend—if he still was a friend—didn't miss the movement.

Ransom kept his rifle at his side, ready to swing into action if needed. "This is going to sound bad at first, but hear me out before you try to shoot me."

"I won't try. I'll do it. Is Jessie up there?"

Starr nodded. "She's up in the dugout, baking a special peach pie."

Cade stared at him in disbelief. Had the whole world gone loco? "Ransom, I'm tired and cranky and want to see the woman I love. My finger is gettin' itchy. Now, tell me what's going on."

"Well, to put it bluntly, I kidnapped her." He held up his hand when Cade lifted the rifle. "To protect her." Cade lowered the gun again. "Why don't you go back and get the rest of your men, and I'll explain it to everybody at once. She's fine...well, almost fine. She has a little cut on her side, but that was an accident. I sure hated it that I hurt her. But we got it wrapped up and stopped the bleeding. All that bouncing around on the road. It's not bothering her much this morning."

Cade's head was practically spinning, and his temper short. He leveled the rifle at the man who once was his friend. "You'd better start making more sense real fast."

Ransom pretty much ignored him. Which was typical. Even when he'd felt threatened, he'd never shown it. His face lit up. "You found the handkerchief and piece of her dress?" Cade nodded. "And where we turned off the road? Couldn't think of any other way to tell you where we were going. Had to make it up as we went along.

"Go get Ty and the others. I assume one of them is Jessie's brother?" He sat down on the rock, and Cade almost punched him. "I'll wait here. It's a long story." He checked his watch again. "And we don't have much time. That pie ought to be ready to eat in about twenty minutes." He met Cade's gaze, his expression growing somber. "I'm still on the right side, Cade. And I'm still your friend. You have my word on both counts."

When it came right down to it, that was good enough.

Cade nodded and turned the horse around, hurrying back

to the others. He quickly told them what he knew while they were mounting up. They reached Ransom, and he explained what had happened. Cade was relieved that he related the situation thoroughly and professionally. He expected it gave the others more confidence in Starr and his almost unbelievable tale. He knew it did him. He was even more amazed to learn of Wyman's involvement than he had been about Doolin.

"You wait on this side of the bend in the creek. I'll walk back over the hill to the dugout. Jessie will give Ira a piece of pie to distract him. I'll whistle and you ride in."

Quint frowned. "How will Jessie's pie distract him?"

"Oh, I forgot to explain that part. She's using salt instead of sugar, so y'all might want to avoid it. Ira tends to shovel in his food, so she figures it will make him choke long enough for me to disarm him and you to reach the dugout. He'll be so busy coughing, he won't have time to think about shooting."

Cade chuckled and pulled Quint's hat down on his face. In a matter of minutes, the nightmare would be over and Jessie would be in his arms. "That sounds like your sister."

Quint pushed his hat back up where it belonged. "She's been hanging around you too much."

He shook his head, anticipation warming his heart. "Not nearly enough."

The baking heated up the small room, so Ira carried the chairs outside. He sat leaning back against the side of the dugout. He kept his seat when Starr approached. "Everything still quiet?"

"Quiet as a sleeping baby. I didn't even see a jackrabbit." Starr met Jessie's gaze. "Is that pie ready to eat? I worked up an appetite sitting there watching the grass grow."

"I think it's cooled enough. Ira, would you like a piece, too?"

"Yes, ma'am. I been looking forward to it all afternoon."

Jessie felt a little twinge of guilt. "I'll bring some out. It's too hot inside to enjoy it."

"Still have any coffee?" Starr followed her inside.

"No, we finished it at dinner." She searched his face. When he nodded, joy and relief took the starch right out of her knees. She leaned against the table, drawing a shaky breath.

Frowning, he sent her a questioning look.

She took a deeper breath and straightened. "Goodness, it's even hotter in here than it was earlier. You don't need to wait inside. I'll bring the pie right out." As he left, she quickly cut two large pieces and put them on plates. Adding forks, she carried them outside.

"Here you are, Ira." Smiling, she handed him a plate.

"Thank you, ma'am." He leaned his rifle against the building, picked up the fork and cut a huge bite. He had to work at it a bit. Jessie wondered how he could get so much in his mouth at one time, then remembered that he had crammed a whole biscuit in at dinner. The bite of pie would be easy for him.

"Sorry the crust is tough. I don't know if the stove was too hot or if it's because I used the skillet." She handed the other plate to Starr.

"It'll be fine." He took his time sawing at the crust, watching Ira out of the corner of his eye.

Ira shoved the bite into his mouth and started chewing eagerly, already cutting the next bite. Suddenly he stopped chewing. His face contorted. His eyes watered. He coughed...and wheezed...and coughed again, spitting peaches and crust everywhere.

Starr let loose with a shrill whistle. He pounded Ira on the back, relieving him of his sidearm at the same time, retrieved the rifle and stepped away from him.

Poor Ira kept coughing and wheezing. Jessie was afraid he'd sucked crust down his windpipe. "Do you need some water?"

He nodded, tears running down his cheeks, finally pulling in a small, gasping breath. "Yes," he squeaked.

Jessie grabbed the ladle in the water bucket and filled it as another fit of coughing hit him. Hearing horses, she looked up to see Cade storming up the creek. Quint, Ty and Asa were right behind him. She thrust the ladle into Ira's hand and scampered away, running to meet Cade.

He jumped off Mischief before the horse stopped, and swept her into his arms, crushing her against him. "Thank God you're safe. Thank you, Lord. Thank you." He held her as if he would never let her go.

And she didn't want him to. When she finally eased back enough to look up at him, she was stunned to see tears making a path through the dust on his cheeks. "Oh, Cade." She wiped his tears with her fingertips, her own eyes filling.

"I thought I'd lost you," he whispered. "I tried not to think about it, but I couldn't help it. I didn't know how I'd live without you."

"You don't have to. I don't care when or where the ceremony is, but we're getting married tomorrow."

A slow smile spread across his face. "Your dress won't be finished."

"I'll wear it to church sometime." She looped her arms around his neck. "I wouldn't keep it on very long on my wedding day anyway."

Heat filled his eyes. "About two minutes after I shut the bedroom door."

She brushed a kiss on his mouth. "That long?"

"Not if you wear an old one." He kissed her tenderly, then glanced up at the five men watching them. "Too bad we have an audience. Looks like Ira is breathing again."

"Poor Ira. I wonder if he'll even try the other pie I made. I used sugar in that one."

Cade curled his arm around her waist, and they started toward the dugout. "Don't tell him. Then I can have his piece."

"Wyman threatened to hurt his mother."

"Does she live in Willow Grove?"

"No. Fort Worth, but Wyman knew all about her. If we could figure out some way to protect her, I think he would cooperate with us."

"We'll see what we can do." He felt the tear in her dress and stopped. She had discarded the pad that morning, but the strip of cloth didn't quite cover up the hole. "That's where Ransom cut you?"

"It's fine now."

"No it's not." Anger vibrated in his voice.

"Let it go, honey. It's as much my fault as his. I hit the knife when I tried to kick him. He was dodging. I'm sure he never intended to hurt me."

Cade scowled and muttered something about drowning him in the water trough.

When they reached the others, Ira glared at Jessie. "That wasn't very nice, Mrs. Monroe."

"I'm sorry, Ira. We had to do something to keep you from shooting at Cade and the others. And we didn't want to hit you over the head."

"Like I did that old lady." Ira looked at Cade, his face full of regret. "She didn't die, did she?"

"No, she's fine. Nola is tough. She said you apologized for hitting her. I think she forgives you, but you'll get the chance to ask her yourself."

Ira slumped down on the ground next to the dugout. "She ain't gonna visit me in jail."

"You might not have to go to jail. Starr told me about how you were tricked into working for Doolin and forced into helping kidnap Jessie. I think we can work something out with the sheriff and the prosecutor if you'll be a witness against Doolin and Wyman."

"I don't know. I'm afraid something will happen to my mother if I do."

"We'll hire someone to protect her," said Cade. "For as long as she needs it. Or if she wants to move to Willow Grove, we'll arrange that. Get her a nice little house in town with someone to watch over her if necessary. I know how it feels to have someone you care for in danger."

Ira looked so woebegone that Jessie's heart ached for him. "I don't have a job anymore. Even if I don't go to jail or prison, nobody will hire me to do a lick of work for them."

"I will," Cade said quietly. "I think you're an honest man who got caught in a bad situation. I can always use a good horse wrangler. And Quint tells me you're good."

"You'd do that for me? Even after I helped take Mrs. Monroe?"

"You can rectify that by helping us put Doolin and Wyman in prison. The choice is yours."

"Then I'll do whatever you tell me to. I've been more scared and miserable these last three months than the whole rest of my life put together."

"Just tell the truth, Ira. Tell the court everything you know about both men."

"I can do that. And I know plenty. I don't talk much, but I listen a lot." Ira stood, his anguish of moments earlier evaporating. "But there's something I don't understand." He smiled and shook his head. "Well, there's a lot I don't understand, but one thing has me completely bumfuzzled. Mr. Starr, are you a lawman?''

"Not exactly. I used to be, but now I'm a detective."

"Well, you ought to go back to bein' a lawman," said Quint. "Willow Grove needs a new deputy sheriff."

"And likely a new sheriff before long," said Ty. "The U.S. Marshal's job is open and Procter wants the appointment. After busting up the rustlers, he'll probably get it. The sheriff's job would be yours for the asking."

"How do you know that?" Ransom leaned Ira's rifle against the dugout.

"Because I'm the new mayor."

"Uh-oh, boys. He's too big for his britches. Better dunk him in the creek," said Cade.

Quint and Asa grabbed Ty, dragging him toward the creek despite his protests that they'd ruin his boots and his pistol. Ransom glanced at Cade and poked Ira with his elbow.

"Shame on you." Jessie laid her head on Cade's shoulder as Ransom and Ira followed the others.

"They won't throw him in." He turned, drawing her into his arms. "But it gives me a chance to give you a real kiss."

"I thought the other one was a real kiss."

"Yeah, but this one will curl your toes."

And it did.

Chapter Twenty-Seven

"Everything is all set." Asa had checked on the status of the trial while everyone else waited outside of town. "They're moving fast. Already tried and convicted everybody but Doolin and Sam. Guess the jury decided the boy had been forced into the gang and acquitted him.

"They're recessed for dinner now, but Doolin's case is up next. It starts again at one o'clock. Sheriff Procter and the district attorney thought a grand entrance is in order. They'll save some seats, but they want you to wait outside and not come in until they call Quint as a witness. He figures the opening statements will take about twenty or thirty minutes. Sam and a couple of the others will testify, too, as long as Quint is there."

"Is Doolin defending himself?"

Asa nodded. "The sheriff said he acts like it's goin' to be a cakewalk. That's one reason they want to surprise him."

"What about Wyman?" asked Ransom. "Has he been at the trial?"

"Every minute. Sheriff figures he'll be sitting right by Doolin since he's supposed to be his assistant."

"Did you ask him about weapons?"

"He isn't allowing any inside the courthouse. Everybody has to leave them at his office if they want to go to the trial."

Ransom frowned and absently rubbed his horse's neck. "You can count on Wyman having a derringer, probably two."

"Procter said they've been checking for them, but he'll pay particular attention to Wyman. And a few others so he won't think he's being singled out." Asa reached in his saddlebag. "The sheriff sent badges for everybody. Said he was deputizing you by proxy." Grinning, he paused. "Guess that's my new name. That way we'll be armed and able to help if there's any trouble. You, too, Ira."

Ira stared at the badge Asa held out to him. "Does this mean I won't go to jail?"

"Yes. And as far as anyone else is concerned, you were helping protect Mrs. Monroe, not actually kidnapping her."

"I'll go along with that if anybody asks," said Ransom.

Beaming, Ira took the badge and pinned it on his shirt. "But after this is over, I'd still like that job you offered me, Mr. McKinnon."

"You've got it." Cade nodded as he pinned on his own badge. He looked at Ty and Ransom. "Almost seems like old times."

They waited until close to one o'clock to go into town, using back streets and leaving the buggy and horses behind McKinnon Brothers. The store, like practically every other business in town except the saloons and restaurant, was closed until the trial ended for the day. They waited inside, watching the front of the courthouse.

A crowd had gathered outside the courthouse because there wasn't enough room in the building to hold everyone. Due to the afternoon heat, the windows and doors were wide-open. Two deputies stood guard on the boardwalk, blocking the doorway. At one-twenty, Sheriff Procter stepped outside and looked toward the store.

"That's our signal." Ty unlocked the front door, locking it again after everyone was outside. They crossed the street quickly, causing a stir as they worked their way through the crowd until the sheriff's sharp "Quiet!" silenced them. Still half a dozen women reached out to touch Jessie's arm, welcoming her home with genuine joy and relief. And even more men gave Cade a slap on the back for rescuing her.

The sheriff held them on the boardwalk until the district attorney's voice rang through the courthouse and out the door. "Your Honor, the prosecution calls as its first witness, Quintin Webb."

Cade watched through the window as Quint walked into the courtroom. Doolin turned around, smiling smugly.

When Quint reached the front of the room, Cade and Jessie went inside. Ty and Asa followed them in, rifles in hand, and took up positions along the wall, guarding the windows.

His hand on her elbow, Cade escorted Jessie to the seats near the front that the sheriff had reserved. He made certain he was on the side closest to Doolin.

Doolin stared at them, his expression dumbfounded. His bewilderment quickly turned to anger, and he leaned over to whisper something to Wyman.

A loud gasp went through the crowd when they spotted Jessie, followed by cheers. When they sat down, he glanced back and saw Ransom and Ira slip inside, guarding the doorway. Ransom had left his rifle at the store, preferring to use his Colt Peacemaker whenever he had a choice. It took several minutes of gavel-pounding before the scowling judge restored order in his court.

He smiled at Jessie. "Mrs. Monroe?"

"Yes, Your Honor."

"I'm glad you're home safe and sound."

"Thank you, sir."

He turned his attention to Quint. "Bailiff, swear in the witness."

"No!" Doolin jumped to his feet, his face contorted with rage. "He's a liar."

The judge pounded the gavel again. "Mr. Doolin, sit down."

"No, I won't." Doolin turned toward the jury. "You can't convict me with one witness. It's his word against mine."

"We have four other witnesses, Your Honor," said the prosecutor. "Men who will not only testify that Doolin was the leader of the outlaws, but that he was also involved in Mrs. Monroe's kidnapping."

"I was in jail." Doolin looked around the room wildly. "I couldn't have been involved."

Cade stood, ready to pounce on him if he needed to. The sheriff worked his way around to the other side of Doolin. Quint stood near the witness stand, also ready to act if necessary.

Doolin spun toward Wyman. "He did it. The kidnapping was his idea. The rustling, too. He was their leader. Not me. I just did what he told me to."

"Be quiet, you idiot."

"You talked me into this. You said Webb wouldn't show up if his sister was taken." He pointed his finger at his so-called assistant. "He's the one you want. And he's a murderer, too. He bragged about how many people he's killed."

"Doolin, shut up!" Wyman reached beneath the table and jumped to his feet, holding a pistol, waving it toward the crowd. Half of them dove to the floor. The other half froze in place. The jury dropped to the floor, hiding behind the waist-high wooden panel in front of the jury box.

Keeping his eyes on Wyman, Cade eased his hand toward his revolver. He figured every other man with a gun was doing the same thing. But shooting him before he hurt somebody would be tricky. Cade hadn't been in this kind of situation in years.

"Put the gun down, Wyman," ordered the sheriff, taking a step closer.

Wyman spun toward the judge, leveling the gun at his chest. "Stay where you are, Sheriff. Don't anybody try to stop me, or I'll shoot him. Judge, you come down here. You and me are going for a little ride."

The judge hesitated, then moved a few feet toward the steps leading from the bench.

"Doesn't take much courage to face an unarmed man." Ransom slowly walked down the aisle, holding his empty hands out to his side.

Wyman tensed. Keeping the gun pointed at the judge, who stood still, he turned so he could see who was talking to him. His eyes widened when he recognized Starr, then narrowed when he spotted the badge on his vest.

"What about O'Malley's wife?" asked Ransom. "Or their son? I doubt either of them had a gun."

"I don't know what you're talking about."

Cade held his breath. Wyman was growing more nervous, which was what Ransom wanted. He had always been at his best in close confrontations. Cade hoped he still was.

"John Michael O'Malley. Denver. Your dealings with him didn't go like you expected, either, did they? You got any family, Doolin? Wyman likes to spread out his revenge." Ransom stopped about twenty feet in front of him. "You went to O'Malley's house for dinner and killed him and his whole family." He paused, studying the other man. "Do you think you can kill me before I shoot you?"

Doolin edged away, crouched down in front of the district attorney's table and crawled under it, alongside the prosecutor.

"You don't even have your gun out of the holster. They'd call it murder." Wyman's gaze darted to the judge and back to Ransom.

"Not if I challenged you. If you kill me, it would be self-defense. Isn't that right, Sheriff?"

"That's right."

"There's only one way to stop me from telling how you hired me to kidnap Mrs. Monroe," said Ransom, his voice calm and firm, "and ordered me to kill her if her brother didn't cooperate."

The sheriff inched forward.

Wyman jerked his head in his direction. "Don't move!"

The judge ducked behind his desk, and Wyman swung the gun around toward the crowd.

Cade and Procter both went for their side arms, but Ransom drew and fired before either of them had their guns out of the holsters.

Ransom leaned over Wyman as he gasped his last breath. "That's for three-year-old Nellie O'Malley. One shot. Right through the heart. Just the way you killed her."

Stunned, the crowd and jury slowly climbed back into their seats. The judge peeked out from beneath his desk, then stood and took his proper place behind the bench. The district attorney and Doolin crawled out from beneath the table.

Sheriff Procter motioned for two men to tend to Wyman's body. They hurried forward and picked him up.

Cade sat down and put his arm around Jessie. She leaned

against his shoulder and closed her eyes when the men carried Wyman from the room.

The judge cleared his throat, his angry gaze focused on Doolin. "Tate Doolin, you made a public confession of your involvement in the rustling."

"It was under duress, Your Honor."

The judge ignored him. "Do you want to change your plea to guilty and save time or shall I have the district attorney charge you with kidnapping Mrs. Monroe, too?"

Doolin glanced at Ira and Ransom, perhaps weighing how much they could implicate him in the kidnapping. "I plead guilty to cattle theft, Your Honor."

"Very well." The judge paused, studying some notes on his desk. "Tate Doolin, I find you guilty on two hundred and fifty counts of cattle theft, one for each stolen cow that ended up on your ranch. I expect there are many more, but this will do to put you away until you're an old man. I sentence you to thirty years hard labor in the Texas State Penitentiary at Huntsville. Sheriff Procter, see to the prisoner." He wielded the gavel one last time. "Court adjourned."

The sheriff called Asa and Ira over to take Doolin to jail. A crowd formed around Cade and Jessie, all talking at once. Holding her to his side, Cade pretty much ignored them, simply nodding politely now and then. He watched the jurors shake Quint's hand and various cattlemen work their way over to thank him. A few of the single ladies made a fuss over him, causing him to blush.

Another crowd surrounded Ransom, including what had to be practically every other unattached female in the county, oohing and aahing about how brave he was. Cade agreed with them. His old friend had grown even better with time, both in skill and steady courage. He smiled as Starr took all the compliments in stride, smiling and chatting a little with each lady and giving them what was probably the thrill of their previously quiet lives.

He glanced back at Ty, chuckling at the consternation on his face as he watched Ransom. Cade caught his eye, and Ty finally smiled. Then he grinned as some of the ladies turned their attention to him.

After five or ten minutes, the sheriff sent folks on their way. "I'm sure Mrs. Monroe would like to get home to her children. Y'all have had enough excitement to last you six months."

Cade and Jessie waited a few minutes more until the crowd thinned out before starting toward the door. The sheriff had stopped to talk to Ransom, and Cade overheard part of the conversation as they walked past.

"It's been a long time since I saw anybody as fast as you," said Procter. "Don't reckon I could talk you into taking a job as my deputy, could I?" He leaned a little closer. "With a move up to sheriff in about a month. I got a telegram this morning appointing me the new U.S. Marshal for this district as soon as the current man retires."

"Congratulations," said Ransom.

Cade stopped and turned around, holding out his hand to the sheriff. "From me, too. You're leaving big boots to fill."

"Talk Starr into filling them," said the sheriff, shaking Cade's hand. "There's nobody in a hundred miles who would be better."

"You don't even know me."

"I watched how you handled a crisis situation. That's all I need to know."

"Let me think about it for a few days. Either way, I have to go back to Colorado and settle some business. Would it be possible for me to search Wyman's belongings to see if there is anything that would prove he was the one who killed the O'Malley family? There was some jewelry missing.''

"I'll tell Miss Flora over at the boardinghouse to let you in his room.''

"I appreciate it." Ransom turned to Cade and Jessie. "You'd better get this lady home to her family.''

"We're working on it. Darlin', I'll go get the buggy and be right back.''

But when they stepped outside, Quint had it waiting for them. "I'll take the horses over to the livery, then be right along," he told them. "Tell Ellie to save some hugs and kisses for her Uncle Quint.''

Jessie laughed. "She has a big supply.''

Cade helped her into the buggy, then settled in beside her, clicking his tongue to the horse. The tired animal started up at a very slow walk. "Don't worry, girl. I'll take care of you in just a few minutes.''

They drove away from the milling throng of people, and he breathed a sigh of relief to see that the street heading to Nola's was empty. "Darlin', about getting married today…''

She looked up at him with a frown. "Don't you want to?''

"Yes. And no. I'd love to go to sleep with you in my arms tonight, but I'm afraid that's just what I'd do. We're both worn-out." He smiled ruefully. "For months, I've dreamed about loving you all night long on our wedding day.''

"Well, I hate to spoil a dream." She relaxed against the back of the seat and yawned. "I am exhausted. I didn't sleep at all night before last and not a whole lot last night. Despite Ransom's clean sheets, that bed was awful.''

When they pulled up in front of the house, Lydia and the children burst out the front door and raced to meet them. Nola followed, walking faster than Cade had seen her move in a long time.

Jessie jumped out of the buggy, kneeling on the street, and pulled Brad and Ellie into her arms, hugging and kissing them. Crying, they both clung to her. Tears poured down her cheeks, too, but Cade knew they were tears of joy.

"Mama, I was so scared you wouldn't never come home," cried Ellie. "But Cade promised he'd find you, and I wasn't so scared anymore."

"How did you get away?" asked Brad. "Did Cade rescue you?"

"Yes, he did. But it's a long story. Let's go in the house and I'll have a big glass of iced tea and tell you all about it." Jessie stood and hugged Lydia, then Nola. She examined the older woman closely. "Are you all right?"

"Still got a lump on my head, but otherwise I'm fine. Now come on inside. Are you hungry? Did they feed you anything?"

Jessie looked at Cade with a twinkle in her eye. "Actually, I fed them. I fried catfish and even tried out a new recipe for peach pie."

"Was it good? You'll have to share it with me," said Lydia.

Jessie looked at Cade again, and they both burst out laughing.

"Only if you want to practically kill somebody." Cade winked at Jessie. "I'll take this poor ol' hoss to the livery and be back in a few minutes."

She nodded, mouthing the words *I love you.*

He said them back, out loud, and made her smile. He drove away, her lovely, tearstained, travel-dusty face lingering in his mind.

How he did love that woman's smile.

Chapter Twenty-Eight

On her wedding day, Jessie sat in front of the dressing table mirror, watching as Lydia pushed the last hairpin into her hair. She had pulled it up in a crown of curls with a braid of white ribbon and honeysuckle woven through, a fancier style than Jessie would have tried.

Lydia sighed, smiling wistfully. "You're a lovely bride, Jessie."

"Thank you. You will be, too. Has Asa hinted at marriage yet?"

"Oh, yes, he's hinted. I think he's been on the verge of asking me a few times but got cold feet." She grinned and stepped back so Jessie could stand up. "I'll wait a little longer before I give him a nudge."

"He loves you. It's as obvious as the nose on his face."

"He's told me so. I suspect he thinks I'll demand that he give up his freedom, but I won't. I know he needs to ride the range as much as he needs air to breathe. As long as he isn't gone for too long at a time, I could handle it."

"Maybe you should tell him that."

"I think I will." She grinned. "It would be nice if our wedding was the next one in town. Now, do you need me for anything else?" When Jessie shook her head, Lydia gave her a hug. "I'll see you downstairs. Cade almost came up here to get you an hour ago."

"Considering I was in my petticoats, that would have been interesting." They shared a laugh as Lydia headed toward the door. "Thank you for helping me. I never would have been able to do up my hair this nicely on my own."

"It was fun."

Jessie looked at her reflection one last time, silently admitting that she did look nice. *Nice* wasn't really the right word, but she couldn't bring herself to say beautiful. Radiant. "Yes, that fits," she whispered. "Because I'm in love." She touched the strand of pearls at her throat, her gaze going from the necklace to the matching pearl earrings, a gift from Cade for her wedding day. Sometimes she still couldn't believe how much her life had changed. She was almost afraid she would wake up and discover it had been a dream.

The diamond in her engagement ring sparkled in the sunlight. It was such a beautiful ring, signifying a precious promise. Thinking of the rings Ransom had found in Wyman's room, and the engraved sentiment on the wedding band, sorrow shadowed her joy. O'Malley had loved his wife, too.

The door creaked open, and Ellie stuck her head around it. Her eyes grew wide. She came into the room, staring at her mother. For once, she was speechless.

"Think I'll do?" Jessie asked softly, sitting back down on the stool in front of the dressing table.

Ellie nodded. "You're so pretty, Mama. Will I be that pretty on my wedding day?"

Jessie's heart gave a little lurch. That day would come all too soon. "You'll be even prettier, sweetheart, because you're beautiful now." She held her arms open wide, and Ellie ran to her. Jessie lifted her up on her lap. "It's the love I feel for Cade that makes me look especially nice today.''

Ellie nodded. ''But the dress and necklace help.''

Jessie laughed. ''Yes, they do.'' She gave her daughter a hug and set her on the floor, admiring her pink ruffled dress. ''You look quite lovely yourself, little miss.''

''I like my new dress. And I put on my company manners all by myself. You didn't even have to tell me to.''

Tenderness and love misted Jessie's eyes. *Oh, dear, if I'm going to get all weepy over company manners, what will I do at the wedding?* She hugged her daughter again. ''Thank you. That makes me extra proud of you.''

''Oh, I forgot. I was supposed to tell you that the preacher is here.''

''Then it must be time for a wedding. You go on down. I think I'm supposed to come down by myself.''

''Okay.'' Ellie skipped to the door and opened it, then looked back at her mother. ''I'm glad you and Cade are gettin' married. He's gonna be a good daddy. And you smile a whole lot more than you used to.''

''That's because he makes me happy.''

Jessie picked up her bouquet of white roses, sent in the day before by train from Cade's friend in Fort Worth, and waited a few minutes before making her way downstairs. When she turned on the landing and saw Cade waiting at the foot of the stairway, she paused to engrave the memory on her heart.

He was quite somber until he saw her. Then his face broke into a beaming smile. His gaze traveled slowly over her, admiration, approval and love in his eyes. He wore a new black suit, pristine white shirt and string tie. His black dress boots had been polished until they glistened.

When she was two steps away, he held out his hand to

her. She clasped her fingers around his, letting him tuck her hand around his forearm when she reached his side.

He leaned down close to her ear. "You're beautiful, and I love you."

"I love you, too." She smiled up at him. "And you're beautiful, too."

"Thank you, ma'am." Still smiling, he escorted her across the room to where the minister stood. Other than Nola, everyone else stood, too. Given that all the men from the ranch had been invited, they never would have been able to seat them all in the parlor.

Brad smiled at her as he and Ellie took their places beside them. He also wore a brand-new suit. Like Cade, he wore his boots, nicely shined. Jessie doubted she'd ever get him to put on another pair of shoes, but that was fine with her.

Quint gave her an encouraging, I'm-proud-to-be-your-big-brother smile. She thought she caught the glint of moisture in Ty's eye as he nodded to her and his brother. Lydia wiped a tear from her eyes, and Asa looked nervous. Ransom grinned and winked.

The preacher cleared his throat. "Dearly beloved, we are gathered here today..."

Jessie heard just enough of the minister's words to respond appropriately. But Cade's voice—deep, firm and filled with resolve—penetrated the daze that had overtaken her. He looked into her eyes and promised to love, honor and cherish her "until death do us part." The pledge, made with love and integrity, resonated in her heart. It would not be broken. Nor would hers to him. He slipped the engagement ring from her right hand and transferred it to the left along with the wedding band.

She slid his wedding band onto his finger, promising in turn to love, honor and cherish him for all her days. He had asked her to change the traditional pledge, leaving out the word "obey."

"It wouldn't be any fun if you obeyed me all the time," he had said. Then he had laughed and added, "Besides, you wouldn't be able to do it."

"I now pronounce you man and wife," intoned the minister solemnly. After a pause, he grinned at Cade. "You may kiss your bride."

Cade kissed her tenderly with a sweetness that touched her soul. But when he raised his head and gazed into her eyes, she saw the promise of waiting passion.

Ellie tugged on Cade's coat. "Are you my daddy now?"

"Sure am, sweetheart."

"Whoopee!!" She jumped up and down and hugged his leg. Laughing, Cade picked her up for a big hug.

Brad was next, and he didn't even mind. He hugged Jessie, too. "This time will be better, Mama," he murmured.

Jessie's eyes misted up again. "Yes, it will be. For all of us."

The others crowded around, offering their congratulations. A half an hour later, Nola and Lydia announced that the food was ready. The cowboys disappeared into the dining room in an instant, quickly followed by the others.

Jessie was too excited to eat much, the daze of the ceremony having evaporated with Cade's kiss. As much as she liked her family and friends, she was anxious to be alone with her husband.

After they ate, Cade caught her hand, leading her out to sit in the front porch swing. "Hello, Mrs. McKinnon."

"Good afternoon, Mr. McKinnon." She stretched up and kissed him, not caring if any of the neighbors saw them. "Did you ask Ty if we can use his house for a few days?"

"Well, no I didn't." He tugged a little on his collar. "I

have something else in mind. But if you don't want to do it, just say so.''

"If you want to go back to the ranch, that's all right." She tickled his chin. "As long as the men know the house is off-limits for a few days."

He chuckled and put his arm around her shoulders. "Well, I wasn't thinking about the ranch. I had thought about throwing a party, bringing in an orchestra from St. Louis, but there wasn't time to arrange it." He leaned down and nibbled on her ear. "So I thought I'd take you to the orchestra. Ever been to St. Louis?"

She stared at him. "No."

"Want to go?" He looked at her hopefully.

"Well, yes. But what about the kids?"

"Nola, Quint and Ty can take care of them for a week. Lydia said she'd be glad to help, too, if Nola needed it. I already talked to Brad and Ellie. Ellie wasn't too sure about it, but Brad convinced her it was a good thing. And I promised to bring her something special."

"You're spoiling her."

"I like to spoil my girls."

"When?"

He pulled out his pocket watch. "The train leaves in about half an hour."

Jessie hesitated. She didn't want to ruin his gift, but she wasn't all that excited about spending what was left of her wedding day—and her wedding night—on a train with dozens of other people. "Would we stop in Fort Worth? Spend the night?"

"Well, we could, but I'd rather not." When she frowned at him, he chuckled and brushed a kiss on her mouth. "I'd rather spend the whole trip making love to you. With a little time out for sleeping and eating."

What had he cooked up? "Well, that would certainly

provide the other passengers with interesting conversation. Might be a little tricky to make love on the seats, though I suppose a sleeping berth might work.''

He threw back his head and laughed. ''It might, but I don't plan on trying it out.'' A train whistle sounded in the distance. ''What I'm proposing, Mrs. McKinnon—dang, I like saying that—is riding to St. Louis in a private Pullman Palace car. Real furniture, including a bed. Complete privacy, unless we ring the dining car for food. Lydia is packing us a picnic basket, so once we get on that train, we won't have to see another soul until sometime tomorrow. Maybe even the next day.''

''It sounds like heaven.''

He leaned down next to her ear. ''With you naked in my arms, it will be.''

Jessie shivered, both at his words and his warm breath on her ear. Then she panicked. ''I have to pack.''

''Nola and Lydia are doing it for you right now. With a little help from Ellie, I expect.''

She relaxed. ''You've thought of everything.''

''I hope so. But we'd better go say our goodbyes so we can head to the station.''

The next fifteen minutes passed in a flurry as Jessie hugged the children, ordered them to behave, mind Nola—and anyone else who watched over them—and hugged them again. Ty brought his buggy to the front gate to transport the newlyweds to the station. Quint drove up right behind him with a rented surrey from the livery to carry their luggage and some of the guests along. The ranch cowboys took off at a quick walk, trying to beat them there.

At the station, they shared another round of hugs and good wishes before boarding the private car. When Jessie and Cade stepped through the doorway, she halted, looking around her in amazement.

The furniture was the finest she had ever seen. A heavy mahogany sofa with thick cushions richly made up in red velvet sat across the car. Two armchairs, made in the same fashion, faced it, with a long, narrow table in between. Two other chairs sat by the window. They were lighter and could be easily moved from one side of the car to the other. Behind the sofa was a table with four chairs. And behind it was a bed, adorned with a paisley bedspread and about ten pillows. There was even a skylight above the bed, and another above the sitting area.

"Cade, it's beautiful. Is it yours?"

"No. Belongs to a friend." He grinned as the porter smiled and closed the door, leaving them in private. She had noticed him slip the gentleman a tip before entering the car. "You'll discover, darlin', that I have a lot of friends. Some of them in high places. The use of his railcar was John Moore's wedding gift to us. He's a cattleman and banker who lives in St. Louis, so you'll get a chance to meet him."

"Will we have to leave this splendor there and ride back in a regular car?" She was only half teasing.

Laughing, Cade put his arm around her. "No, he said we could use it for the trip home, too. But I had to promise to send it back to him."

The whistle blew, and the train started to slowly move. Cade and Jessie went to the open window, waving to their family, friends, and about half of the town who had come to see them off.

When they cleared the station, he tugged off his tie and shrugged out of his coat, unbuttoning the stiff high collar on his shirt. "That's better. It's too hot to wear that getup all day."

Jessie peeked into a couple of cabinets and the closet,

stopping by a window to look at the passing countryside. "I've never ridden on a train before."

Chuckling, he came up behind her. "Not bad for a first trip." He leaned down and kissed the nape of her neck, sending goose bumps down her arms. "Do you have any problem making love in the daylight?"

"Not if the drapes are closed."

"I'll take care of it. Maybe you could do something with those pillows."

"I see an empty corner." She tossed the pillows into the corner and folded back the bedspread, nervous anticipation making her hands shake slightly. The bright sunlight in the car slowly dimmed as he closed the curtains, leaving some of the windows open at the top to let in air. He moved to the other side of the bed and helped her fold up the bedspread, setting it on a high shelf in the closet.

He drew her into his arms, kissing her slowly, his fingers working the buttons at the back of her dress. She unbuttoned his shirt, tugging the shirttail from his trousers, splaying her hands across his broad chest. He edged the dress off her shoulders, slipping the sleeves down her arms, and took a step back as the gown slid to the floor.

Feeling a little self-conscious, she picked up the dress and draped it over a chair. He tossed his shirt on another chair and caught her hand, drawing her back around so he could look at her. His gaze caressed her, then his hands— so gentle, so loving, with each touch vanquishing the hurts of the past.

He carefully pulled the pins from her hair until it fell across her shoulders and down her back. Starting at her temple, he threaded his fingers through it and smoothed his hand all the way down to her waist, letting the ends curl around his fingers. "I've wanted to do that since the first night I met you. I wanted to kiss you, too, in the worst way."

Smiling, he brought his hand up and lightly brushed the edge of his thumb across her lips. "But I did this instead."

Jessie sighed softly. "It felt like a kiss. I could still feel your touch the next morning."

"And you will tomorrow morning, too."

They undressed each other slowly, treasuring the freedom—and the blessing—to do so, to love the way they wanted to. He carried her to the bed, laying her down with exquisite care, and stretched out beside her. Then he showed what making love truly meant.

Afterward, lying in his arms, being gently rocked by the motion of the train, Jessie finally accepted the fact that she had never been lacking as a woman. She only needed a good man who loved and respected her. Looking up into the beloved face of her husband, she breathed a soft sigh of contentment. This strong yet gentle man had done what she had feared impossible.

He had mended her broken heart and healed her battered soul.

*　*　*　*　*

SHARON HARLOW

lives near Seattle with her husband of thirty-five years and one very spoiled doggie. Their twenty-three-year-old son has his own place, but he's close enough to drop in for dinner a few times a week, much to his mama's delight. Originally from Texas, she says her writer's heart dwells in the rolling plains of west Texas, mainly in the 1880s and 1890s. But she occasionally hops in her time machine and travels across the ocean to England and Scotland during the Regency period. This is her eighth historical romance in the regular market. She has also written five books in the inspirational market under the name Sharon Gillenwater.

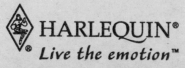

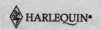

COMING NEXT MONTH FROM

HARLEQUIN HISTORICALS®

BEAUTY AND THE BARON
by **Deborah Hale,** author of LADY LYTE'S LITTLE SECRET
Lucius, Lord Daventry retreated from society after being disfigured in the war. But in order to satisfy his grandfather's dying wish, Lucius proposes a temporary engagement to Angela Lacewood, with the understanding that she'll break it once his grandfather dies. When the old man rallies, will their engagement become a reality?
HH #655 ISBN# 29255-4 $5.25 U.S./$6.25 CAN.

• **SCOUNDREL'S DAUGHTER**
by **Margo Maguire,** author of NORWYCK'S LADY
When prim and proper Dorothea Bright comes home to reconcile with her estranged father, he is nowhere to be found. Instead, she encounters Jack Temple, a handsome archaeologist who is intent on dragging her along for the adventure—and love—of her life!
HH #656 ISBN# 29256-2 $5.25 U.S./$6.25 CAN.

• **WYOMING WIDOW**
by **Elizabeth Lane,** author of NAVAJO SUNRISE
Desperate, widowed Cassandra Riley Logan claims that the missing son of a wealthy Wyoming rancher is the father of her unborn child. His family takes her in, and Cassandra finds herself drawn to Morgan, the missing man's brother. But when her secret threatens to tear them apart, will their love be strong enough to overcome Cassandra's reluctant deception?
HH #657 ISBN# 29257-0 $5.25 U.S./$6.25 CAN.

• **THE OTHER BRIDE**
by **Lisa Bingham,** Harlequin Historical debut
Though Lady Louisa Haversham is married by proxy to a wealthy American, she isn't ready to settle down. Instead, she convinces her maid, Phoebe Gray, to trade places with her. As Phoebe, Louisa must now masquerade as a mail-order bride. Gabe Cutter, the trail boss escorting several mail-order brides to their grooms, proves to be a thorn in her side—and a constant temptation!
HH #658 ISBN# 29258-9 $5.25 U.S./$6.25 CAN.

KEEP AN EYE OUT FOR ALL FOUR OF THESE TERRIFIC NEW TITLES